Shadow Redemption

REBECCA DEEL

Copyright © 2019 Rebecca Deel

All rights reserved.

ISBN-13: 9781689601016

DEDICATION

To my amazing husband, the love of my life.

ACKNOWLEDGMENTS

Cover by Melody Simmons.

CHAPTER ONE

Ruth Monihan shivered in the bright sunlight, goosebumps surging across her skin despite the soaring heat of the August day. She stopped for the third time in as many minutes and looked over her shoulder.

No one paid attention to her on the crowded Nashville street. She must be imagining things. Again. Understandable considering a few months earlier she'd been kidnapped by a terrorist. Revulsion filled her at the memory of Hugo Torino's hands and mouth on her. But that episode of her life was in the past, Ruth reminded herself. Hugo would be locked in prison until he was an old man.

She still couldn't shake the feeling that someone was watching her. Ruth continued forward. She should be used to it since she made her living in front of a camera. At least for now. Three more jobs and her supermodel alter ego, Roxanne, was retiring. It was past time and Ruth wanted a normal life beyond a spotlight and runway. These days, standing in front of a camera made her skin crawl and her anxiety skyrocket, a legacy from her time as Hugo's prisoner.

Ruth crossed the street to Vanderbilt Children's Hospital with a gift bag in hand. She had a plan for life after she finished the last contracted job and the money to make her plans come to fruition. She had no debt and had taken advantage of her financial advisor's wise counsel over the years.

She walked into the hospital lobby, a sigh escaping. Her sister, Bridget, was blissfully happy with her hunky husband, Trace, a super soldier with muscles to spare, lethal sniper skills, and a heart that beat for his wife. Ruth was thrilled for her sister and loved that her brother-in-law was so besotted with Bridget. Watching them together, though, highlighted the lack of someone special in her own life.

The mental image of Trace's dark-haired teammate, Ben Martin, popped into her mind, a fascinating man who made time to train her in self-defense when they were in town at the same time, and who always made time to talk on the phone in the middle of the night when memories plagued her the most. Although he watched her when they were in close proximity, he'd never acted on those tantalizing hints of interest.

Ruth stepped into the elevator and pressed the button for the correct floor. She leaned against the wall. Maybe Ben considered her tainted. She blinked back the sting of tears and chided herself for being ridiculous. The handsome operative didn't shy away from her when she'd been rescued from Hugo's clutches. Although he hadn't asked questions, Ben must have known or suspected the truth.

That left the inevitable conclusion that Ben wasn't interested in her as more than a casual friend. Man, that thought hurt because the mysterious, quiet operative with shadows in his eyes intrigued her.

By the time the polished silver doors opened, Ruth had her game face on. After an inquiry at the nurses' station, she knocked on Trinity Edwards' door and walked into the room.

An auburn-haired woman stood, her jaw dropping. "Oh, wow. I can't believe you're here. I thought someone would bring a signed picture. I'm Anita, Trinity's mother."

Ruth smiled. "Since I was in town for a few days, I thought I'd drop in to see your daughter."

"I can't thank you enough." Her voice sounded choked. "You're all she talks about."

"Who is it, Mama?"

The soft voice drew Ruth further into the room. On the bed lay a young girl with a knitted hat on her head to cover her baldness. "Hello, Trinity."

The girl stared in disbelief before a wide smile curved her mouth. "Roxanne! You came. Mama said you would be too busy."

Ruth sat in the empty chair beside the bed. "I'm between jobs at the moment and thought I would surprise you. I brought you a gift." After a glance at Trinity's mother for permission, she gave Trinity the doll she'd mentioned saving up for in the letter she sent to Ruth. Although she felt weird about giving a Roxanne doll as a gift, she wanted Trinity to have another incentive to fight the disease attacking her fragile body.

"What is it?" Trinity's eyes lit as she accepted the gift bag.

"Open it and see. If you don't like it, I'll find something else for you that you'll like better."

"Go ahead, baby," Anita said.

The girl opened the bag and reached inside. When she pulled out the Roxanne doll, Trinity squealed in happiness. "Look, Mama. It's the Roxanne doll I wanted! Thank you, Roxanne."

Ruth grinned, some of her dark mood lifting. "Your email said that you are saving for the doll. Now, you can use the money to buy outfits or maybe a handsome escort for your doll."

She spent another ten minutes with Anita and Trinity when Ruth noticed the child's eyes were drooping. She rose and laid a hand on Trinity's shoulder. "I'd love to keep in touch with you. Is it all right if I email you once in a while to see how you're doing?"

The girl gave a sleepy smile. "I'd like that."

"I'll give your mom a card with an email address where you can contact me directly. I'll let you rest now."

A small nod and the child was asleep.

Ruth handed Anita a business card.

"Thank you so much for stopping by," Anita said, accepting the card. "Your visit means the world to both of us. My husband will be sorry he missed you. He's also a fan of yours."

"Maybe I'll have a chance to meet him the next time I see Trinity." She glanced at the sleeping girl. "What are the doctors saying about her?"

"They're optimistic. Even though this is her second bout with cancer, her body is responding very well to treatment."

"I'm relieved to hear that." After another minute, Ruth left the room and made her way to the parking garage where she'd left her SUV. Her lips curved. An SUV a certain mysterious operative had insisted she drive instead of the sweet little red sports car he'd labeled a deathtrap. She didn't know where he'd special-ordered the vehicle, but it felt heavier and more secure than anything she'd driven, and she loved it. Ruth frowned. Now that she thought about it, the SUV looked and rode like the one her sister and Trace drove. A month after she escaped Hugo, Ben had parked the SUV in her driveway and handed her the keys without an explanation.

As she walked toward her SUV, Ruth's skin pebbled again. Scowling, she spun, determined to find the person watching her and saw no one. For the first time, she feared that her time with Hugo had broken her in ways that couldn't be fixed. Was she going crazy despite her counselor's efforts to help her?

Gritting her teeth, Ruth clutched her purse close to her body and moved at a quick clip toward the darkened corner of the garage where she'd been forced to park. As she neared the SUV, she noticed a white envelope on the windshield.

A parking ticket? Couldn't be. This was a free parking garage provided courtesy of the hospital. Had someone dented her SUV? She circled the vehicle, looking for signs of damage. Nothing. Huh. Ruth unlocked the SUV and tossed her purse inside, then reached for the envelope.

Lifting the flap, she peered inside and gasped, horror filling her. Fighting not to throw up, she scrambled into her vehicle, locked the doors, and cranked the engine.

Gaze firing all around, she grabbed her purse and felt around the interior for her cell phone. Hand shaking, she pulled up her contact list. She would call Trace, but his team was out on a job somewhere and Bridget didn't know when they'd return. That meant Ben was also out of reach.

She selected the next best option on her call list and prayed as she drove from the garage. Looked like she wasn't crazy after all.

CHAPTER TWO

Ben Martin eased his Go bag from his shoulder and unlocked his SUV. Man, he was glad to be home. Three weeks in a cesspool chasing another scumbag human trafficker was three weeks too long. At least the outcome had been good.

He snorted. Right. Shadow, his black ops team, had freed the sex slaves, most of them children, but the damage had already been done. Some kids looked at him with terror in their eyes. The most damaged ones were resigned to yet another encounter with a child abuser.

Ben swallowed hard, shoving the painful memory behind an impenetrable wall to deal with later. He drove from the Fortress parking lot at John C. Tune Airport.

His cell phone rang. Frowning, he glanced at the readout on the dashboard and sighed. If the caller was anyone else, he'd let the call roll into voicemail. You didn't ignore the boss if you wanted to keep your job, and he definitely did. He loved working for Fortress. He tapped the screen. "Yes, sir?"

"My office, now."

Hands clenching the steering wheel in a white-knuckled grip, he said, "Shadow just got off the jet. I'm not good company right now." Understatement, that. He was lousy company. The thing he needed most was a hard, pounding workout, a long hot shower, and about twelve hours of uninterrupted sleep, provided the nightmares didn't catch up with him.

"Tough." Brent Maddox ended the call.

Ben growled and accelerated onto the interstate. Whatever the CEO of Fortress Security wanted better be quick to handle. Ben wouldn't be able to fake civility more than a few minutes without biting someone's head off or ending up kicked out on his butt. Maddox didn't put up with insubordination.

Forty minutes later after fighting through ugly Nashville traffic, Ben parked in the underground garage at Fortress headquarters and slammed his door, temper close to boiling over. He needed to wrangle the temper under control or his boss would do it for him after handing Ben his head on a platter.

He punched the elevator call button and stepped into the car. While the elevator rose to the appropriate floor, Ben took a minute to shove the temper and foul mood behind lock and key.

When he walked into Maddox's outer office, his assistant waved him through. Ben gave a perfunctory knock and opened the door. He pulled up short when he spotted the distinctive blond hair of the woman sitting in front of Maddox's desk. He stiffened, steeling his resolve yet again to resist the magnetic pull of the most beautiful woman he'd ever seen in his life.

Maddox motioned to the remaining empty chair. "Sit."

"What's going on?"

A scowl. "I'll explain when you sit down."

Jaw clenched, Ben dropped into the chair, aware of Ruth Monihan as he was of no other woman on the planet. He was also aware that she hadn't lifted her head to look at him since he arrived. What was up with that? He and Ruth were late night calling buddies, not strangers.

Although he wanted to demand answers from his boss, Ruth's continued silence concerned him. "Are you all right?" he asked her.

Ruth shook her head, arms crossed over her stomach as though protecting herself from a blow.

Not good. Adrenaline zipping through his veins, Ben looked at Maddox. "What happened?"

His boss slid an envelope across his desk to Ben. "Someone left this on her windshield today. We tested for fingerprints and found none except Ruth's."

Ben withdrew a single sheet of paper from the envelope. His eyes widened and his mouth grew dry at the picture of Ruth in a revealing long white dress. He frowned. Ruth looked like she was wearing a wedding dress. Where was this taken? This wasn't a photo shoot. She was walking into a room filled with people, her arm in the grip of a big bruiser.

Ben sucked in a breath as recognition hit him. The bruiser was one of Hugo Torino's men. Torino, a wannabe gunrunner, had kidnapped Ruth with the intent of forcing her to marry him. Ben and his teammates had freed Ruth, captured Torino, and tossed him to the feds. "Is Torino still locked up?"

A nod. "Zane checked with the feds and the prison. He's in isolation, unable to communicate with the outside world. This isn't his work."

"Doesn't mean one of his flunkies isn't out for revenge on his behalf."

Ruth shuddered.

"How did he or she get this picture?" The paper crinkled in Ben's fist.

"Z's working on it."

If anyone could nail the leak, it was Zane Murphy, Fortress Security's tech wizard and communications guru.

"I thought he was trolling the Internet for these pictures and deleting them."

A muscle in Maddox's jaw twitched, a sure sign of his growing irritation with Ben's questions or the edge in his voice. Probably both. "Ice it down, Martin."

Ben looked at Ruth. "Is this the only threat?" When she didn't respond, his suspicions rose. "Give us a minute, boss."

An eyebrow rose. "This is my office."

He glanced at Maddox. "Please."

The CEO stood. "Make Zane's job easier," he murmured and walked out, closing the door behind himself.

Ben watched Ruth for a moment, willing the model to break her silence and look at him. But the woman was stubborn, a trait he'd praised her for in the past few months. When Torino tried to break her down, Ruth refused to cede any ground to the creep. Although she'd never admitted it, Ben knew she paid a heavy price for refusing to cooperate with Torino's agenda. He hoped she shared the details with her counselor.

"Ruth, look at me."

She turned her face away.

Alarmed, he stood, reached down, and drew the model to her feet. With a gentle touch, Ben cupped her chin and tilted her face toward his. The fear and defeat in her eyes gutted him. "Talk to me. You've had other threats, haven't you?"

"Yes."

"Why didn't you tell me?"

"You've been gone. I didn't want to distract you. Your work is dangerous and I didn't know when you would return so I went to Brent. I knew he would help me."

He slid his hands down to hers and squeezed, shocked at the icy feel of her skin. "I'm always available to you unless I'm in the middle of an active operation. If I am, I'll call you as soon as I'm clear. You come to me if you're in trouble, Ruth." Ben didn't want to look deeper into his own motives for insisting that she turn to him first.

"I thought I was doing so well, and look at me. A picture made me panic and run."

"Hey, don't do that. You have legitimate reasons to be afraid after what happened with Torino. Remember what I've repeated to you since you escaped from that creep?"

She nodded. "Always trust my instincts."

"That's what you did. Your instincts told you this was a real threat and you listened. Being embarrassed because you overreacted is better than ignoring the danger and suffering the consequences. Tell me what I need to know to help you."

"I've been receiving email threats. Well, Roxanne has."

Ben scowled. "You have an agent. Why aren't your emails going through him?"

"They are, Ben, but he's overworked and just glances through things, then forwards them on to me. He didn't see these as threatening."

"You need someone to vet your email. You must receive hundreds of messages a week from your adoring fans."

Hurt flashed through her eyes at his acerbic comment. "There's no point in hiring anyone."

He blinked. "Why not?"

She waved his question aside. "It doesn't matter. I just want the threats to stop."

"Oh, they're going to stop, all right. I'll take care of it." And her, he silently vowed. No way was anyone going to threaten Ruth Monihan and get away with it.

"You're too busy, Ben."

"We just came off a three-week assignment. We're due for a break in another week." Sooner, if Ben had any say so in it. He didn't want to leave her vulnerable while Shadow was deployed on another mission. He couldn't protect her from halfway around the world. "Did you keep all the threats?"

She nodded.

"Good. We'll talk to Zane and let him work his magic." He hesitated. "Unless you'd rather have Bridget do the work." Bridget Young was Ruth's sister and newly married to Ben's teammate, Trace. She also worked in the Fortress research department.

"No. I don't want her to worry."

"She'll find out and be hurt that you didn't come to her with this. She's a good researcher. Bridget could have tracked down the sender or enlisted Zane's help if she ran into a roadblock. Because you're at risk, Trace will want to know, and he doesn't keep secrets from his wife."

Ruth sighed. "I know. The pictures bothered me, but I didn't feel like I was in danger until I found that last one on my SUV. I planned to tell you when you returned."

"How long have you been receiving threats?"

"They started right after you left on this latest assignment."

"Where were you parked when you received the latest threat?"

"In the parking garage at Vanderbilt Hospital."

He stilled. "Why were you there? Are you sick or hurt?" Ben scanned her quickly and saw nothing he didn't usually see. Perfection.

"I'm fine. I was visiting a young girl with cancer. She wrote to Roxanne and Rich, my agent, forwarded the message because I have a soft spot for kids."

A kid. Ben's gut twisted. "What are her chances?"

"Good, I think. The doctors are optimistic."

He relaxed. Ben refocused his thoughts. "This is the first time you've received a threat aside from email?"

Again, she hesitated.

Seriously? "Ruth."

"I can't swear that the other threats were meant as one."

He scowled. "Details, Monihan."

That brought a small smile to her lips. "Someone left a gift on my dressing table at the photographer's studio in New York."

"What was it?"

"A beautiful basket of strawberries."

"Why is that a problem? You eat fruit all the time." He didn't know how she had enough energy to live and work based on what she ate every day. Rabbit food and fruit with a little lean protein thrown in to liven things up. He'd starve on that boring diet. His taste buds needed pizza and hamburgers to stay engaged. Lasagna was also high on his list of favorites. All those choices were things that Ruth couldn't eat because of her job's weight constraints.

"I don't eat strawberries. I'm allergic to them."

Huh. How did he not know this? He'd been talking to her for months, yet she had never mentioned the problem. "A severe allergy?"

"I carry an epinephrine pen wherever I go."

"What did you do with the strawberries?"

"Added them to the community food table." Her beautiful mouth curved into a full-blown smile. "You wouldn't be surprised to know that the food consisted of fruit and vegetables. The strawberries fit right in."

He rolled his eyes. Of course they did. "What else have you received?"

"A dozen roses." Her smile faded and she dropped her gaze to his chest.

Jealousy flared inside Ben. "I thought all women liked to get flowers."

"Not black roses."

His eyes narrowed. Black, as in a death threat. She deserved bright yellow roses, the color of sunshine. "Was there a card attached?"

She shook her head. "I thought the card fell on the ground, but I couldn't find one."

"Anything else?"

"No. I was going to tell you everything when you returned home, Ben."

He squeezed her hands again. "I believe you." And because he did, some of the tension that had been eating a hole in his stomach since he walked into his boss's office began to melt away. Although he wouldn't tell Ruth the truth, Ben needed her trust. "We should let Maddox back into his office," he said and released Ruth's hands with more reluctance than was wise for either of them. "Have a seat. We'll be here a while." His boss would mine for more gems of knowledge as long as he thought there was useful information to find.

Ben opened the door, signaled his boss, and returned to his seat beside Ruth. As soon as Maddox sat in his desk chair, Ben said, "We need Zane, too."

His boss flicked a glance at Ruth, then called the communications expert and asked him to join them. That done, he asked Ruth, "Do you need anything? Water, herbal tea, a soft drink?"

"Herbal tea sounds perfect. No sweetener. I don't think I could stomach water or a soft drink." She wrinkled her nose. "I don't have soft drinks often anyway."

"Nothing with strawberries," Ben added. "She's allergic." Might as well let the people who would be around Ruth know about the problem.

"Good to know. Coffee, Ben?"

Thinking of the potentially sleepless night ahead if his plans proceeded like he thought, he nodded his acceptance.

Maddox stepped to his office door and spoke to his assistant, then moved back to admit a dark-haired man in a wheelchair.

Zane Murphy smiled at Ruth. "Good to see you again. I didn't know you were in town."

"I'm only here for another day. I have a photoshoot the day after tomorrow."

Ben frowned. She couldn't be serious. Someone was stalking her, and she was going to pose in front of a camera?

Zane shifted his attention to Ben. "Glad you're back in one piece, Ben. Heard it got hot."

He wasn't talking about the weather though that was hot as blazes as well. Ben hated jungle missions with a white-hot passion. "We handled the heat. It's what we do."

"Why do I have the feeling you're not talking about the weather?" Ruth muttered with a cute scowl on her face.

He was saved from having to think up a neutral response by the arrival of the drinks. Ruth wrapped her hands around the mug of tea and sipped the weak-looking brew with evident pleasure.

After a sip of his coffee, Maddox set his mug on the desk and leaned back in his chair. "Let's hear it, Ben."

He recounted all the information Ruth had shared with him in the past few minutes and waited.

"Stalker," Zane said, eyes glittering.

"Maybe. There are other possibilities, including one of Torino's crew looking for payback." Maddox pinned Ben with his gaze although he addressed Ruth with his next question. "You have any unwanted male attention coming your way, Ruth?"

Ben straightened. Maddox thought he might be the stalker? His cheeks burned, temper spiking again. He held it in check. Barely. A heavy workout couldn't come fast enough although he most likely wouldn't have a chance to get one in now. "Thanks for the vote of confidence, Brent."

"Zip it. Ruth, answer the question."

Ruth's gaze shifted from Brent to Ben and back, uneasiness and the beginnings of fear in her body language. "I always have unwanted attention. It comes with the job."

"You sidestepped my meaning on purpose. Try again, Ruth. Are you receiving unwanted attention from Ben?"

"No! We're friends."

A nasty mix of bitterness and disappointment brewed in Ben's gut. Being relegated to the friend zone hurt although that's all they could ever be. Anything more would put her in the crosshairs of his enemies. He couldn't be in her world and she didn't belong in his. End of discussion. So why did he want to argue the point?

"Ben would never stalk me," Ruth insisted. "If he was interested, he'd come right out and stake his claim."

Zane chuckled. "Subtlety is not his one of his strengths."

"Not helping, Z," Ben said.

"What are friends for?"

He ignored the tease and focused on his boss. "Ruth needs a protection detail. The stalker is growing bolder. The first threats were emailed pictures. The flowers and strawberries were delivered to the studio where she was working." He tapped the picture from her SUV. "This last picture was placed on her personal vehicle. The stalker is actively following her. He's escalating." Ben had to stop him before the stalker did more than scare Ruth. The likelihood that sooner or later he would hurt Ruth was unacceptable.

"Agreed. As of this moment, your new assignment is to serve as Ruth's bodyguard. Coordinate with the other members of Shadow. They're due to arrive in the conference room in thirty minutes."

Ben froze. Dismay filled him. He couldn't be Ruth's bodyguard if he wanted to survive.

CHAPTER THREE

Drawing in a careful breath, Ben looked at Zane. "Would you escort Ruth to the conference room? I need a minute with the boss."

"Sure." Zane scooted his chair back to allow Ruth to go ahead of him. "While we're waiting for the others, you can give me your email address and password and I'll start tracking the threat sender." He closed the office door.

"Assign someone else to protect Ruth." Ben's hands fisted. Although handing responsibility for her safety to someone else was the last thing he wanted to do, it was best for them both.

"Why?"

He scowled. "You know why. I have a long list of enemies."

"We all do, including your teammates."

"They don't have a price on their head at the moment. I do. I can protect Ruth from her stalker, but who will protect her from my past?"

"She needs you, not some other operative."

"I wouldn't hand responsibility for her safety to just any operative. I planned to handpick the candidate."

"No."

Anger flashed through Ben. "I'm better off in the shadows, Brent. Why are you being unreasonable?"

"You know why. No one else will be able to secure her cooperation like you, not even Trace. Every male operative who knows what happened in Mexico treats her as though she's the walking wounded and they're afraid to tell her no, even if it's for her own protection."

"I'll talk to her. She'll cooperate with the bodyguard."

"You have an advantage over everyone else."

His eyebrow rose.

"She trusts you."

"She shouldn't."

"It's necessary for the success of this op."

Ben tilted his head, analyzing the overtone in his boss's voice. Maddox's skill at strategy was legendary. He had something planned, something he hadn't shared yet. Whatever it was, Ben was positive he wouldn't like it. "What haven't you told me?"

"You're going into this mission as more than a hired bodyguard."

Dread coiled like a snake in his gut, waiting to strike. Ben already knew where Maddox was headed with this discussion. He wanted to refuse and walk out, but that would leave Ruth more vulnerable. "How much more?"

"You're going undercover as her boyfriend."

And there it was. The one thing he knew was the worst-case scenario for Ruth's wellbeing. "No."

Maddox frowned. "You don't get a vote, Martin. Find a way to make it work. The assignment stands as is."

He sighed. He'd lost this battle and knew it. That tone of voice brooked no more argument. How would he survive the coming days? More important, how would he protect an innocent like Ruth Monihan from him and his enemies? "You heard her. Ruth has a photoshoot in two days."

"Then you and your teammates have plans to make. Dismissed."

Jaw clenched, Ben left the office before his fury and frustration spilled over onto his boss and cost Ben a job he loved, one that kept him sane. Maddox's assistant tossed him a sympathetic look as she answered an incoming call.

In the hallway, he turned away from the conference room and headed for the breakroom instead. He needed a minute to get himself under control before he joined Ruth.

When he walked into the breakroom, Ben snagged two bottles of water and a banana. Ruth probably hadn't eaten anything in hours. Since she was working in front of the camera soon, he wouldn't ply her with fattening food, but he would insist that Ruth eat something.

Before he left the room, he took a minute to shore up his control and stuff the demons of his past behind an impenetrable wall. A temporary fix, but that's all he had time for. Anything more extensive would have to wait a better time. When that would be was anyone's guess.

Ben knew exactly what Maddox hoped for. If the stalker wanted Ruth for himself, he'd see Ben as a rival. If he was enraged enough at the challenge to his perceived territory, he'd make a run at Ben. Fine. The sooner that happened, the better for all of them. He was meant for the shadows, not the light. The sooner he crawled back where he belonged, the better for all of them, especially Ruth.

Enough stalling. His teammates would gather in the conference room soon and Ben needed a minute with Ruth before they arrived. He strode to the conference room, nodding to a colleague who greeted him in the hall.

Ruth glanced at Ben when he walked in. Relief and a warm welcome filled her gaze.

That look hit him straight in the heart. Man, this was a disaster in the making. He wasn't good enough for this woman. "I brought you a snack."

She smiled. "You're always feeding me."

"You need to eat more."

"Not if I want to keep my job."

A job he hated. Probably made him a Neanderthal of the lowest order, but he hated knowing men across the world were looking at Ruth and wondering what it would be like to have her for their own.

"I have to return to the comm center," Zane said and spun his wheelchair toward the door. "I'll get back to you about the origin of the emails when I come up with anything."

"Thanks, Z." Ben closed the door behind his friend and crossed the space that separated him from Ruth in a few long strides. He set the water and banana on the table and turned to her. "We need to talk."

What little color she had in her cheeks drained away. "What's happened?"

"Nothing yet."

Her brows knitted. "You're not going to act as my bodyguard, are you? I could tell you didn't want the assignment." Her voice carried disappointment and worry.

"I'm going to protect you. I don't trust anyone else to do it."

"But you don't want to do it."

"No, I don't."

She started to turn away, her expression revealing her hurt.

He caught her by her upper arms and turned her to face him. "Don't. It's not what you think."

"What's to misunderstand? You've made your feelings clear. You don't want to be around me."

"That's not the issue."

"Then what is?"

"I'm not safe to be around, Ruth."

She stared. "That's ridiculous. I only feel safe when I'm with you."

His grip tightened. "I have a lot of enemies. Any number of them would love to put a bullet in my head. I don't want you caught in the crossfire."

Harsh laughter burst from her. "Looks like I'm already in someone's crosshairs. What's a few more? Ben, I trust you to keep me safe."

"I hope so because this assignment will require that you trust me implicitly."

"What do you mean?"

He edged a little closer, watching for signs of fear or distress. Relieved when there weren't any, he said, "Maddox knows you trust me, and he chose me for a specific role in addition to bodyguard for that reason."

"I don't understand."

But she did. The knowledge was in her eyes. "Yes, you do. The boss wants me to act like I'm your boyfriend."

Ruth dragged in a ragged breath. "No!"

Ben let go of her. This wasn't going to work, no matter what his boss wanted. If she was terrified of him, he couldn't do the job properly. Maddox would have to come up with something else, maybe assign a female bodyguard to protect Ruth. Ben would return to the shadows and do what he did best. Hunt in the darkness.

He started to turn away when Ruth's hand on his arm froze him in place. This was the first time she had reached out to touch him of her own volition.

"Ben, please, look at me."

His gaze locked with hers.

She closed the gap he'd created. "Any woman would be honored to have you for a boyfriend, including me. I don't want this arrangement because I'm in the spotlight all the time. You just said there are people who want to kill you. As soon as the media gets wind of a man in my life, they'll be relentless. Your face will be splashed all over the world. I don't want you to die protecting me. You mean too much to me."

His heart skipped a beat at that last statement. What did that mean? "A boyfriend is the best way to flush out your stalker. He'll come after anyone he sees as a challenge to his claim. If you won't accept me at your side, will you be comfortable allowing another male operative in that role?"

She flinched. "Don't ask me to do that. I can't. Not after...."

Not after the abuse she'd suffered at Tornio's hands. Moving slowly so he wouldn't spook her, Ben wrapped his arms around her and tucked her against his chest.

Mistake. Such a huge mistake. Ruth fit against him like she'd been made for him. How would he place distance between them when her stalker was caught and the mission ended?

"What are we going to do?" she whispered, her head resting over his heart.

"Whatever is necessary to flush out your stalker. In order to carry off this ruse, I'll have to touch you when we're in public. People expect certain behavior between dating couples. Will you be able to tolerate my touch?"

Her mouth curved a little. "I'm not having a problem now, am I?"

Yeah, but how long would it last and would she be able to handle more than one touch? "If we do this, I'll be holding your hand and touching your back, arms, and shoulders as often as possible for the next two days. We have to make sure you don't flinch away from me. Someone will notice and report the odd behavior. That will torpedo our plan before we have a chance to spring the trap."

"I still don't like it," she murmured.

He stilled. His touch? "What don't you like?"

"Putting you in danger."

Ben tapped her nose in a gentle reprimand. "Ruth, my job is dangerous. Dealing with a stalker is less problematic than running down terrorists and human traffickers."

She gave a huff of laughter. "Well, when you put it that way, this situation doesn't sound all that bad."

Yeah, except for the part where he would have a target on his back from the moment his face appeared in the media. Ben cupped her cheek. "I've missed hearing your laughter the past three weeks," he murmured.

The conference room door opened and Trace walked in. He stopped, eyebrows winging upward. "Something I need to know about?"

Ben shifted to stand beside Ruth. "I only want to give an explanation once. We'll wait until the others arrive." He pulled out a chair for Ruth and seated her.

Within minutes, Nico Rivera, his team leader, and Joe and Sam Gray joined them. When they were seated around the table, Nico said, "Sit rep, Ben."

He unfolded the picture that had been left on Ruth's windshield and slid it across the table. Trace's hands fisted as he stared at the picture.

"Where did you get that?" Joe asked.

"Someone left this on Ruth's windshield this afternoon."

Sam's eyes narrowed. "Did he or she leave a note?"

He shook his head. "This is only the latest in a string of contacts, each one more unsettling or threatening."

Trace scowled at Ruth. "Why didn't you tell me?"

"They started right after we left for our latest mission," Ben said. "Ruth's been receiving emails with pictures of her. The first three were photos of her taken at a distance. The quality is lousy so I'd say they were probably taken with a cell phone camera. The next three were pictures of her while she was at public events."

Nico tilted his head. "You're sure this isn't the work of an ardent fan? Ruth is well known all over the world."

"Roxanne is well known," Ben corrected. "Ruth is a small-town Tennessee girl, not a supermodel."

Joe's fingers played with his wife's hair. "To the public, there's no difference."

"We're not talking about an overly enthusiastic fan." Trace's words came out measured. "You think Ruth has a stalker."

"She also received two gifts, each delivered to the photography studio. The first was a basket of strawberries."

A snort from Trace. "Not exactly dangerous, Ben. Bridget eats them all the time."

"They can be deadly when you're allergic to them."

His teammates shifted their gazes to Ruth. "You're allergic to strawberries?" Sam asked.

She nodded. "I carry epinephrine with me at all times."

Trace whistled softly. "Your co-workers know about the allergy?"

Ruth shrugged. "Word gets around when you refuse all strawberries, but eat other types of fruit."

"What was the second gift?" Nico asked.

"A dozen black roses."

His teammates exchanged grim glances. "What do you need?" his team leader asked Ben.

"Backup. Maddox assigned me as Ruth's bodyguard." He slid a glance at Trace. "And as her boyfriend."

The silence was so absolute, the tick of the clock on the wall sounded loud.

Her brother-in-law stared hard at Ben, then shifted his attention to Ruth. "Look at me, sweet lady." When she complied, Trace asked in a soft voice, "Are you okay with this arrangement?"

"It's what Brent wants."

"That's not what I asked. If you're not comfortable with this, I'll talk to Maddox and we'll come up with a different plan. So I'll ask you again. Are you okay with this arrangement?"

Ruth's chin lifted, that familiar stubborn glint in her eyes. "I trust Ben. It's him or no one. The rest of the men in Shadow are married and it would be too uncomfortable to play out that role with you, Trace."

"What about another operative, one we trust?" Nico asked. "Cal Taylor, Rafe Torres, and Curt Jackson are in town without assignments."

She shuddered. "Ben or no one,' she repeated.

Ben wrapped his hand around Ruth's and squeezed in silent support. "Zane is already at work tracking down the emails. We have plans to make. Ruth has a photoshoot in two days. Everything needs to be in place before then."

A slow nod from Nico. "Let's get started."

CHAPTER FOUR

Ruth sat back after the brainstorming session, relieved the grilling was over for the moment. She hadn't been able to provide many satisfactory answers. As far as she knew, she didn't have enemies.

That left a stalker who wanted her for himself. Weren't stalkers the hardest to find? Dismay filled her at the prospect of not knowing who was after her for the foreseeable future. Ben and his friends couldn't protect her in the long term. They had more important jobs to do than babysitting a model receiving threatening pictures and questionable gifts.

If that wasn't enough to handle, her head ached and she was hungry. The banana Ben brought her was long gone. Being this hungry made her cranky. Sometimes she hated her job. Good thing a change was coming.

"Where is your photoshoot?" Nico asked.

"Puerto del Sol, Mexico."

The members of the Shadow team groaned. Trace dragged a hand down his face. "Of course it is." He glanced at Nico. "Why can't we take assignments in other, more friendly countries? I hear Switzerland is a beautiful place to visit."

The other man lifted one shoulder. "We go where we're sent."

Ruth frowned. "What's wrong with Mexico? The country is beautiful."

"Parts of it are beautiful," Joe agreed. "The problem is Fortress has a reputation in Mexico."

"What kind of reputation?"

"The kind that will get us killed if the wrong people find out who we are and who we work for." Ben's voice was rough, his expression resigned. "Shadow doesn't have friends in certain parts of the country."

"At least we're not going to the Chihuahua province," Joe said. "Is the photoshoot at the beach?"

She nodded. "We're doing advertisements for a new line of casual clothes."

"Swimsuits, too?"

Sam elbowed him.

Joe chuckled, rubbing at the spot she'd jabbed. "I was thinking about finding a new suit for you, Sparky."

"Good save," she muttered.

Ruth smiled, longing for that kind of close relationship with someone special in her life. With her job, though, men were more interested in her as an arm ornament than a true friend or potential mate. Aside from her sister, Bridget, Ruth's friend list was pitifully short. "We're modeling swimsuits, all sorts of casual clothes, and shoes. Beach wear for the best-dressed vacationer."

Ben looked at her. "How long is the job?"

"Three or four days. Depends on how fast Scott gets the perfect shots. He usually takes the full time allotted, if not more." Although the photographer was a tyrant on photoshoots, he was the most sought-after photographer in the business and brought the best out of his models.

"Scott?" Nico raised an eyebrow.

"Scott Barber. He's one of the few photographers that I work with."

"Don't you have to work with whoever is chosen for the job?" Sam asked.

"In the beginning of my career, I did. At this level, there are very few photographers chosen for the top models. I'm familiar with most of them. Scott is the best."

"I'll ask Zane to run his background." Ben grabbed his cell phone and set off a text. When he was finished, he said, "Do you know where you're staying while you're in Puerto del Sol?"

"Casa del Mar."

A soft whistle. "Nice hotel. Does someone make reservations for you?"

"My agent, Rich Eisenhower."

"I'll arrange for us to have a suite." Ben looked at Joe and Sam. "I'd like you to stay with us to help with guard shifts and to watch our backs."

"Be happy to stay in a luxury suite." Joe grinned. "Sure beats the accommodations we've had for the past three weeks."

Ruth twisted to face Ben. "Where were you?"

He snorted. "The hot, stinking jungle."

She blinked. "I'm not a fan of the jungle."

Nico chuckled. "Believe me, we aren't fond of it, either." He glanced at his team. "Go home and get some rest. I'm going to re-introduce myself to my wife. We'll meet tomorrow to analyze the security at Casa del Mar. We need to know the locations of your photoshoot, Ruth. Give Ben whatever information you have and he'll pass it along to the rest of us. I'll talk to Z about reserving a room for me and Trace at Casa del Mar."

Ben grabbed the empty water bottles and tossed them in the recycling bin before assisting Ruth to her feet. For a man who swore he was bad for her, Ben Martin always behaved like a gentleman and treated her with respect. He pressed his hand to the small of her back to guide her from the room, intentionally touching her so she would grow used to the contact.

Would he ever touch her voluntarily outside of this assignment? She shoved the thought aside. What she wanted didn't matter. What she needed was for Ben and his friends to smoke out the stalker and free her from his threats so she could get on with her life without fear.

They rode the elevator in silence. When they exited in the underground parking garage, Ben steered her toward his SUV.

"I drove myself here."

"You're not driving yourself anywhere else until the threat is neutralized." He glanced at her. "Do you need anything from your vehicle?"

She shook her head.

After helping her into the passenger seat, Ben circled the hood and climbed behind the wheel. "You hungry?"

"Starving."

"So am I. I know the perfect place to take you. It's quiet and exclusive, so we won't have to worry about any news media stalking you just yet." He held up his hand before she could say anything. "Don't worry. The restaurant has selections that will fit your dietary restrictions and mine."

She rolled her eyes as he drove from the Fortress compound. "You don't have dietary restrictions. I don't know how you eat so much and yet never seem to gain an ounce of weight."

He flicked her a glance. "I'm not worried about a few extra ounces on my frame. We train for hours a day and burn a lot of calories on missions and off. We have to be in top shape to do our jobs."

"Must be nice."

"You don't have to model, Ruth. There must be something else that interests you."

She twisted in her seat to study his profile. "Several things. What about you?"

He frowned. "What about me?"

"Are you interested in another job?"

"No. This is what I'm trained for and I'm good at it."

She believed that after seeing what he was capable of when he and his teammates rescued her. "Have you always worked for Fortress?"

Another quick glance before he returned his attention to the road. "No. Fortress is only a few years old. Maddox started the company when he mustered out of the Navy."

"Brent was a sailor?" He seemed more than that to her, but what did she know about black ops work?

"He was a SEAL."

Ruth's breath caught. "Are you serious?"

"Oh, yeah. He was one of the best of Tier 1 operators. There aren't many like him."

Something in Ben's voice sparked her suspicions. "What about you? Were you in the military before you signed on with Fortress?"

"Yes, ma'am. I was a SEAL for ten years."

She sat in silence, stunned at the revelation. How had she never figured out that the man she called in the middle of the night when she couldn't sleep was one of the most elite warriors on the planet?

"Does that bother you?" Although Ben's voice was soft, his white-knuckled grip on the steering wheel told Ruth her answer mattered.

"Why should it? You gave ten years of your life to protect our country. You deserve accolades for your sacrifice."

"Don't make me out to be a hero. I'm the farthest thing from a hero than you can imagine."

"I don't believe that."

"Do you know what my specialty is?"

"How could I? You never talk about your work."

"I'm an EOD man."

"EOD?"

"Explosive ordinance disposal."

"You handle bombs?" Her heart skipped a beat. Dangerous work. One slip and he would be blown to tiny bits. She could lose him in a heartbeat if he made a mistake. The void his loss would leave in her life was unspeakable. Her hand fisted. "I assume you're good at what you do."

"Very."

Despite her uneasiness at his admission, Ruth had to smile at that simple statement of fact. "Were you EOD as a SEAL?"

He nodded. "My secondary specialty was K-9." A smile curved his mouth. "My German shepherd, Daisy, had the best nose. She could sniff out explosives better than the other military working dogs."

"What happened to her?"

"She was retired four years before I left the SEALs. After that, I worked without a furry partner."

"Do you know what happened to her?"

"She went to live with her former handler in California. He sent me pictures of her lazing around in the sun and running through a field. She lived a good, long life before passing away from old age in her sleep." He slid her another glance. "I defuse bombs, Ruth. I can also construct them."

"I imagine that skill comes in handy on your missions."

A huff of laughter escaped. "Yes, it does."

After that, conversation remained in neutral territory while Ben drove to the restaurant. Ruth relaxed when he parked in the lot of Damien's, a high-end steak house. Perfect. She loved this place although she didn't often have the time to stop here and eat. The food was excellent and the service superb, the whole experience unhurried. And best of all, the food selection included things that fit in her diet plan. "Thanks for bringing me here. I love Damien's."

Ben smiled. "It's good to see you smile." He came around the vehicle to open her door.

Inside the restaurant, they were seated at the corner table in the back and were soon ordering their meals. Once the waiter left, Ben covered Ruth's hand with his own. "Tell me about Scott Barber."

"You asked Zane to run a background check on him."

"Tell me what you know and your impressions of him. Every scrap of information will make our job easier."

She frowned. "You think Scott is behind the threats?"

"Everyone is a suspect until we rule them out."

His thumb brushed the back of her wrist, distracting her. Why did his touch send sparks flying through her veins? "Scott is the top fashion photographer. He's a little quirky, but he gets results."

"Quirky?"

"Scott doesn't like extra people around when he's working a photoshoot. He's hands-on with the models."

His hand tightened. "He puts his hands on you?"

"Just to move us around if we don't understand what stance he wants."

"Are you okay with that?"

She shrugged. Not really, but how could she complain? He wasn't singling her out and he never placed his hands in inappropriate places. Before her experience with Hugo, Scott's quirkiness hadn't bothered her. Now, however, she struggled not to jerk out of his hold. Of course, that was true for any man who touched her except for Ben. She didn't have trouble with his touch, even when they were doing self-defense training.

"What else do you know about him?"

"He's been divorced four times."

Ben's jaw dropped. "Are you serious?"

"Scott's a charmer and loves women, especially models. All four of his wives modeled for him. He has a problem with fidelity. He's surrounded by beautiful women all the time and can't resist when one of them makes a play for him."

"Has he shown that kind of interest in you?" he asked, voice gruff.

"Not since the first time I modeled for him. He seemed puzzled when I turned him down."

"Did he accept the shutdown?"

"I haven't had any problems with him."

"What about your agent? Tell me about him."

"Rich is a great guy. He's been my agent since the start of my career."

"Married?"

"Yes, for more than thirty years to an interior designer. They have three kids, all adults, and four grandchildren with a fifth on the way. He's a good man, Ben. Rich and Amalie, his wife, were some of the first people to reach out to me and Bridget when our parents died. He rearranged my contracts to allow me time to grieve their loss, then helped with the details of their estate. I'm telling you, he's not the stalker. He's like a father figure to me."

"How did you meet him?"

She smiled. "My friends and I went to the mall at Green Hills to shop. Rich was there to scout for new talent. He saw me and convinced me to pose for a few pictures. Things just snowballed from there."

The waiter brought their orders soon afterward. By the time they finished their meals, the tension that had gripped Ruth from the moment she spotted the envelope on her windshield had melted away. As they walked from the restaurant, Ben wrapped his arm around her shoulders, his touch light.

He guided her toward his SUV. Somewhere close, an engine idled. As they made their way down the aisle, the headlights of a vehicle flashed on, the beams on high. The driver gunned the engine. Tires squealed.

Ruth squinted at the oncoming headlights as the vehicle barreled down on them.

CHAPTER FIVE

Ben grabbed Ruth and leaped away from the path of the oncoming car. Still holding tight, he flipped their positions as they fell to ensure he hit the ground first. Immediately, he rolled to cover her body with his in case bullets started to fly.

The car zoomed past, the front end clipping bumpers of cars on either side of them, and raced from the lot.

He lifted his weight from Ruth. "Are you okay?"

"I'm good. You?"

"Same. I'd call that a win for the good guys." He grabbed his phone as he extended a hand to help her sit up. When his call was answered a moment later, he said, "I need you to access traffic cams at 10th and Sycamore Drive."

"Hold," Zane said. The sounds of his keyboard clicking drifted from the phone's speaker. A moment later, "Got it. What am I looking for?"

"A dark green car, four doors, fairly new. The driver tried to run us over and sped off going east on Sycamore. I want the plates so we can find this clown." He wanted to have a discussion with the driver that might or might not include the use of his fists.

More keys clicking, then, "No plates."

Ben growled. "Track it as long as you can. Maybe we'll get lucky." He wasn't holding his breath, though. His luck was never that good.

"Copy that. Any injuries?"

"We're fine."

"I'll get back to you when I have something."

Ben slid his phone away and helped Ruth stand. "Let's get out of here."

"What about the damage to these cars?"

"I'm more concerned with your safety than sticking around to be a witness on a hit-and-run in a parking lot." Determined to get Ruth into the safety of his vehicle before any other mishaps befell them, he wrapped his arm around her waist and tucked her tight against his side. If he'd been a step slower in recognizing the danger bearing down on them, the green car would have hit Ruth.

Had the stalker escalated or was this about Ben? He scowled. This was exactly the reason he didn't want to be assigned as Ruth's bodyguard/boyfriend. He was just as much a danger to her as her stalker. The thought of another man taking on this role with Ruth made Ben grit his teeth in frustration with himself and the situation. He couldn't have it both ways. Ruth wasn't for him. She deserved better than a man with his background who might cost Ruth her life.

Ben hurried her across the lot, unlocked his SUV, and breathed easier after enclosing her inside his reinforced ride. He slid behind the wheel and drove away from the restaurant as patrons streamed from the building to investigate the commotion.

He took Interstate 40 and headed for Ruth's home. Noticing her trembling, Ben warmed the temperature to help her combat the shock and threaded his fingers through hers. "You'll be okay in a few minutes."

"I can't stop shaking." Her teeth began to chatter.

"It's adrenaline dump. We have to deal with it on missions."

"I'm not a f-f-fan."

He chuckled. "I hear you." He turned on the heater in her seat. Three exits later, he saw a coffee shop that served hot tea and took the exit and pulled into the shop's drive-thru lane. He ordered hot tea for her and black coffee for himself. He was dealing with his own case of adrenaline surge and knew he'd need caffeine to keep himself awake through the night. Didn't help that he couldn't sleep on the jet on the way home.

Ben sighed. Looked like he would have to call on one of his friends to help him keep watch. He preferred one of the Shadow unit, but they were as tired as he was.

Two minutes later, he accelerated onto the interstate and resumed his journey toward her home. "I'll be staying with you tonight, either on the couch or in my SUV in front of your house. It's your choice where I stay, but you don't have another option. After this incident, I won't leave you alone."

"I have the alarm system that Trace had put into the house. He told me it was the best Fortress had to offer."

"No system is foolproof. Won't hurt to have your own personal guard dog as extra insurance."

"Don't be ridiculous, Ben. You must be exhausted. Go home to sleep. I'll be safe."

He shook his head. "This isn't negotiable, Ruth. I'll need someone to help me keep watch. He's a good friend, someone I trust at my back."

She sipped her tea. "Who?"

"Either Rafe Torres or Cal Taylor."

"I've met Cal. He used to be a cop, right?"

He relaxed. Good. If she knew Cal, having him in her home should be easier to handle. "A detective with Metro Police. He's just returned from a short assignment and should be available to give me a hand. Will you be comfortable if I call him in?"

Ruth glared at him. "I'm not that fragile. I'll be fine, especially if he spells you so you can sleep. Otherwise, you'll be awake all night to protect me."

He kissed the back of her hand lightly. "Sorry, sunshine. I forget about that steel spine of yours."

"I'll be sure to remind you when the occasion calls for it. Why did you call me sunshine?"

"You remind me of a beam of sunlight spearing through the clouds on a gloomy day." He wanted to laugh at himself. Listen to him waxing poetic. The truth was, Ruth was the sunshine to his darkness. She lit up a room when she walked in.

Her fingers tightened on his. "I like it. No one's called me by a nickname that meant something since I lost my father." Ruth settled deeper into the seat and sipped her tea as the minutes passed in silence.

Ben divided his attention between her, the road in front of him, and the mirrors. Although it wouldn't be a stretch to realize he was taking her home, he didn't like surprises. He activated his Bluetooth and called Cal.

"Yeah, Taylor."

"It's Ben. I need a favor."

"What do you need?"

"Help with a night shift."

"When and where?"

He gave his friend the details and received immediate agreement to lend a few hours to keep watch. "Thanks, Cal."

"Yep. See you in a few minutes." He ended the call.

"He must be a good friend." Ruth set her tea in the cup holder.

"Why do you say that?"

"Cal agreed to help without any convincing or asking who he was guarding."

"He's a good man."

"Why did he apply to Fortress?"

He glanced at her. "No one applies to work at Fortress. Maddox approaches you after a careful vetting process. Cal has had an open invitation to join Fortress for five years."

She frowned. "Why?"

"He was one of Maddox's teammates. He resigned from the police department and threw in with us full time when he'd had enough of working within the confines of the law."

When she lapsed into silence again, Ben retained his hold on her hand. He rationalized it as helping her become used to his touch. While it was true, his real motivation was pure pleasure in the connection. Her skin was like living silk. Warm, soft, delicate. He figured indulging himself for a short time wouldn't hurt.

He checked on her a short while later and saw that she was asleep. Good. Maybe by the time they reached her home she'd feel better.

Thirty minutes later, he parked in the driveway of Ruth's house and scanned the area. Nothing looked disturbed, but he wouldn't allow her too far into the house until he'd checked the rooms for intruders.

He exited the SUV and circled the vehicle to open Ruth's door. "Hey, Sleeping Beauty. Time to wake up."

Ruth raised her eyelids and looked around in confusion. "We're home already?"

Ben chuckled as he escorted her to the front door. "You slept for almost an hour. Feel better?"

She nodded. "I'm sorry I didn't help you keep watch for someone following us."

"Figured out what I was doing, huh?"

"Hard to miss the vigilant super spy routine."

When they reached her porch, Ben held out his hand. "Keys. I want to clear the house before you go beyond the front door."

She handed over the keys without argument and told him the alarm code. Nudging her behind him, he unlocked the door. Sig in hand, he entered the house and keyed in the alarm code. He was almost sure the house hadn't been breached, but he wouldn't take chances with Ruth's safety.

He returned to the porch and tugged her inside. After closing the door, he whispered, "Wait here until I return." Remembering the layout from the night he'd been Trace's backup while protecting Bridget, Ben cleared her colonial-style two-story house room by room and found it empty of threats. Nothing appeared disturbed.

Returning the Sig to his holster, he retraced his steps to Ruth. "It's clear."

Relief shone in her eyes. "Good." She went to the kitchen and began to make coffee. "I'm assuming either you or Cal will want coffee to help you stay awake tonight."

"Smart lady."

When the doorbell rang, Ruth's hand jerked and spilled coffee beans on the counter.

"Easy. That's probably Cal. Your stalker would have to be deranged to announce himself by ringing the bell." He squeezed her shoulder as he moved past her.

After checking the peephole, Ben opened the door to the former police detective. "You made good time."

A snort from his friend. "For once, there wasn't a traffic accident to work around. Who's the principal?"

Ruth's soft voice sounded from the kitchen entrance. "I am, Cal. Thanks for agreeing to help out tonight."

Cal turned, a smile curving his mouth. "Good to see you again, Ruth, although I'm sorry it's under these circumstances." He turned back to Ben. "What are we dealing with?"

"Stalker."

The smile faded. "You have leads?"

"A few. He's been sending pictures to her email, a delivery of strawberries, a fruit she's allergic to, and a dozen black roses. Today, he left a picture on her SUV's windshield and we were nearly hit in the parking lot of Damien's tonight."

A scowl. "He's escalating."

"Zane is tracking the car as far as he can with traffic cams, but the car didn't have plates."

"What about the emails?"

"The Internet search is in progress as we speak."

A slow nod. "When did Shadow return?"

"A few hours ago."

"Ah. I'll take the first shift and stick around in case you need an assist."

"Appreciate it." Ben looked at Ruth. "Will the coffee be ready soon?"

Her eyes narrowed. "Is that a hint to leave the room so the super operatives can confer with each other without alarming the fragile victim?"

"It's a request for your magic elixir, Ruth, not a comment on your spine or your courage."

"Why don't I believe you? Your magic elixir will be ready in a few minutes." She whirled and disappeared into the kitchen.

"Whew. The lady is seriously irritated. I don't envy you at all. Now, tell me the rest," Cal murmured, his gaze locked on Ben's.

In as little detail as possible, he relayed her experience with Torino and Maddox's order for Ben to act as Ruth's boyfriend to draw out her stalker.

"What do you know about her personal life?"

He shrugged. "We're friends. We talk." A lot. Hours at a time, hours that he was able to relax and let down his guard.

"Does she have a boyfriend or an ex who doesn't want to let go of one of the most beautiful women on the planet?"

"She hasn't mentioned one." He shoved the jealousy behind a mental wall, reminding himself again that she wasn't for him. Ruth deserved someone better.

"Find out everything about her dating history."

Ben eased the curtain aside from the front window. So far, nothing had changed since he and Ruth arrived at the house. "You think it's someone she knows?"

"It's a good place to start from this end while Z tracks the Internet trail. Did you spot a tail going to Damien's?"

He flashed his friend a pointed look.

Cal held up his hands. "I had to ask. I'm assuming you didn't announce in public where you were taking her for a meal. If you weren't followed, how did the stalker know where Ruth was?"

"I don't know. I drove my SUV. The only thing Ruth brought with her was her purse. Her vehicle is in the underground garage at Fortress. Are you thinking a tracker?"

"Makes the most sense unless you missed a tail." Cal leaned one shoulder against the wall on the opposite side of the window and eased the curtain aside to peer through the window. "There's only one way to find out."

Hoping he wasn't about to make Ruth more angry, Ben walked to the entrance of the kitchen. "Do you mind if I search your purse?"

The model spun around, eyes wide. "Why?"

"Eliminating the possibility that someone planted a tracker in your bag. Dinner at Damien's was a spur of the moment decision and I didn't spot a tail going to the restaurant."

She waved him on. "I don't have anything to hide. Go ahead."

"Thanks."

He snagged her bag from the couch where she'd tossed it. Unzipping it, he dumped the contents on the coffee table and sifted through the contents. A packet of tissues, three tubes of lipstick, a compact of pressed powder, pens, gum, a small mirror, brush, keys, two epinephrine pens, and her cell phone. When he turned her cell phone over, the screen lit up with a picture of him.

Ben froze. When did she take that? Frowning, he studied the shot. This was taken at Nico and Mercy's house last month before Shadow was deployed. The couple had invited the unit plus Bridget and Ruth, since she was in town that weekend. Why did she have his picture as her screen saver? Never mind that he had a picture of her on his phone, too. Like he'd told her, Ruth was a ray of sunshine in his dark world. Sometimes when the missions were ugly or the nights hard, he took a minute to enjoy the sunshine before he got on with what had to be done.

"Find anything?" Cal asked.

Nothing he wanted to discuss with the other operative. "Not yet." Ben checked everything, including Ruth's cell phone cover, for a tracker, leaving the packet of tissues for last.

He picked up the folded pack and separated the sections. After pulling the tissues out, he checked inside the compartments. In the left one, he found a small black disk. "Cal."

His friend crouched in front of the coffee table and examined the disk. "This tracker is available for purchase on the Internet. Cheap construction, but it works."

"Think we can trace it?"

Cal picked up the tracker and turned it over. The surface near the bottom of the disk was scratched. "Nope. The number we could have used to trace the origin is defaced. At least you know how the stalker found you tonight."

"We also know he had access to her purse. I want to know how long he's been keeping track of her movements."

Ruth walked in with a mug of coffee in each hand. "The coffee is black. Do you want cream or sugar?"

Both men shook their heads. "We don't have access to sugar or cream when we're on missions," Cal said. "Thanks for making coffee."

"Sure." She handed Ben his mug. "Did you find anything?"

"Take a look." He indicated the black disk.

Ruth frowned. "What's that?"

"A tracker. Someone has been keeping tabs on your movements. That's how he found us at Damien's."

She paled. "Then he knows we're here. Should we go somewhere else for the night?"

"No need. That's why we have Cal with us. Besides, after that miss in the parking lot, I doubt he'll regroup fast enough to try again tonight. When are you supposed to leave for Mexico?"

"Tomorrow night."

"Did your agent handle the arrangements?"

She nodded.

"Send him a text. Tell him you're going to make alternate arrangements. You'll fly down on a Fortress jet. I don't want you on a commercial plane."

"He'll want to know why."

"Tell him you're flying down with your boyfriend. Word will get around faster. That's what we want." Ben handed over her cell phone and grabbed his own, sending a text to Nico about the timeline for leaving.

His team leader acknowledged the text a minute later, promising to relay the news to the rest of the team.

Ruth picked up her cell phone and called her agent. After convincing Rich to cancel her plane ticket, she spent several minutes discussing the upcoming photoshoot and children's charity event.

Ben frowned. Bad enough that she would be on Casa del Mar's beach in plain sight of anyone with a scope. Protecting her on that beach would be a nightmare. Now, he had to factor in security arrangements for a children's charity fundraiser. The only bright spot was the fundraiser was being held at Casa del Mar.

He shot another text to Nico and Zane with the new information. Shadow would be studying schematics for the hotel plus analyzing the route to and from the airstrip, looking for security threats. Ben rubbed his jaw, bristles rasping against his fingers. He'd need an army to do this right and blanket Ruth with enough coverage to satisfy his driving desire to protect her from anyone out to hurt her.

As Ruth ended the call with her agent, her text signal chimed an incoming message. She looked at the screen and gasped, blood draining from her face.

Ben moved to her side and took the phone from her unresisting fingers. He growled.

"What is it?" Cal asked.

"A text from a blocked number. 'You won't be so lucky next time.'"

CHAPTER SIX

Ruth patted her face dry and stared at her reflection in the mirror. She flinched. Who was that woman with the haunted shadows in her eyes? She thought when Hugo was locked up in prison that her anxiety and fear would disappear.

Right. The person stalking her wasn't Hugo or someone in Hugo's employ. No, this was a whole new nightmare. Lucky her. Standing in the bathroom and brooding wouldn't solve the problem. She needed to sleep although she believed that was impossible.

Ruth twisted the knob and opened the door. She stopped abruptly when she saw Ben leaning against the wall across from the bathroom. He straightened.

"We need to talk about tomorrow. What's on your schedule?"

"An appearance at a charity luncheon."

He shook his head. "The risk is too great. We don't have time to check the security setup as thoroughly as we need to."

She narrowed her eyes. "I appreciate that you're concerned for my safety, but this is part of my job. I make public appearances. In this case, the charity is one I support with donations. I'm not going to hide in my house because a creep has fixated on me."

"Again."

"That's right. Just my luck to have more than one jerk decide I belong to him. This is one of the most important fundraisers of the year for Children's Rainbow. I'm supposed to deliver a short speech. My participation in this event has been scheduled for months. I'm not going to disappoint them. You'll have to work out the security arrangements."

"I'm trying to keep you safe."

"And I'm trying to live my life without fear that another monster will hurt me." Her voice broke. Ruth closed her eyes and drew in a slow breath. Yelling at Ben wouldn't solve the problem or reveal the stalker in the next twelve hours. All she would do if she continued her diatribe was hurt Ben with her lack of faith in him and his ability to protect her. That was the last thing she wanted.

She opened her eyes. "I'm sorry. I didn't mean to yell at you."

He studied her face for a moment. "Are you sure there isn't a way to bow out of this thing?"

"Positive. This means too much to me, Ben. I won't cower behind a locked door."

"Protecting yourself and your security detail isn't cowering. It's called being smart."

She scowled. "Are you calling me stupid?"

"I didn't say that and would never call you anything but what you are."

"Which is?"

"Gorgeous, sexy as sin, tough as nails, and courageous as a lion with a heart of gold."

All the umbrage he'd stoked settled down to a low simmer. "Thank you."

He inclined his head. "This charity thing means that much to you?"

Ruth laid her hand on his chest over his heart. "Please understand. I have to attend this luncheon. Can you make this happen without risk to yourself or anyone else?"

He sighed and trailed the backs of his fingers down her cheek, his touch gentle. "I'll do it, but you'll do exactly as I tell you. If I think it's time for us to leave, we leave."

"As long as I've finished my speech. I promise, Ben. After that, I'll make my excuses to leave as soon as you think we should go."

Ruth moved past him to the door of her bedroom.

"Will you be able to sleep?"

No. She turned back. "I hope so," Ruth hedged.

The operative moved to stand in front of her, so close that his body heat warmed her skin and stole her breath.

Ruth tilted her head back to look into his chocolate-brown eyes. She could spend hours just looking into the fathomless depths of his eyes.

"If you can't sleep, come to me. I might be able to help."

"How?"

"Let's just say I have my own issues sleeping most nights." He cupped her cheek, his thumb brushing lightly over her bottom lip. His eyes seemed to heat as he watched the progress of his thumb across her mouth.

Ruth's breath stalled in her lungs. What did this mean? Was it simply a way to help her overcome her skittishness about a man touching her? Didn't he understand that she never minded his touch?

"Where is this luncheon?" he murmured.

"The Garden Hotel in Murfreesboro. The luncheon starts at noon."

Some of the tension left his muscles. "Perfect. I'm familiar with the hotel." He locked his gaze with hers. "I want to kiss you," he said softly.

Her eyes widened.

"Are you going to stop me?"

"Depends."

"On?"

"Whether or not my bodyguard is kissing me or my boyfriend."

He inched closer. "Let me kiss you, sunshine. Yes or no?"

"Yes." Please, yes. She'd dreamed of his mouth on hers ever since he'd helped rescue her.

Ben's hand slid from her cheek to her nape and his mouth slowly descended to hers, giving her a chance to step back if this wasn't what she wanted. She didn't move.

The moment his lips touched hers, heat exploded in Ruth's gut and her blood turned to honey. Although she half expected Ben to take her mouth with a demanding kiss, his touch remained as light as a feather, coaxing her mouth to respond to his. A soft moan escaped. He was driving her crazy.

"Easy, baby," he whispered, his hold on her nape tightening as though he was afraid she'd wrench herself from his hold. "I'd never hurt you." Ben's other hand rested at her waist. No pressure, just warmth.

Ruth wanted to stay in his gentle hold for hours, soaking up the warmth and safety he offered. She was in so much trouble. This man was addictive and he viewed himself as a loner. What chance did she have of convincing him to give them a real chance at a relationship? He needed someone strong to stand with him, not a woman who was still piecing herself back together.

Minutes or hours later, Ben lifted his head without initiating the deeper kiss that Ruth craved, his dark eyes glittering with a strong emotion she couldn't identify. "If you can't sleep, come to me. I'll be downstairs. You're safe here. No one will get to you on my watch. You have my word." He lifted her hand, pressed a kiss to her palm, and nudged her inside her room. "Dream of me," he whispered, and shut her door.

She listened to his retreating footsteps, turned and pressed her back against the door. Holy cow. Ben Martin went straight to her head and her heart. How would she survive until Ben found the stalker? She might lose her heart to a man capable of breaking it into a million pieces.

Ruth got ready for bed. In case she had to run in the middle of the night, she opted to wear her yoga gear and left her running shoes beside her bed.

She turned out the light and prayed for sleep. An hour later, she threw off the covers and sat up, shoving her hands through her hair. This was hopeless. Every time she closed her eyes, she saw that horrid picture on her windshield and memories of her captivity plagued her.

Ruth slid her feet into her shoes. Maybe a cup of herbal tea would help. If she didn't sleep, Scott would have to retouch her photos, something that would tick him off. Listening to him rail against her for not taking better care with her appearance was difficult to take.

She went downstairs as quietly as possible but she shouldn't have bothered because both operatives heard her coming. Cal turned from the window, his eyebrow raised. Ben sat up on the couch where he'd been sprawled.

He met her at the bottom of the stairs. "Can't sleep?"

Ruth shook her head.

"Come sit with me."

"I was going to make herbal tea."

He grimaced. "I've heard it helps, but I can't stand to drink the stuff. Go make your tea."

She rummaged through the kitchen cabinet to find the stash of chamomile tea Bridget had left behind. She dropped a tea bag into the mug and nuked the water. When the heating cycle ended, Ruth carried the mug into the living room.

Ben patted the cushion beside him. When she sat, he wrapped his hand around her free one and grabbed the television remote. Scanning through the channels, he chose one airing episodes of people building cabins.

"Are you interested in building your own cabin?"

"Not a chance. I couldn't build a bird house much less a cabin. I like to watch how the cabins come together, though."

"Is this what you watch when you can't sleep?"

"Sometimes. Other times I choose a sports channel. I didn't think you would appreciate a baseball game."

She squeezed his hand, glad she had something else in common with him. "Actually, I love baseball."

His head whipped around. "Seriously?"

Ruth smiled. "Why is that so surprising? My dad is the one who got me hooked on baseball. We used to go to the Nashville Sounds games. Whenever we traveled at night, Dad would listen to a baseball game to keep himself awake. Those are some of my favorite memories of him." Her smile faded as her heart ached anew at the loss of her parents. "I haven't been to a game since he and Mom died."

"Would you like to?"

She nodded. "I think it would be fun."

"Good. We'll plan on attending a game when we return from Mexico."

"What if we haven't uncovered the stalker by then? Will it be safe to attend a game?"

"I'll work something out." With that cryptic comment, Ben channel surfed until he found a baseball game to watch. Setting aside the remote, he released her hand to wrap his arm around her shoulders. "If you get tired, lay your head on my shoulder and close your eyes."

"You won't be comfortable."

"Who says?"

"Promise you'll send me to bed if I conk out and you need to stretch out for a while."

"Watch the game, Monihan."

"Yes, sir," she snapped out in her best imitation of a soldier.

Cal glanced over his shoulder with a twinkle in his eyes.

After Ruth finished her tea, she took the mug to the dishwasher and returned to her place beside Ben.

He spread a blanket over her lap and tucked her close to his side, arm once against draped over her shoulders. "Comfortable?"

She nodded.

"Good. Just relax and enjoy the game."

Ruth settled deeper against the cushion and focused on the slow-paced game. After three innings, her eyes grew heavy and her head wanted to loll against Ben's shoulder. She rested her head against the back of the couch and closed her eyes. As she drifted, the noise of the game faded into the background and she felt a gentle pressure against the side of head, urging her to lean against Ben's shoulder. Too tired to resist, Ruth gave in, sighed, and let her body slip into sleep.

CHAPTER SEVEN

When Ben was positive that Ruth was asleep, he reclined with his feet propped on the coffee table and shifted the woman in his arms so she slept with her head on his chest. His heart lurched when she snuggled closer and went boneless in his arms.

He was getting in too deep with Ruth, but he couldn't seem to stop himself. She felt perfect in his arms. How would he give her up when the mission was complete? No matter what his battered heart told him, he couldn't keep her.

Cal looked at him, a smirk on his face.

"Shut up."

A soft chuckle. "I didn't say a word."

"But you were thinking it." He was, too. Didn't make the words more comfortable to think about or say.

His friend turned back to the window. "Sleep, Ben. I've got this."

"Wake me in three hours." If he didn't wake himself up with nightmares or the internal alarm clock in his head.

"No need. I don't have another assignment yet. Take the chance to sleep while you have it."

Although he wanted to refuse the offer, Cal was right. When this case heated up, and it would sooner rather than later, he'd be short on sleep. All the shuteye he banked now would keep him on his feet while protecting Ruth. "Thanks."

Unsure if he could sleep with someone other than his teammates close by, Ben was surprised to find himself going under easily. Sometime later, he woke when Cal said his name.

Alert, he looked at the other operative. "Problem?"

"Maybe. I need to scout around outside."

"Go. I'll take the watch." He glanced at his phone. Four hours of sleep. Not bad.

After Cal left by the back door, Ben eased Ruth to the couch cushions, lips curving when she frowned and moaned. She sounded like a grumpy kid.

He tugged the blanket over her shoulders and allowed himself to stroke her silky blond hair once, then walked to the window and eased the curtain aside. A black Camaro was parked across the street three houses away with the engine running and lights off.

Might be a neighbor going to work early. If so, why sit with the lights off? The car was a newer model, one with automatic lights. The driver turned them off deliberately.

Nothing else had changed on the street except lights were beginning to glow in windows at houses up and down the street.

A dark figure walked around the corner of a house one block up the street and walked down the sidewalk toward Ruth's home. Cal moved closer, cell phone in his hand, screen lit up as though checking or surfing the Net while he walked. When he drew closer, the operative adjusted the positioning of his phone without slowing and walked past the idling car. He glanced at the car as he continued down the sidewalk.

Headlights turned on and tires squawked as the driver raced away from the curb, hung a fast right at the next corner, and disappeared from view.

Cal jogged across the street toward Ruth's home, and Ben unlocked the door to let him inside. "Did you get the plate?"

"Of course. Windows were tinted too dark to see the driver. No passengers from what I could tell."

"Send me and Zane the plate picture. We'll see what he turns up."

A minute later, Cal said, "Done. If you want to shower, I'll stay until you're finished."

Ben glanced at Ruth, still asleep on the couch. "Yeah, I'll do that. Thanks." He grabbed his Go bag from behind the couch and took the stairs two at a time. Fifteen minutes later, he returned to the first floor dressed in black cargo pants and t-shirt and his tactical boots to find that Cal had brewed another pot of coffee and was sipping a mug filled with the steaming liquid.

He dropped off his bag and detoured to the kitchen for his own mug. After downing several sips, he stood beside his friend. "I've got this if you want to go home now."

Cal yawned and finished the remaining coffee in his cup. "Call me if you need me." After taking his mug to the kitchen, the operative left.

Ben stayed at the window, watching the sunrise and the neighborhood stir to life. He'd replenished his coffee one more time before Ruth stirred.

He turned from his vigil. "Good morning."

"Where's Cal?"

"He went home. How do you feel?"

She smiled. "Good considering a car tried to run me down yesterday. I can't believe I slept last night."

"I'm glad you did. You needed it. I know you have to be at The Garden Hotel by noon. Is there anything else on your agenda?"

"Working out and packing."

"Shadow is meeting at 3:00 p.m. at Fortress headquarters. Have you talked to Bridget or Trace since the parking lot incident?"

Ruth grimaced. "I didn't want to worry them."

"Be ready for recriminations. They won't be happy that you didn't call."

"They're newlyweds. They need time together, and I trusted you to take care of me."

He squelched the grin threatening to form on his mouth at her snippy tone. "Still, they'll gripe." Ben didn't blame them. He wouldn't be happy if she kept him in the dark. "There's coffee in the pot if you want it."

"Maybe a little. I can't work out with anything much on my stomach."

"What about food when you're finished?"

"I don't have much in the house. I'm not good in the kitchen and I've only been here a couple of days."

"After you work out and pack, I'll take you to breakfast. We can check in with Zane on our way to the hotel."

A moment later, she stood beside him with a mug half-full of coffee. "Anything happen while I was asleep?"

He glanced at her, wishing he could keep the truth from her. She didn't need anything else adding to her stress level. However, Ruth needed to know she could trust him to tell her information that might keep her safe. "We noticed a black Camaro idling a few houses away with the lights off around five this morning. Does the car sound familiar?"

Ruth shook her head. "I'm not here most of the time, though. One of the neighbors might have purchased a new car although I can't see them buying a sports car. Soccer moms and gray-haired grannies live around me. Did you or Cal confront the driver?"

"What makes you think we would?"

"You aren't one to sit back and wait."

He grinned. Smart woman. "We didn't confront the driver, but Cal took a picture of the license plate and sent it to Zane to trace."

"What was the result?"

"The car and the plates don't match."

"What does that mean?"

"Someone attached the license plate of another vehicle to the Camaro."

"We're at a dead end."

"For now."

"Someone was watching my house. With your SUV in the driveway, he knew I was home. Unless he followed us, he wouldn't know you were here, too. Why didn't he come after me again?"

"Your sister and brother-in-law drive the same SUVs as you and I do. With Cal's SUV in front of the house, the watcher could have mistaken his vehicle for your sister's. If this guy watches you much, he'd know Bridget stays here sometimes when Shadow is gone and you're in town."

Ruth smiled. "It's like old times. I miss my sister the most when I'm here alone. Don't get me wrong. I'm happy for her and it's obvious Trace is head-over-heels in love with Bridget. I love that they're together, but I miss spending time with her."

"Life is about change. Some good, some not. You'll adjust. One day, you'll have a man in your life and Bridget will have to make the adjustment herself."

Her smile faded. "Maybe."

"Definitely." Man, why did that thought make his heart hurt? "Any man lucky enough to win your heart will have a treasure worth protecting, Ruth." Ben cupped her cheek and brushed his thumb over her bottom lip. "Do what you need to. I'll be here if you need me."

She pressed her cheek into his hand for a moment before turning away and going to the garage which had been turned into a workout room.

The heat of her skin still made his palm tingle by the time Ben finished the mug of coffee. He rinsed the dregs from the pot and switched the machine off. Assuming they wouldn't return to her home after the meeting with Shadow, he checked her refrigerator for food that might spoil while she was in Mexico.

His eyebrows shot up when he saw the empty interior aside from a few condiments and bottles of water. Wow. The lady hadn't been kidding when she said she wasn't a cook. Curious, he peeked into the freezer. At least that was well stocked with frozen dinners. Looked as though Bridget had cooked and frozen individual portions for her sister.

Satisfied that she wouldn't return to a science project in the fridge, Ben returned to the living room window. When the sun rose high enough, he slipped out the front door to scout around the perimeter.

He didn't like that someone had been watching Ruth's house. Yeah, he knew Cal would have sounded the alarm if the driver exited the vehicle and walked around the neighborhood or the house. Didn't matter. He wanted to see that nothing had been tampered with for himself.

Ben walked the perimeter, looking for signs of egress, but found nothing that raised an alarm. As he returned to the house, Zane called "You're at work already?"

"Claire had an early morning photoshoot. Since I was already up, I decided to come in."

"Have anything for me?"

"I tracked the green car on traffic cams until the driver exited Interstate 40 at Mt. Juliet. I lost the car when the driver went into a residential neighborhood."

"Any chance of narrowing down the house?"

"Slim to none. It's a big subdivision, Ben. I could try to narrow down the potential residences, but it would take too much time."

He grimaced. "Don't bother. He could have driven through the subdivision on the way to another part of the city. Anything pop on the fake plates?"

"The plates belong on a red minivan driven by a mom of four rambunctious boys who are into baseball. She was horrified to realize her license plate was missing. The Camaro driver stole hers without swapping with another vehicle."

"All right. Any new activity about Roxanne on the Net?"

Zane grunted. "Her public relations people are working overtime to promote the new line of clothing she's getting ready to model in Mexico."

Ben grimaced. Great. That would generate a lot of attention to Casa del Mar. A boost for the hotel and a nightmare for Shadow. This was turning into a circus. "Anything out of line?"

"Not so far. I expanded the search perimeter for the bots. I'll know within minutes if we have a new threat on that front. I traced the origins of the emails going to Roxanne. They came from different accounts. All of them were throwaway accounts closed immediately after the emails were sent. I can't trace them any further."

"Any new threats aimed at me?"

"Not yet."

He sighed. "It's coming."

"As soon as the news media realizes you're with Ruth," Zane agreed. "I'll let you know when the activity picks up."

"Thanks."

"Yep. Watch your back, buddy."

"Always." He ended the call, glanced over his shoulder, and froze. "Ruth. How long have you been standing there?"

CHAPTER EIGHT

Ruth drew in a ragged breath. How could Ben stand there, calm and collected as though she'd heard nothing out of the ordinary? "Long enough to know I have to fire you."

His eyebrows rose. "Why?"

"How can you ask me that? You were talking to Zane about threats to your life. Who wants to kill you?"

A small smile. "Several people, most of them terrorists."

"Don't you dare joke about this. I'm in front of a camera ninety percent of my time in public. Your handsome face will be plastered all over the news media as soon as they realize you're more than just a bodyguard " He would always be more to her battered heart.

His lips curved into a grin. "You think I'm handsome?"

"Ben."

He held up his hands. "I'll handle it. Trust me."

The man was so infuriating. "You're risking your life to protect me."

"Any man who serves as your bodyguard will be at risk."

A dodge. She wouldn't let him get by with it. "How serious is the threat to you?"

The operative shrugged. "No more than it usually is."

"At least, not yet," she added, her gaze locked on his.

He inclined his head.

Ruth's heart sank. "I can't let you do this." No matter how much she wanted him with her in Mexico, she wouldn't risk his life. He meant too much to her. "It's too dangerous. I'm sorry to do this, but you're fired and off duty as of this moment."

"My job is dangerous all the time." He left his vigil at the window and crossed the space separating them to stand in front of her. "You can't protect me by firing me. Besides, you didn't assign me to this task. You don't have the authority to relieve me of my duties."

"Then I'll ask Brent to assign someone else to the job."

"No, you won't."

She scowled. "You can't tell me what to do." Especially not this. She wouldn't sacrifice his life for hers.

"In this case, I am. I'm not stepping down, Ruth."

"There must be other Fortress bodyguards who can do the job."

"Many," he conceded. "I won't let them take over."

"Why not?"

Ben's large, rough-skinned hand curled around the back of her neck and drew her forward until she stood a bare inch from him. He tipped her chin up with his other hand. "You know why," he murmured.

"Spell it out."

"This." He captured her mouth with his, the touch hard and hungry. Heat spread through her veins like liquid lightning, weakening her knees. Ben closed the scant distance between them and wrapped his strong arms around her as he explored her mouth with a thoroughness that stole her breath.

Holy cow! He'd been holding back. Last night's kiss had been tame compared to this one. This kiss smacked of possession in capital letters. Was Ben trying to gain her cooperation or was he finally letting his real feelings escape that quiet reserve he showed to the world?

The long, deep, drugging kisses made it impossible for her to think, to reason. She wanted to stay sheltered in his arms forever. A soft moan escaped her throat as her arms encircled his neck.

Minutes passed as the kisses went on and on. He broke the kiss long enough to drag in a breath, then pressed more kisses to the side of her throat, down along the curve of her shoulder, and back up to plunder her mouth again. Heat blasted through her, obliterating the chill that had sunk deep into her bones when she'd overheard his comments to Zane.

When Ben eased away, Ruth dragged him back for another kiss. Addictive. Ben Martin was more addictive than her love of chocolate.

He gave in for a minute, then broke the kiss and pressed his forehead to hers. "We have to stop, baby. I'm hanging on to my control by a thread." While waiting for their breaths to slow, he ran his hand slowly up and down her back.

Minutes later, he leaned back to look her in the eyes. "I won't step aside, Ruth. Don't ask that of me. We'll deal with whatever comes. Asking me to leave your safety in the hands of another operative?" He shook his head. "Won't ever happen."

Stubborn man. Didn't he understand why she was afraid to keep him by her side? Evidently not. Fine. He could deal with the truth. "How can I protect you?"

He looked stunned for a second, then rallied. "Do everything I tell you to do when it comes to your safety. Give me your trust."

This wasn't the first time he'd mentioned trust. "You have to know that I trust you." How could he think otherwise? If another man had kissed her, Ruth would have panicked. The kind of kisses she and Ben had shared? They were more meaningful than Ben realized. The handsome operative had strong feelings for her despite not wanting to feel anything. At his core, he was a protector.

Satisfaction flashed in his eyes. "I won't let you down."

"I never doubted that for a minute, but I want you safe. If something happens to you...." She trailed off.

"I'll be fine. Shadow has my back."

Ruth did, too. She would protect him, no matter the cost to herself.

She stepped out of his hold. "I'll shower and pack." Although she longed to dive back into his arms for more blistering kisses, that wasn't fair to him and would torture her. She made herself head upstairs.

After showering, she dressed for her luncheon and packed a suitcase. When she'd double-checked her makeup supplies to be sure she had everything along with her toiletries, Ruth called it done and locked her suitcase. She set the case on its wheels and rolled it from her room.

Ben must have been waiting for her because he hurried upstairs to take the case from her. "Need me to carry anything else?"

She shook her head.

"You travel light."

"The clothes for the photoshoot don't belong to me so I don't have to transport them." She followed him to the first floor. "Talk about traveling light. You have one bag."

"Two. My equipment bag is in the SUV."

"What kind of equipment?"

He grinned at her. "The fun kind. Guns, bullets, knives, C-4, detonators, grenades, RPG, plus a medical kit. It's not as fancy as Sam's mike bag but it will do in a pinch."

Ruth stared. He was kidding, right? "RPG?"

"Rocket-propelled grenade launcher." He slid her a pointed glance. "You saw the kinds of weapons we carry when we freed you in Mexico."

"I knew what Trace carried. I didn't realize you all had the same equipment."

"Not exactly the same. The others don't carry C-4 and only Joe and Trace carry sniper rifles. Does it bother you?"

Did it? She examined her response and realized she was surprised rather than upset by his revelation. If having the equipment kept Ben safe and brought him home from his missions in one piece, she was in favor of him carrying whatever he needed. "Not upset, no. I'm surprised by how extensive your supplies are." Another question occurred to her. "Are you always armed?"

"I never leave home without weapons."

His gentle voice caused a shiver to race along her body. Man, he was potent. Even his voice did things to her that should be illegal. "Why?"

"Bad things happen all the time. I protect innocents. That's my job. I can't do that as effectively if I'm not armed and ready at all times."

"Would you have shot the driver who tried to run us down?"

"If I didn't have another option, yes. I would have done anything necessary to protect you. I always will." He dropped a quick kiss on her mouth and got them moving toward the front door. "I've already checked the windows and doors. Everything is locked down. Do you leave a light on when you're out of the house?"

"The living room light."

After turning on the lamp and setting the alarm, Ben ushered Ruth from the house and escorted her to the SUV.

Once she was inside, he stored her luggage in the back of the SUV and circled to climb behind the wheel.

The journey into Nashville was uneventful. Ben drove to Fortress headquarters and parked in the underground garage.

"Why are we here?" Ruth asked.

"I need to restock my supplies and since we have a little extra time, I'd rather do it now. This will take about five minutes. Do you want to visit with Zane while I go to the weapons vault?"

"Is it against the rules to show me the vault?"

"You want to see it?"

"I do."

He gave her a considering look. "All right. Whatever you see inside the vault can't be discussed with anyone."

"I'm a vault with secrets." She smiled.

Ben chuckled as he exited the vehicle.

Success. She'd made the taciturn man laugh. Her job was done for the moment. Her new mission was to bring a little laughter into his life. He deserved that and so much more.

After a short elevator ride down two levels, they arrived at a floor with multiple steel doors on either side of the corridor. "You weren't kidding about calling them the vaults, were you?"

He shook his head. "The vaults are exactly what the name implies. They hold Fortress weaponry and medical supplies as well as uniforms and tactical boots."

"Uniforms. The black cargo pants and shirts?"

"We have lighter-colored camouflage if the terrain calls for it. Most of the time, Shadow doesn't need it. We do much of our work at night." He carded in, keyed in a code, and submitted to a retinal scan before opening the door of the closest vault.

"Is this the only floor with the vaults?"

He shook his head. "There's another floor below this one." Ben slid his bag from his shoulder and led Ruth inside.

She slowly scanned the shelves and hooks filled with weaponry of all types. "This is incredible. You could start a war with the supplies inside here."

"Not hardly. We could stop a skirmish if we were careful."

She'd never seen so many weapons in one place. "Do you know how to use everything in here?"

"We're well trained."

A non-answer, but it was telling enough to know that he could utilize everything in this vault. She continued her perusal as Ben restocked his equipment bag, amazed at the variety of weaponry on display. How much money had Fortress spent to arm the operatives?

Her gaze shifted to Ben. How much of his work required this kind of heavy artillery? She worried about the cost to Ben mentally and emotionally. The big, tough SEAL might deny that he paid a price for his work. She knew better. Considering that he was always awake when she called at odd hours of the night or early morning, Ben didn't sleep much. That wasn't good for his health.

She knew her lousy sleep habits impacted her body. Photographers harped at her constantly now. Before Hugo, she'd rested well. Now, nightmares invaded her dreams and jarred her awake, skin clammy and heart racing.

Ben was the one she turned to when memories pressed too close. He always took her calls, a true gift from what she'd learned from Bridget. Ben didn't hand out his personal number to anyone but his teammates and a few select colleagues from Fortress.

Ben turned, an unspoken question in his eyes when he caught her watching him.

She shook her head. "Sorry. I was thinking about...things."

He closed his bag and hoisted it to his shoulder. "Torino?" he asked, voice soft.

Ruth turned away. She didn't want Ben to think she was weak.

Catching her arm, he turned her back to face him. "Don't."

"I need to get over this." She wouldn't let Hugo ruin her life. She refused to give him that power.

"You're talking to the counselor I recommended, right?"

"Every week. Marcus Lang is a good man. He's helping me work through everything." Although not fast enough to suit her.

Ben cupped the side of her neck, his touch heating her skin and flooding her body with a sense of comfort and security. How did he do that with one touch?

"You suffered a serious trauma. Recovery takes a long time. Distance from the event will help."

Conviction rang in his voice. "You sound as though you know that from experience."

"I do."

"I'll recover." She wouldn't allow any other outcome.

"Triggers will still be there, Ruth. Years from now, a man will do or say something that brings all of it back. When that happens, you'll beat back the nightmares again and get on with your life. You're strong. You'll defeat Torino every time he pops up in your mind." He pressed a soft kiss to her mouth and slid his hand from her neck down to her hand. "Come on. It's time for a light breakfast and then you can wow the crowd at your children's charity."

CHAPTER NINE

Ben polished off the last of the rubbery chicken, scanning the packed banquet room at The Garden Hotel from his seat at the side of the room near the dais. At least his back was to the wall and Ruth was tucked away in the corner beside him, the safest place she could be under the circumstances. When it was time for her to speak, he'd escort her to the platform.

Knowing Ruth wouldn't be comfortable with a stranger sitting close to her, Ben had removed the chair on the other side of her and added it to the nearest table along with the place setting. The reward for his thoughtfulness was a beaming smile and a hand squeeze under the table. Good enough. For now. He intended to collect another kiss later for his trouble.

He frowned. When had he been this taken with a woman? Thinking back through his spotty dating history, the answer to his question was never. None of the other women had been that important to him, at least not enough to occupy his thoughts, waking or sleeping. Ruth Monihan was special, and he couldn't keep her.

That thought jarred him enough to refocus on his job instead of his principal. So far, he hadn't seen any suspicious activity or unusual attention. The truth was, everywhere they went, Ruth generated a lot of interest. Went with the territory when he was with one of the most beautiful women on the planet. She was every inch a supermodel without having the prima donna attitude.

He was grateful that Ruth had managed to secure a ticket for him without difficulty. Who knew that Ben Martin would ever be a plus one for Roxanne? She'd also insisted on sitting in the audience rather than on the dais with the other guest speakers, the host, and event organizer. She was still visible, but not on a raised platform in full view of the entire room, a setup that would have made her a bigger target. The organizer seemed surprised that Ruth didn't want to be in the spotlight although he didn't complain about the change.

At that moment, the organizer walked to the podium. Conversation in the room slowly petered out. He welcomed the patrons to the fundraiser and thanked them for their generosity. "I hope you brought your wallets and checkbooks. We have a silent auction going at the back of the room. The grand prize is a four-day getaway for two to Jamaica. We hope you bid often and large to treat someone special in your life to an unforgettable weekend."

He smiled as the audience laughed at his comment. When the audience quieted, he introduced the founder of Children's Rainbow who took her place at the podium for a few remarks.

Ruth leaned close to Ben. "I'd like to place a few bids on items in the auction. Want to go with me?"

"Sure. Don't you need to be close to the stage?"

"I have a few minutes before it's my turn to speak." She smiled. "Some of the speakers go over their allotted time. We have the same speakers each year."

"Does that present a problem?" he whispered as they walked toward the back of the room.

"Not really. The patrons came to support a good cause."

Ben stayed close as Ruth bid on several gift baskets and the Jamaica getaway package. His eyebrows rose at the amount she bid on each. "What happens if you win all of the auction items you bid on?"

She grinned. "I'll be gifting them to friends and family."

"And the Jamaica getaway?"

A shrug. "I don't know. I may not win any of these items. This room is full of generous people with a soft spot for kids."

Maybe. He didn't think any of them were as generous with their wallets as Ruth was with hers. After she'd placed her last bid, Ben escorted her to their table in time for her introduction as the next speaker.

"That's your cue," he murmured and walked with her to the stairs leading to the dais. While she spoke to the audience, thanking them for their generosity to the cause and explaining why their help was critical in saving the lives of critically ill kids, Ben kept his attention on the audience, scanning for trouble. When Ruth finished her remarks to a rousing round of applause and left the dais to return to his side, he held out his hand to help her down the stairs. When she stepped on the carpeted surface, Ben lifted her hand to his mouth and kissed her palm.

Ruth's breath caught as murmured conversations filled the large room.

He winked at her and led her to their table. This was as good a time as any to start the media machine rolling. Someone here would remark on the mysterious stranger with Roxanne at a luncheon. Hopefully, no picture of him would appear on the social media sites yet and give him a few more hours without escalating danger from his background circling them although he knew his luck wouldn't hold. Sooner or later, his past would come back to bite him. He prayed Ruth wasn't caught in the crossfire when that happened.

During the next few minutes, Ben sat beside Ruth with his hand wrapped around hers. Surprised to feel her trembling after a speech where she gave no hint of her nervousness, he squeezed her hand and leaned close to whisper, "You've been holding back on me."

Her brows knitted. "What are you talking about?"

"You're a good public speaker, sunshine. You made me want to reach for my own wallet to contribute to this charity."

"Do you think anyone knew my knees were knocking?"

"Not a chance." If he weren't holding her hand, Ben wouldn't have known how afraid she was. The lady was a class act.

Turning his attention to the audience, he noticed several cell phones aimed their direction and sighed. So much for not having his picture in social media. His face would be plastered all over the Internet in a matter of minutes.

Ben slid his phone from his pocket and sent Zane a text, alerting him to the newest development and asking him to monitor the Net closely after the pictures hit. He needed to know about new threats as soon as they appeared, and still believed Brent made a mistake assigning Ben to this task.

He glanced at Ruth and found her watching him instead of the latest speaker. Ben admitted to himself that he wouldn't have been happy to have another operative watching over her, especially after those incendiary kisses she'd shared with him. The chemistry between them was so powerful he was amazed that he hadn't burned to ashes on the spot.

The thought of another man having the right to kiss and hold Ruth Monihan made Ben see red. Not good. He needed objectivity to do his job right and protect his heart.

He reminded himself that this was just a role he'd been assigned. She was a job and he was only acting the part of the besotted lover.

Right. If that was true, why did this feel real enough to trigger his protective instincts and make him want to mark Ruth as his?

Finally, the interminable speeches were finished and the auction winners were announced. "And for the grand price of a four-day getaway to Jamaica, the winning bid belongs to Roxanne." The organizer grinned at her as the audience clapped. "Congratulations, my friend. See me after the luncheon and I'll give you the information you need to enjoy a long weekend away with a friend."

Ten minutes later, the luncheon ended and patrons trickled out of the banquet room. A few people stopped by the table to congratulate Ruth and compliment her on the speech before leaving.

The event organizer broke away from a small group and walked to their table. "Congratulations, Roxanne."

"Thanks, Charles." She smiled. "Great luncheon, as always."

"Better than great, thanks to you and your promotion efforts for this event." The middle-aged man turned to Ben with a smile and held out his hand. "I'm Charles Haywood. I'm glad you could join us today."

"I'm Ben, Roxanne's boyfriend. I appreciate you finding a place for me. I wasn't sure my schedule would allow me to join her today. She speaks highly of Children's Rainbow."

One of Charles's hands fisted. "I wasn't aware that Roxanne was dating anyone. My congratulations to both of you."

Ben slid his arm around Ruth's shoulders. The organizer's words said one thing, his body language another. The man appeared to be ticked off that Ruth was in a committed relationship. Was it possible good old Charles was interested in being more than an acquaintance? Could he be Ruth's stalker? "Thanks."

Charles shifted his attention to Ruth. "When did you start dating?"

"Recently. We've known each for months, but with his schedule and mine we haven't been in a place where we could spend much time together."

"But now you can," he said flatly.

"We're making time," Ben said. "The perfect time will never come, not with our jobs."

That drew the organizer's attention back to Ben. "Oh? What do you do for a living?"

"I'm in private security."

A frown. "You're a sales rep for a security company?"

That made him smile. "I specialize in hostage retrieval."

Alarm shown on Charles's face. "You're a mercenary." He turned to Ruth. "I need to speak to you for a minute." Another glance at Ben. "Alone."

"Not going to happen," Ben said before Ruth could answer. "Whatever you have to say to her can be said right here."

"It's all right, Charles," Ruth said. "You can speak freely in front of Ben."

"Fine. You shouldn't be with him. He's dangerous."

She laughed. "You're right about that. He is dangerous but not to me. He's exactly what I need."

Ben's heart turned over in his chest even as he warned himself not to get caught up in the fantasy she spun for the other man. This wasn't real.

"He's only after your money."

Eyes narrowed, Ben said softly, "I care about her, not her money." He flicked a glance at Ruth. "It's time for us to go, baby."

She stood immediately and slid the long strap of her purse diagonally across her body. "It was good to see you again, Charles. Take care."

"Wait! I haven't given you the information you need for your prize."

"Email it to her." Ben ushered Ruth from the room before Haywood could do more than sputter a protest. He steered her toward the stairs to the underground garage rather than the elevator.

"Where are we going?"

"SUV by way of the stairs."

"You have something against elevators?"

"Stairs are safer. If someone attacks us while we're in an elevator, there's nowhere to go to escape. In the stairwell, we have options."

She stared at him a moment. "I'll never feel safe in an elevator again, thanks to you."

Ben shrugged. "I won't apologize if the precaution keeps you safe." He opened the door to the stairwell, checking the interior before tugging Ruth inside. Although he wanted to demand answers to his questions about Charles Haywood, this wasn't the time or place to pursue the information. The sooner she was safe in his SUV, the better he'd feel. His gut was telling him that trouble was coming, fast.

As they walked down the stairs, Ben kept Ruth on his left side, leaving his weapon hand free. When they reached the door to the underground garage, he nudged her back against the wall. "Wait while I see if the coast is clear," he murmured. She nodded and, with a final glance up the stairwell to confirm no potential threats were near, opened the door to the cavernous concrete interior of the garage.

He eased into the open, keeping his body between the garage and the stairwell. No cars or people moved on this level. On another level of the garage, a vehicle's engine cranked and footsteps sounded.

Ben waited in the shadows, senses on alert, the skin on his nape prickling. He remained still, quartering the area, searching for the threat he felt but couldn't see.

Behind him, he heard footsteps on the stairwell. He held out his hand to Ruth. "Let's go. Stay right beside me."

When she hurried to his side, Ben wrapped his arm around her waist and urged her into a fast walk. His gaze continually scanned the garage as they moved toward his SUV.

Fifteen feet from their destination, a car alarm went off at the other end of the aisle. Ben slid the Sig from his holster and moved to block any shot that might be aimed her direction. "Run!"

Ruth sprang into motion. Ben clicked the remote on his SUV and covered her when she yanked the door open and dived inside.

Weapon still up and tracking, he circled to the driver's door and climbed inside. A split second after the door closed, a shot rang out.

CHAPTER TEN

Ben cranked the engine and sped from the hotel's garage, tires squealing as he rounded corners. More shots rang out and peppered the passenger side of his vehicle. "Get down." His vehicle was armor-plated and the glass bullet resistant, but that didn't mean his ride was bulletproof. If enough bullets hit the same place in the windows, eventually the glass would break. He'd rather have Ruth a little uncomfortable for a short time than risk her being hurt or, God forbid, killed.

Ruth hunched over, her face toward him. "The stalker is trying to kill me now?"

Thank goodness she sounded ticked off as opposed to panicked. "Not you. He was aiming for me. If he takes me out, you're more vulnerable to attack or being kidnapped."

She scowled. "He could have killed me."

Still might if he couldn't shake the SUV on their tail. Ben activated his Bluetooth system. His call was answered seconds later.

"Yeah, Murphy."

"It's Ben. You're on speaker with Ruth. We're coming in hot."

"Location?"

He maneuvered around a slow-moving car as he accelerated onto the interstate entrance ramp. "Just got on I-24 westbound at Medical Center Parkway, heading for headquarters. Do we have assets in the area?"

"Checking now." The sound of Zane's fingers flying over the keyboard. "Eli Wolfe is ten miles from your location. He's working his way to you now. Description of the vehicle?"

Excellent. Eli Wolfe used his southern charm with the same skill and expertise with which he wielded his Ka-Bar and Sig. If he couldn't have Shadow at his back, he'd gladly have this fellow SEAL on his six. "Black SUV, late model Explorer. Tell Wolfe there are two men in the SUV, both trigger happy."

"Copy that. Need me to stay on the line with you?"

Ben reached a relatively open stretch of interstate and pressed the gas pedal to the floor. The SUV's powerful engine responded quickly. He eyed the sea of red lights about a mile ahead. "As long as you can. We have traffic ahead of us. I'll have to exit the interstate."

"I'm sending Wolfe your SUV's GPS signal so he can track of your location."

"Copy."

A pause, then, "I have another call coming in. I'm putting you on hold for a minute."

Ruth said, "Is it okay for me to sit up?"

Although Ben didn't like it, he nodded. The Explorer was a quarter of a mile behind them. Traffic was slowing and bunching up which meant he would have to take the exit just ahead. He couldn't afford to let the Explorer catch them without Wolfe to lend a hand. The last thing he wanted was for these bozos to run him off the road with Ruth in the vehicle. "If the Explorer gets too close...."

She held up her hand. "You don't have to say it. If they get too close, I'll fold myself in half again like a cheap suitcase." Ruth flashed him a grin as she sat up.

He laughed. "You have a wicked sense of humor. I like it." How did he not know this about her? He'd obsessed about her for months yet still missed this.

For some reason, Ruth looked pleased with herself, as though she had an agenda, but he couldn't figure out what her plan was. As long as she wasn't in a panic or crying, he'd count himself blessed. He could handle anything except her tears.

"Who is Eli Wolfe?" she asked.

"Another one of Maddox's teammates. He's one of the best operatives I've ever seen in action. He and his friend, Jon Smith, aren't men you want on your tail. They never give up."

"Jon Smith? Really?"

That brought another short laugh. "That's his real name. Jon has a well-worn driver's license to prove it. He's a quiet, intense guy, a man that smart men don't cross if they know what's good for them."

"He's that dangerous?"

"Oh, yeah. Smith has a soft spot for women and children, though, so you're safe."

"Is he married?" She sounded as though she didn't believe any woman would trust her own safety to Jon.

Ben nodded. "His wife's name is Dana, and he adores her and their daughter. He's fiercely protective of his family. Anyone who threatens them winds up in prison or dead. He's not particular about which option is chosen."

"Wow."

Did she realize Ben would be just as fierce a protector for her? She couldn't or Ruth wouldn't be nearly as comfortable in his presence.

"What about his partner, Eli?"

"Same with his wife, Brenna, and their daughter. He's a full-on southern gentleman as long as you're no threat to his family. Eli is as dangerous as his partner, but he always catches people by surprise because of his easy-going demeanor."

"Did you work with them in the military?"

"Their SEAL team and mine completed a couple of missions together. I've worked with them more since we joined Fortress. Shadow worked several operations in conjunction with Wolfe and Smith. They're dangerous, driven, and the perfect duo to give us an edge on our missions."

"Do they have a team?"

He thought about how much to reveal and, in the end, decided to go with part of the truth. "They've worked with the Zoo Crew since Fortress began. I've been hearing rumors that Maddox is forming another team with Wolfe and Smith and a few other operatives."

"Is that a good thing?"

"We need them. Fortress is short-handed. Our rest rotations are becoming shorter and that's not safe for any of the operatives." Especially Shadow. They tracked down and freed victims of human trafficking in between hostage retrievals and tracking terrorists. The almost constant missions were taking a toll on all of them. His own coping skills were fraying at the edges. In the battle for his sanity, the nightmares were winning.

Ben cut across three lanes of traffic without signaling a change and exited the interstate. He took a quick right and raced down the two-lane road, heading for a subdivision with many houses and roads, an easier place to lose the Explorer.

He randomly made turns, sped up to corners, took them at speeds most drivers would never be able to negotiate, and raced down another street. Winding his way through the subdivision, he noted that there were now more children and caregivers enjoying the warm sunshine on this June day. He couldn't keep driving at these speeds in an area where a kid might dart out into the road after a ball or a pet.

On a straight stretch, he checked the mirrors and spotted the chasing vehicle. The gap between them was slowly closing. Scowling, he turned left onto a road out of the subdivision that led to a winding road with many places where his SUV would be out of sight for a few precious seconds. One of those places would be the perfect location to turn off the road onto a side road and disappear. Maybe.

He hadn't had time to check his vehicle for a tracking device. His goal had been to get Ruth to safety and out of the line of fire. Ben drew in a slow breath. All he had to do was keep the goons off them until Wolfe joined the party. The two of them should be able to handle the thugs if things went bad.

He coaxed a little more speed from the SUV as he struggled to put more distance between them and the Explorer.

"Do you know where we are?" Ruth asked. "I don't have breadcrumbs to toss out the window to find our way back." Her knuckles were white where she gripped the seat with one hand and the door's arm rest with the other.

"No need for breadcrumbs. I've been in this area many times over the past few years." This was one of his favorite places to drive at night when he couldn't sleep. Wide, open spaces kept Ben from feeling trapped.

Memories from his time in the hands of a sadist tried to crowd to the forefront of his mind. He ruthlessly shoved them back into the mental box where he kept the disturbing images of his childhood. This wasn't the time to wrestle those demons. Driving at these speeds required all his concentration.

"Thank goodness because I lost track of where we were several minutes ago. Is there anything I can do to help?"

"Keep an eye on our friends back there while I call Wolfe and find out where he is. Let me know if the Explorer starts gaining ground on us again."

Ruth twisted in her seat and peered through the back window.

Ben placed the call to his fellow operative.

"Sit rep," Wolfe said instead of a greeting.

"We're driving north on Forest View. Just passed Willow Pond. The Explorer is about 100 yards back. The goons seem pretty determined to stick with us, but they aren't aggressive yet."

"That will change soon enough. I'll intersect with Forest View at Blackberry Lane and get these guys off your six."

"Be careful, Eli. These guys are trigger happy."

"No worries, Shadow Man. I have my own trigger-happy friend two minutes behind me, and I'd bet on my friend to defeat your goons any day of the week. Jon and I stopped in to check on Sophie Winter since Micah's out of town, so we were in the area. We're happy to lend a hand. Jon's been bored of late."

Huh. Guess that was a good thing if he planned to join the regular mission rotation. "Once we're clear, I need you to stay with us to run interference until we're at headquarters. I didn't have the chance to scan my ride for a tracking device before bullets started to fly and my gut says I have unwanted electronics on board. I was more interested in getting Ruth to safety."

"I hear you. See you in two." Eli ended the call.

"The Explorer is staying with us. I don't think they've moved any closer."

A glance in the mirror confirmed Ruth's assessment. Although the road snaked through the countryside in a series of tight twists and turns, Ben pressed the accelerator closer to the floor. Eli needed room to work. If Ben's SUV had a tracker on it like he suspected, he'd need help to keep these guys his back long enough to reach headquarters without them shooting out the tires or forcing Ben off the road.

"The Explorer is gaining ground," Ruth said.

He glanced in the rearview mirror and scowled. Hopefully, Wolfe and Smith were closer than their estimate.

Zane's voice filled the cabin. "Sit rep, Ben."

"The goons shifted to aggressive pursuit. Wolfe and Smith aren't close enough to help." Ben checked that Ruth wore her seatbelt. "The ride will be rough, Ruth."

"I'll handle it."

He reached for her hand, squeezed, then released her to grip the wheel. After another glance in the mirror, he said, "Get down and hold on."

The Explorer rammed the back of his SUV. Ben wanted to check on Ruth, but the Explorer surged forward again. With this harder jolt, Ben wrestled with the wheel to keep his SUV on the road. He shoved the gas pedal to the floor. The tires squawked as the vehicle leaped forward.

Half a mile ahead, Forest View intersected with Blackberry Lane where Eli Wolfe waited. The SUV skidded as he took a curve too fast. Ben compensated without easing up on the gas. He prayed no innocent civilians were in the area. At the speed he was driving, he'd have no time to take evasive action if someone pulled out in front of him.

Although the Explorer put on a burst of speed, the vehicle couldn't close the gap between them. Excellent. Wolfe would have just enough time to cut off the Explorer.

Ben rounded another large curve and spotted two sets of headlights 300 yards ahead on Blackberry Lane. He sped down Forest View, passing Blackberry. Eli and Jon pull out behind the Explorer.

The Explorer's passenger leaned out the window with a gun in his hand.

"Stay down, Ruth!"

Gunshots rang out. Bullets pinged off the back of the SUV.

"They won't give up, will they?"

"Jon and Eli are almost in position."

"I wish they'd hurry. It's hard to breathe. I'd prefer to be short of breath for a better reason than this."

He glanced at her. "Like what?"

"Receiving a sizzling kiss from a certain hot operative named Ben Martin."

Zane chuckled.

Ruth groaned. "Oh, man. I forgot Zane was listening in."

That made the tech wizard laugh.

Hot operative? Ben grinned, amazed that he could under the circumstances. "Once we're safe, I'll see what I can do about that."

More bullets slammed into the back of the SUV. Seconds later, he heard a loud boom. The SUV lost speed and pulled hard to the right. Ben gritted his teeth as he fought to control his vehicle.

"What was that?"

"A bullet punctured our tire."

The Explorer rammed into the back of his SUV again.

Ben growled. Bear, the Fortress mechanical genius, would be furious at the damage to the SUV. He took damage to the Fortress fleet personally.

"What will we do?"

"Pull over and have a heart-to-heart talk with them."

"Are you nuts?"

"Not today, sunshine." Probably.

"Ben, they have guns and aren't afraid to use them."

He flashed her a look. "I have more weapons and training than they do, and I have backup."

Ben steered the hobbled SUV to the side of the road, aiming the nose toward the rocky hillside. "Stay down. No matter what you hear, don't move until I tell you it's safe."

"Be careful."

Right. As if his job was ever safe. "Z, monitor us. Ruth has her cell phone with her if something happens to me."

"Copy that. I'll keep track of her."

After parking the SUV, he released his seatbelt, and scrambled into the cargo area. Ben kicked out the compromised safety glass. He aimed his Sig at the Explorer that skidded to a stop behind his SUV. "Come on," he murmured. "Let's finish this so I can take my woman to safety."

He blinked. His woman? Ben blew out a breath. She wasn't his, he reminded himself for the thousandth time. He couldn't keep her, and she deserved better than a half-crazy EOD man with a questionable life expectancy. Being an operative was more dangerous than working as a cop, even though he was better trained and equipped. Considering what she'd already been through, Ben didn't know if she wanted to deal with the constant worry and long absences that accompanied involvement with a Fortress operative.

"Z, wait ten minutes, then call for a wrecker. My ride isn't drivable."

"Copy."

The Explorer doors flew open and two men spilled from the vehicle, weapons aimed at Ben. "Get out of the vehicle. Now."

"Not going to happen."

The driver scowled. "You don't have a choice unless you want to die. We just want the girl."

"Over my dead body."

"That can be arranged," the passenger growled. "Throw down your gun and get on the ground."

Eli parked at an angle behind the Explorer and exited his vehicle, smile on his face, southern charm in full force. "Looks like you're having car trouble. You boys need help?"

The driver glared at the operative. "Scram before you get hurt."

"Sorry, buddy." Eli raised his Sig and aimed for center mass, good-old-boy charm morphing into his SEAL all-business mode. "Can't do that."

Driver started to shift his aim toward Eli when a dark, low-voiced warning sounded from the passenger side of the Explorer. "Pull that trigger and you'll be dead before you draw another breath."

CHAPTER ELEVEN

Despite Ben's warning to stay out of sight, Ruth wanted to know what was happening. She raised up high enough to watch the drama unfolding outside the vehicle.

Two men dressed like Ben aimed weapons at the Explorer thugs in what looked like a wild west standoff.

The Explorer passenger sneered at one of the operatives. "You won't pull that trigger."

"Want to bet your life on that?" the soft-spoken operative behind him said. "I'll be glad to rid the world of one more piece of slime."

Those quiet words sent a shiver through Ruth. She suspected the speaker was Jon Smith. Ben was right. She wouldn't want him tracking her. Something about him said he wouldn't quit until he cornered his prey, or miss a target if he pulled the trigger.

The tone of the man's voice and his total lack of fear registered with the passenger because his face lost all trace of color. He slowly lowered his gun to his side.

"Drop it and get on your knees."

As he complied, the other operative tilted his chin at the driver. "You know what to do unless you prefer a bullet." The words were light, almost playful. His tone was calm, eyes watchful.

With multiple vicious curses, the first thug tossed his gun aside and dropped to his knees.

The quiet operative with death in his voice covered the two creeps while his friend used zip ties to immobilize them. When he finished, the first man tossed his SUV keys to Ben who snagged them in mid-air.

He turned to Ruth. "Come around the front of our SUV and wait for me. Z, send the wrecker now."

"Copy that."

She clambered from the vehicle with her purse. Pausing by the driver's side door, Ruth waited for Ben to turn off his SUV and transfer their bags to the other vehicle. When he escorted her to the new ride, Ben kept himself between her and the two thugs.

"Find out what you can," he said to his friend.

A sunny smile curved the operative's mouth. "Won't take long. We can be very persuasive."

Ben tucked Ruth inside and climbed behind the steering wheel. He drove away as Jon and Eli marched the two thugs into a thick stand of trees.

"Where are Eli and Jon taking the two men?" Surely they wouldn't kill them in the trees. Too many people could have witnessed the breakneck chase through the subdivision and onto this winding cow path masquerading as a road.

"Into the trees to interrogate them."

"Interrogate?" She twisted in her seat to stare at Ben. "Is that a euphemism for killing them?"

He flashed her a grin. "What an imagination you have. They'll question the bruisers who ran us off the road and got me into trouble with Bear."

Her brows furrowed. "Who is Bear?"

"A Fortress mechanical genius. He's the one who upgrades our vehicles with armor plating and bullet-resistant glass."

"Why will you be in trouble?"

Ben grimaced. "Bear takes it personally when one of his vehicles comes back to the shop damaged. Usually the operative guilty of not treating his handiwork with the respect it deserves pays a hefty price to appease the big man."

"Big?"

"Oh, yeah. He's the size of a Grizzly. Hence, the nickname Bear. He also has the personality of a grouchy bear woken too soon from a long winter's nap." Ben glanced at Ruth, eyes narrowed. "That's not to be repeated in Bear's hearing. You better not rat me out, Monihan."

Ruth grinned. "You better make it worth my while to remain silent."

"Blackmail, huh? How much will your silence cost me?"

She pretended to think about that when in reality she knew what she wanted. Ruth tapped her chin. "I don't know, Martin. This is a big secret. My price must be steep enough to reflect the value. I'm not sure you can afford it."

He snorted. "Please. If you're thinking of a monetary reward, you're in for sad surprise. You make more with one job than I'll earn this year."

"Then it's good I wasn't thinking of a dollar figure."

"What do you want?"

"Five kisses."

He glanced at her, lips curving slightly at the corners. "Just five?"

"Hmm. You have a point. This is a big boon I'm granting you. Ten kisses. Ten excellent, melt-my-fingernail-polish-from-the-heat kisses. Do we have a deal?"

"You drive a hard bargain, but I don't have much choice if I want to keep my hide intact. Deal." He synced his phone to the Bluetooth and called Zane. "It's Ben. Eli and Jon intercepted the Explorer and are chatting with the two thugs. I'm in Eli's SUV with Ruth."

"Copy."

"Keep track of us, Z. Since I don't know if those thugs had friends in the area, I have to assume we have hostiles looking for us."

"I'll monitor your progress. The boss wants an update. I'm transferring you now."

Silence, then Brent Maddox's voice filled the cabin. "Sit rep."

Ben reported everything to his boss, using what sounded like military jargon.

"We need to check your SUV for a tracking device. Are you driving it now?"

"Rear passenger tire was shot out and the SUV has rear end damage."

A soft whistle from Brent. "Hope your medical insurance is up to date."

Ben scowled. "I'm tempted to ship the two idiots to east Tennessee with my ride to explain the damage to Bear themselves."

His boss chuckled, then said, "Ruth."

She straightened. "Yes, sir?"

"Are you all right?"

She was shaking and cold. Adrenaline dump. Again. Definitely not her favorite thing to weather. Maybe this would be the last time. Right. Pipe dream, that. "I'm not hurt, just dealing with adrenaline dump."

Ben adjusted the temperature in the SUV and turned on her seat heater.

"That will pass soon. Ben, what should Eli and Jon do with your two friends?"

"If they tell us what we want to know, turn them over to the cops. If not, dump them in a black site until they do."

"And after they're persuaded to tell us what we need to know?"

"I don't care what happens to them as long as they're no threat to Ruth."

"What if they won't talk?" Ruth asked.

"We don't have to worry about that," Brent said, his tone wry. "Jon's the best interrogator we have. Those boys don't stand a chance against his skills."

She swallowed hard. How dangerous was Jon Smith?

"How soon will you arrive, Ben?"

"Barring any more trouble, about forty-five minutes. We're coming in hot. I don't know if the Explorer guys had friends close."

"We'll be ready." Brent ended the call.

"What did he mean by that?" Ruth asked.

"He'll have reinforcements at the gate to discourage a tail from following us onto Fortress property. If they're stupid enough to try for us anyway, they'll regret their choice." He slid her another glance before returning his attention to the road. "Is the heat helping with the shakes?"

"Some. I'd feel better with you holding me."

He reached for her hand. "If I knew you were safe, I'd pull over in a heartbeat."

She squeezed his fingers. "I'll stop whining now, but I hate that we were in this situation because of me."

"We don't know that."

She heard what that creep said. They had come for her. "Brent said Jon is good at interrogation."

"Not just good. He's amazing."

She would probably regret asking her next question, but Ruth needed the answer. No more hiding. She'd survived an ugly experience and was slowly pulling herself back together. She could handle the truth. She hoped. "Will he kill the men?"

Ben shook his head. "He'll make them think he is."

"Why?"

"They'll talk to bargain for their lives."

She listened to what he said and what he didn't. He was holding back information. Did she really want to know the whole truth? "Talk isn't all he'll do, is it?"

"Jon uses a variety of methods to obtain information we need to protect our principals. Sometimes those methods are unpleasant."

Ruth stared. Oh, man. "He'll hurt them?"

"If they leave him no choice. We need the information, sunshine. Your life might depend on it. Don't feel guilty about Jon's work. The thugs made their choices. They can deal with the consequences."

The idea of anyone being hurt on her account caused her stomach to tighten into a knot until she remembered that Ben's life was at stake, too. He'd stand in front of her in an attack. Ruth's hands fisted. She wanted the danger gone. If Jon Smith's skill at interrogation made that possible, she would deal.

Ben returned to the interstate and resumed their journey to Fortress headquarters. As the miles passed, he retained his hold on her hand, occasionally lifting it to his mouth to press a kiss to her palm or wrist.

Goosebumps surged up her spine. Ben was potent. Would he ever consider a real relationship with her? Who was she kidding? Why would a man as amazing as Ben want a woman broken by a monster? The kisses, hugs, and hand holding were designed to help with their cover. Ben hadn't hinted that he was interested in her in the real world despite off-the-charts chemistry between them.

Ben must have sensed something amiss because he squeezed her hand. "Are you okay?"

"I'm fine." A whopper of a lie.

"Why don't I believe you?" Another squeeze. "Come on. We've been middle-of-the-night phone buddies for months. Talk to me."

She wanted to but feared broaching a subject that could lead to the end of their friendship. "I can't talk about this right now." She didn't want to lose him. As ashamed as she was of her own weakness, Ruth needed Ben to protect her from the stalker.

After her final modeling job, she wouldn't be in the limelight as much. Maybe her stalker would decide she wasn't worth his time anymore. Ruth sighed. Right. In her dreams. Real life wasn't so kind.

"Will this impact your safety?" Ben asked.

Ruth shook her head. If he bailed on her, Maddox would assign someone else to act as bodyguard.

Ben considered her a moment, then said, "All right. I'll let it slide. For now. But we'll come back to this soon. I want the truth. No hedging. We've come too far for that." He flicked her a pointed glance. "I won't let you retreat behind your walls, Ruth."

She prayed she found the courage to ask for what she wanted and needed in her life. Ben.

CHAPTER TWELVE

Ben remained vigilant throughout the rest of the drive to Fortress headquarters, alternating between checking the mirrors and watching Ruth with his peripheral vision. Something was bothering her, but what?

Although he longed to badger her into revealing what troubled her, he wanted to fully concentrate on the discussion. Concerned that the constant threats to her safety were causing memories of her time with Torino to resurface, Ben would encourage her talk to Marcus Lang before the jet left for Mexico tonight.

His thumb skimmed over the delicate skin of her wrist, lips curving when she shivered in reaction to his touch.

When Ben checked the rearview mirror again, his eyes narrowed. An old green truck weaved through traffic, edging closer to them. Gut tightening, he changed lanes and increased his speed. The truck surged forward, shifting into the lane a few car lengths behind his SUV.

Not good. He squeezed Ruth's hand before releasing her to get a better grip on the steering wheel. "We have company."

Ruth twisted to look out the back window. "Which vehicle?"

"Old green truck. We're ten miles from Fortress. By the time Zane dispatches operatives to intercept, we'll be close to the compound."

"So, we're on our own?"

"For now. I don't want to use evasive maneuvers. Traffic is too bad."

"Will they run us off the road?"

"Not on the interstate. Too many witnesses with cell phones to call the cops. They'll wait until we get off the interstate."

"Let's give ourselves some room, then. I'd prefer not to travel to Mexico with whiplash injuries."

He glanced at her, concerned. "Are you hurting?"

"Nothing that an over-the-counter pain medicine won't cure. Don't worry about me, Ben. If I was injured, I'd tell you."

"You have to be truthful with me at all times, Ruth."

"I don't make a habit of lying." Her voice sounded snippy.

No, but she withheld information when a subject made her uncomfortable. "Let's hope these goons don't bash into us or Bear will come down even harder on me." Ben didn't want to be on the receiving end of Bear's temper and tongue-lashing if he was involved in damaging two Fortress SUVs. He'd never hear the end of it from the mechanical genius.

"I can't wait to meet this guy."

"He's a character. Bear has a soft spot for women in danger. It's why we always ask him to beef up the safety features on SUVs for the wives and girlfriends of operatives."

She went quiet.

Ben chanced another glance her direction and noted the thoughtful look on her face. "What is it?"

"My SUV looks and feels exactly like the Fortress fleet."

He should have told her the truth before now. His hands tightened on the wheel. Ben hadn't wanted to give Ruth an excuse to reject his gift to her. Yeah, the price had been steep, but when Bear learned why Ben had asked for a rush job on the SUV, the grouchy mechanic had given a short nod and fast-tracked the vehicle through the process.

"Did Bear work on my SUV?" Ruth asked.

If he insisted on the truth from her, he couldn't offer her any less. "Yes."

"You arranged that for me, didn't you?"

And paid for it. He gave a short nod. Would she be angry? "It was the best way I could think of to protect you." When he wasn't with her which was most of the time. Ben had never been dissatisfied with his work. Until now.

A soft sigh. "Thank you for taking care of me even when I'm unaware of your efforts, Ben."

"You're not angry with me?"

"How could I be? You're a protector. This is more evidence to prove it."

Protector? Ruth viewed him through those rose-colored glasses. Ben was a stone-cold killer, a role he'd been forced to accept from the time he turned twelve and escaped the horror of his childhood.

His lip curled. The SEAL trainers had honed his skills to turn him into a lethal killing machine. If Ruth knew the truth, she would run from him, screaming in terror. In comparison, Ben made Hugo Torino look like a tame tabby.

He didn't want Ruth afraid of him. Ben swallowed hard. Her fear would shatter what remained of the broken shards of his heart.

Another glance in the mirror revealed the green truck was now three car lengths back. Ben sped up the Harding Place exit ramp. The green truck swerved onto the ramp in their wake. If he had any doubts about the truck and its occupants, the latest move settled the issue.

Ben threaded through Nashville traffic, keeping at least two vehicles between his SUV and the truck as he fought to lengthen the distance between the vehicles.

When they were one mile away from the compound, Ben called Zane. "It's Ben. We're five minutes out, still coming in hot. A green truck is in pursuit."

"Copy that. We're ready. Go to the east gate." He ended the call.

The green truck put on a burst of speed.

Ben scowled, turned a sharp left, and slammed the accelerator to the floor. The SUV sprinted ahead, creating a larger gap between the vehicles. Wouldn't last. The creeps in the truck were determined to catch up and force them to the side of the road to kidnap Ruth or kill Ben. Maybe both.

As Ben guided the SUV around another curve, the truck's passenger lowered the window and leaned out with a gun in his hand. "Get down!" he ordered as the first bullet pinged against the back of the SUV.

Ruth bent over, face angled toward him. Her hands gripped the passenger seat to keep herself steady, a necessity with Ben weaving around the light traffic on the road leading to the warehouse district where Fortress Security headquarters was located. "Will we make it?"

"Of course." He wouldn't allow anything else. Ben didn't want Ruth in close proximity to thugs who wouldn't quibble about hurting her, especially if he was the target.

The length of the pursuit and the determination of these goons to run them off the road convinced Ben that he was the ultimate target. Whether or not the goal was to get rid of him to reach the woman in the passenger seat or just to wipe him out of existence was the question. Somehow, though, Ben didn't see a run-of-the-mill stalker having the resources to hire this many hoods to pursue Ruth. The stalker would come after her himself in the darkest hours of the night.

Another frown. Unless Torino was behind the attacks. His men could have a long-standing order to make Ruth pay for her escape and for crippling his organization. But what satisfaction would that bring the wannabe gunrunner? He would be in prison until he was an old man. His men couldn't hold Ruth until he was released.

More bullets struck the back window while others bounced off the SUV. Another round of gunfire caused the back window on the passenger side to spiderweb.

Half a mile more and they'd have backup. "Not much farther."

She flinched when more bullets struck the vehicle.

Ben sped around a slower-moving vehicle and surged ahead when the truck had to wait for an oncoming car to pass before dodging around the slower-moving vehicle and resuming pursuit.

The Fortress compound came into view. Ben raced toward the open gate and zoomed between two Fortress SUVs. A third raced in to fill in the gap as soon as Ben passed through the gap, providing a barrier between the closing gate and the truck. Operatives poured from the vehicles and took up position with weapons in their hands.

As Ben sped toward the underground garage, the truck skidded to a stop. The driver threw the vehicle into reverse and backed up until he reached a side street, turned and sped away. One of the Fortress SUVs pursued the thugs.

When Ben parked in the garage, Ruth sat up, her face drained of color. Furious at the men who scared her, Ben hurried around the hood to the passenger side. He had to hold her and assure himself that she was safe in his arms.

He opened the door and Ruth dove into his arms. "I've got you. You're safe now," he murmured, arms tight around her, grateful beyond words that she was turning to him instead of panicking and shoving him away.

"Who is doing this?" she whispered.

"I don't know, baby, but I'm working on it. I'll help you reclaim your life." Even if it meant giving her up to protect her from him and his past.

He stilled. When had he decided to claim her? He couldn't. His past could cost Ruth her life and she meant too much to him to risk that.

The elevator arrived at the garage level with a soft bell. Footsteps drew close. "You two okay?" Shadow's medic, Sam, asked as she drew near.

Ben kissed Ruth's temple before glancing over his shoulder at his teammate. "No serious injuries, but Ruth had quite a scare. She's in pain from the hits my SUV took."

"I'll find a blanket and pain medicine, and prepare a mug of tea with sugar in it. As soon as the rest of Shadow returns from the east gate, we'll meet in the conference room."

"Thanks, Sam."

"Yep." She returned to the elevator and seconds later, the doors closed, whisking her to the sixth floor.

Ben continued to hold Ruth while the shakes worked their way through her system. He murmured encouragement in her ear and pressed an occasional gentle kiss to her temple while waiting.

Ten minutes later, the trembling ceased, and Ruth leaned heavily against Ben. He swept her into his arms, used his hip to close the vehicle door, and strode toward the elevator.

"I can stand," Ruth protested.

"Can't a man sweep his lady off her feet?"

"Ben, I'm too heavy."

He stepped into the elevator car with a chuckle. "I've packed heavier gear into the field and hauled it around for miles. Let me hold you."

She sighed and pressed her face against the side of his neck, resting against him.

Ben drew in a deep breath, amazed at her absolute trust in him. He prayed he never destroyed that fragile bond between them.

When the elevator stopped, Ben carried Ruth into an empty office three doors down from the conference room. What he was about to do was beyond stupid and would only make things harder on both of them. Didn't change his intention.

Ruth glanced around. "Why are we in here?"

He set Ruth on her feet, then closed and locked the door. Turning back to her, he said, "I need a minute." Or ten. "Come here." Ben spread his arms, waiting for her to make the decision about the next move.

She moved into his embrace without hesitation, wrapping her arms around his neck. "Ben?"

"Shh. I need this." He needed her. His mouth came down on hers and took control of the kiss from the first touch. On every mission, ice water ran through his veins. Nothing rattled him. He'd had fear drummed out of him in BUD/S. The events of the past hour, though, had shaken Ben to the core.

He shuddered. One bullet penetrating the SUVs safety features and Ben could have lost Ruth. He deepened the kiss, twining his tongue with hers in a slow, sensual dance that spoke volumes about feelings he didn't dare verbalize.

Although he lost himself in the kiss, he was aware enough to maintain a hold on Ruth that she could break at will. He didn't want her to feel trapped. When he knew his control was seconds away from collapsing, Ben broke the kiss.

"No, not yet. Please."

"Shh. Let me hold you for a few minutes."

"What about the meeting with Shadow?"

"They'll wait." He trailed his fingers along her spine while his other hand cradled the back of her head. As their breaths settled into a normal rhythm, he eased away to lock his gaze with Ruth's. "You amaze me, sunshine."

She blinked the last of the dazed look from her eyes. "Why?"

"You could have panicked during those two attacks. Instead, you followed my instructions, making it easier for me to concentrate on protecting both of us."

"I was equal parts terrified and furious."

"Furious?"

"That you were in danger again because you're protecting me. I don't want to lose you."

"If I'm out of commission, other operatives are capable of protecting you."

Ruth scowled and thumped his chest with her fist. "No. You don't understand."

Ben's mouth grew dry. "What are you saying?"

She opened her mouth to say something, then closed it again and started to turn away.

He caught her upper arms and held her in place. "Don't run. Talk to me."

"I don't want anyone else protecting me."

A truth, but not all of it. He waited, willing her to open up to him. She stayed silent, unease flickering in her eyes. What was wrong? Afraid he'd pushed her too far, too fast, he slid his arms around her again, drew her against his chest, and lowered his head until his mouth was against her ear. "What do you need, Ruth?" As far as he was concerned, anything Ruth wanted, she could have.

She edged closer. "You," she whispered. "I need you."

He froze. "As a bodyguard, a friend?" Please, not the friends-only talk. That might kill him despite the fact it was safer for her.

"More."

His heart rate spiked. "How much more?"

"Whatever you'll give me."

Ben cupped her chin and tilted her head back. "Tell me."

Ruth shook her head. "It's a ridiculous fantasy. I should go find my sister and assure her I'm safe. She must be frantic."

"Bridget will wait another few minutes. In the darkest hours of the night, what is your fantasy, Ruth?" Was her fantasy the same as his improbable dream?

She took a deep breath. "That you and I are a real couple."

Oh, man. Never in his wildest dreams did he think Ruth would consider a real relationship with him. "Why do you think us dating is a ridiculous fantasy?"

Sadness filled her beautiful eyes. "Because you deserve a woman who isn't tainted and broken."

CHAPTER THIRTEEN

Shock held Ben immobile as he stared at Ruth who looked as though she would burst into tears any second. "You aren't tainted or broken. You're perfect."

Ruth tore herself from his arms, the expression on her face highlighting her inner grief and turmoil. She spun and would have dashed to the door if Ben hadn't stopped her by wrapping his arms around her from behind. She tried to wrench away from him.

Ben tightened his grip. "You had enough courage to tell me what you wanted." She'd spilled a truth that had literally taken his breath away. Although he longed to grab onto her with both hands and never let go, he couldn't have her. Could he? "Tell me the rest." Perhaps if she couldn't see his face while she talked, saying what was on her mind and heart would be easier. Did she mean what she said? Did she want him in her life long term?

Ruth shuddered.

Fear or attraction? When she pressed her back more firmly against his chest, the constriction around Ben's heart eased. Attraction. Thank God. The chemistry between them was combustible, making her almost irresistible to him. He was in so much trouble.

"I haven't told you what Hugo did to me," Ruth whispered. "I couldn't."

He closed his eyes as pain for her rocketed through him. He wished he could go back in time and prevent Hugo from kidnapping her, but it was impossible. "I have a pretty good idea. He raped you, didn't he?"

A slight nod. "I feel dirty inside and out." Her voice broke. "Even though I know what happened wasn't my fault, I can't help how I feel."

"I understand." More than she or anyone else knew.

"You can't."

Ben turned her to face him. "Actually, I do."

Ruth stared, then understanding dawned in her eyes. A second later, blood drained from her face and she gripped his upper arms. "Who hurt you?"

No time to discuss this right now. He also had to prepare himself to bare his worst nightmare. If anyone else asked that question, he'd shut them down, cold. But this was Ruth. If he shut her out of this portion of his life, he'd lose her. "We don't have enough time for that story. We need to go to the conference room before someone looks for us."

Her hands tightened around his arms. "You promise to tell me the truth?"

"I will."

"When?"

"When we're alone and not worrying about interruptions." He cupped her cheek with his palm. "You're the strongest woman I know, Ruth Monihan. You don't have broken pieces."

She looked uncertain. "What about my ridiculous fantasy?"

He pressed a light kiss to her mouth. "We'll talk about that, too. But you should know the feelings are mutual."

When she gasped, Ben knew they had to leave this room before he launched into a lengthy discussion or yanked her into his arms for more sizzling kisses.

They needed the soul-baring discussion before he allowed himself to touch her like that again. She deserved the truth and a choice about whether to risk the danger.

He threaded his fingers through hers, unlocked the door, and led her to the conference room where his teammates were seated around the table.

Trace scowled. "Where have you been? Doesn't take 20 minutes to get from the garage to the conference room."

"I needed time to get rid of the shakes," Ruth said before Ben could tell his best friend to back off.

The fierce look in the sniper's eyes shifted to concern in an instant. "You're okay? No injuries?"

"I'm fine, thanks to Ben. He saved my life twice in the past ninety minutes."

"Any word from Jon or Eli?" Ben asked Nico.

His team leader looked grim. "Yeah. They called the cops a few minutes ago. Law enforcement should be on scene soon."

"The two idiots talked."

A nod.

Ben frowned. "Well?"

"You won't like what they had to say." Nico's gaze flicked to Ruth before returning to him.

Oh, man. Dread coiled in his gut like a viper readying itself to strike a death blow. When Ruth's hand tightened on his, Ben pulled out a chair and seated her. Might as well hear the bad news sitting down. He dropped into the chair beside Ruth's. "Let's hear it."

"Bridget wants to see Ruth," Trace interjected.

"She'll wait." Ruth stared down her brother-in-law. "I'm stronger than you think, Trace."

"This doesn't concern you."

"Can it, Trace." Ben sent him a pointed glance as he wrapped a blanket around Ruth and pressed the insulated cup into her hand. "No more secrets." Keeping something this vital from Ruth would be an epic mistake. Ben wanted her to choose him with full knowledge of the risks involved.

He wrapped his hand around Ruth's free one. Even considering a relationship with her was foolish. He knew the people who had a price on his head. Ruth didn't understand. Between the two of them, she wasn't the broken one. He was. Ben shifted his attention to Nico. "What did Jon learn?"

"The two thugs in the Explorer weren't after Ruth."

That's what he'd been afraid of. "They were after me."

"I already informed Zane and Maddox. They're looking into it."

He rubbed the back of his neck, frustrated and angry. Which ghost from his past was coming back to bite him now? Didn't really matter, he realized. They were all deadly and wanted revenge against him and anyone who meant something to him. Shadow unit could take care of themselves. Ruth, on the other hand, would be helpless against the violence and murderous rage of his past.

"What will we do?" Ruth asked, voice soft.

"Deal with it when we find out who is behind the attack." He turned back to Nico. "What about the troublemakers in the truck?"

"Lost them at a traffic light. Zane is checking the security footage. Hopefully, we'll find the truck and the drivers and have a chat with them."

"Will Jon question these men, too?" Ruth asked.

Joe's eyebrows rose. "What do you know about Smith?"

"Only what Ben told me. He says Jon's very good at his job."

Sam exchanged glances with her husband, then said, "Trace and Nico have serious interrogation skills as well. If Z identifies the truck guys before we leave for Mexico, they can question the men if Jon's not available."

Nico grabbed a remote and pointed it at the wall screen. "We have a few hours before we head to the airport. Let's talk about hotel security while we wait for word from Z. We need the hours on the jet to recharge." He brought up the hotel schematics. "Ruth, this would be a good time to go see your sister. Bridget wants to see you."

She was silent a moment. "Are you trying to get rid of me?"

Shadow's leader grinned. "No, ma'am. I know firsthand from my wife that these discussions are boring as dirt to anyone not involved in the security end of a mission. All you have to do in Mexico is model and follow our recommendations for your safety."

Ruth looked at Ben.

He leaned close and brushed her mouth with his. "Go. You'll feel better after talking to your sister and so will Bridget." Satisfied that she'd be safe inside Fortress headquarters, he remained seated as she left the conference room with her blanket and cup of tea.

When he turned back to his teammates, all of them were staring at him, various degrees of surprise or shock on their faces. "What?" His tone came out curt.

"I thought this dating relationship was to satisfy the media and draw out the stalker," Trace said, his voice dead even. "Something you need to tell me, buddy?"

"It's none of your business."

His friend's eyes narrowed. "Try again, Martin. She's my sister-in-law. I have a vested interested in her wellbeing."

"Enough." Nico rose to his feet, glaring at them. "We can't have division on this op, Trace, so either deal with what's happening or walk away from the assignment."

"That's Bridget's sister he's kissing like she's his flavor of the week. She's fragile."

Hands fisted, Ben said, "She's stronger than any of us. Don't underestimate her. You know better than to think I would toy with her emotions. Make another crack about Ruth being my flavor of the week and you'll be sporting a black eye on this assignment." After five years as teammates and best friends, Trace's belief that Ben would treat Ruth with anything less than respect ripped a gouge in his heart. Guess he didn't know Trace as well as he thought.

"Enough, Ben. This is your last warning, Trace," Nico said.

"I have to say one more thing, then I'll shut up until we're back on US soil." Trace glared at Ben. "If you hurt her, you'll answer to me. Friend or not, you'll pay. Hard."

"Understood." If he hurt Ruth, Ben would deserve whatever Trace dished out. Knowing how protective Maddox was of the supermodel, he suspected his boss would weigh in as well. Despite his vow not to hurt Ruth under any circumstances, he didn't want to be on the receiving end of his boss's fists. Maddox wouldn't hold back.

"If you're finished drawing your battle lines, let's get to work," Nico said.

While Shadow debated the strengths and weaknesses of Casa del Mar's security, Ben kept tabs on the length of time that Ruth was absent. When an hour passed without her making an appearance or sending him a text, he couldn't stand sitting there any longer. He didn't understand it, but he had to see for himself that she was safe. He knew the urge was irrational since Fortress headquarters was a high-security facility. Didn't matter. Seeing her for himself had shifted to the top of his priority list.

He stood. "I'll be back in a few minutes." Ben pointed at Trace. "Don't."

His friend's lips tipped up at the corners as he held up his hands in mock surrender. "Who, me?"

Without giving anyone else a chance to comment or stop him, Ben left the conference room and headed to the research division on the third floor and Bridget's office.

He gave a perfunctory knock and opened the door. Both women turned. Alarm roared through Ben when he noticed Ruth's wet cheeks. She'd been crying.

Ben crouched beside her and cupped her cheek. "What's wrong?"

"Nothing. I'm decompressing. I'm allowed to cry."

He wiped the remnants of tears from her face. "No, ma'am. You aren't."

"Why not?"

"I can't take it. Your tears kill me."

As he'd meant for her to do, Ruth laughed. "Tough luck, buddy. You'll have to get over it. I cry occasionally."

"Not often, okay? Tears send me into a panic."

She rolled her beautiful eyes. "You build and dismantle bombs for a living."

"Your tears are more dangerous that any IED I've ever come across."

Ruth laughed, the last of the sadness leaving her eyes.

Mission accomplished, Ben glanced at Bridget and noticed the same wetness on her cheeks. He flinched. "Your tears are Trace's problem," he muttered. "I'm not up to the task on your behalf."

"My hero," she said in a dry tone. "Bailing at the sight of a little water."

He ignored Bridget and refocused on Ruth. "Do you need anything before I head back to the conference room, sunshine?"

Ruth shook her head. "I'm fine. Really."

He dropped a quick kiss on her lips. "Stay inside Fortress headquarters. I'll check on you again in another hour." He forced himself to leave the office although for the first time in his career at Fortress, he longed to blow off his job in favor of holding Ruth in his arms for a long time.

Ben returned to the conference room and took his seat again.

"Nice of you to rejoin us, Ben." Nico gave him a hard look. "Stay focused."

Right. Would Nico remain focused if Mercy was in danger and out his line of sight? He didn't think so. "Yes, sir."

The security plans with multiple contingencies progressed with Ben sneaking surreptitious glances at his watch every few minutes. Another hour passed and Ben was ready to make another trip to the research division when Ruth returned to the conference room.

He was on his feet the next instant. "What happened?"

She handed Ben her phone. He glanced at the screen to see an email sent to Roxanne. Ben scanned the contents and scowled.

"Problem?" Nico asked.

"Ruth received another threatening email."

Trace frowned. "What does it say?"

"If you want to live, stay away from Mexico."

CHAPTER FOURTEEN

"When did you receive this email?" Ben asked.

Ruth hid her hands under the table. With a room full of operatives who dodged bullets for a living, she didn't want to appear weak and afraid even though that's how she felt. Would this nightmare never end? "Ten minutes ago. I showed it to Bridget. She's tracing the sender's IP address."

"I doubt she'll have much luck," Joe said. "The other threatening emails came from throwaway accounts that were closed as soon as the message was sent."

Sam frowned. "Are you sure your stalker sent that email?"

"Why wouldn't he be the sender?"

"What are you thinking, Sparky?" Joe asked his wife.

"Stalkers usually send pictures or verbal threats if the object of his obsession shows affection to another man. That email doesn't sound like it came from a stalker."

Nico looked thoughtful. "Sam has a point. Any chance it's from a professional rival?"

Another model? "It's possible," she admitted. "The modeling business is competitive. Supermodels don't stay at the top of the profession for long."

"Why not?"

"Age and time work against you. The window of opportunity is a short one."

"How long have you been a model?"

"Long enough that my career is winding down." Sooner than anyone realized except for her agent. He wasn't happy with her decision, insisting that she was still a hot commodity since she still received offers for many plum assignments.

But Ruth had made more money than she could spend in ten lifetimes over the course of her modeling career. Through judicious saving and investing, she never had to work again. However, she was too young to sit on a rocking chair on the front porch of her home for the rest of her life. Good thing she had ambitious plans in the works.

"That's crazy." Under cover of the table, Ben's hand covered hers. "You're one of the most beautiful women in the world."

She grinned. "Thanks for the vote of confidence."

"Focus," Nico said.

Right. "To answer your question, yes, I do have professional rivals who would do almost anything to take over my contracts."

"Would they kill for the opportunity?" Trace asked.

Ruth thought about that for a moment, then shrugged one shoulder. "A few would happily gouge my eyes out if they could get by with it. I don't know about murder, though."

Joe shook his head. "Cutthroat competition."

"We need a list." Nico slid a small pad of lined paper across the table to Ruth along with a pen.

"You don't know how many men and women that will include."

"Focus on those who will be in Mexico with you. The threat specifically mentioned that location."

"Is this photoshoot that important in the industry?" Nico asked.

"It's for the top fashion designer in the world. This is the job every model wanted."

He inclined his head toward the notepad. "Make your list. We'll run the names."

Ruth freed her hand from Ben's to make the list. According to her agent, four other models were joining her for the Casa del Mar photoshoot. Any of them could be a potential threat. Or not. She hated for Shadow to invade their privacy if they were innocent.

On the other hand, if one of these models was responsible for the black roses and strawberries, he or she might do something even more risky that could hurt Ben. She couldn't allow what was happening to her to cause him harm.

She slid the pad of paper back to Nico. "Other models may be on site. These are the ones my agent mentioned. They are chief rivals for most of my jobs, though."

"Then it's a good bet if a model is responsible for part of your trouble, one of them is to blame." Nico scanned the list. "We'll divide up the names and dig into the background of each model. The jet leaves in two hours. Don't be late." He dispersed assignments to each member of Shadow. "Ruth, we'll do our research and discuss our findings when we're in the air. You can add your insights then. The rest of you, check your gear bags and replenish whatever you need. Pack heavy. We don't have many friends where we're going."

Aside from Ben, the operatives exited the conference room, leaving Ruth alone with him. "Are we going back to the weapons vault?"

He smiled. "In a few minutes. I want to check in with Zane first." Ben stood and tugged Ruth to her feet. He led her from the conference room to the communications center at the opposite end of the hallway.

Zane manned the center alone. Several computer screens were lit up, data scrolling on one, maps of different locations on two others, and yet a fourth screen had some kind of tracking system engaged.

Ruth scanned the room, awed by the amount of electronics housed inside the four walls. Now she understood why Zane Murphy was known as the communications guru and tech wizard for Fortress.

Zane spun his wheelchair around to face them. "How are you, Ruth?"

"Becoming an old pro at handling adrenaline dump."

He chuckled. "Let's hope you've experienced the last one for a while. What do you need, Ben?"

"Information and a phone for Ruth."

Zane zoomed across the room to a cabinet. He opened one of the steel doors and reached inside for a phone plus a cover.

"I have a cell phone, Ben." She looked at him. "It's brand new."

"This one is better. We use satellite phones that are heavily encrypted. No one will be able to eavesdrop on your conversations or intercept your messages." He brushed a soft kiss on her mouth, sending fire shooting along her nerve endings. "It's the only way I'll be able to communicate with you while I'm deployed."

Did that mean he wanted to text and talk to her while he had downtime on his missions? She hoped so. She missed him like crazy when he was gone. "All right."

Relief gleamed in his eyes. "Thank you." He turned to Zane. "What cover did you find for her?"

"Something I hope she enjoys." He handed the covered phone to Ruth.

She flipped it over and burst into laughter. Zane had found a glittery cover with different kinds of dolls scattered over the surface. This was perfect, especially in light of what she wanted to do with the rest of her life. The choice made her wonder if Zane Murphy knew more than he let on about her future plans. "I love it. Thank you, Zane."

"My pleasure." He looked pleased with her response to his choice.

"Any news on the truck?" Ben asked.

"Stolen from Mt. Juliet. The police report it's been wiped down so no usable prints. And, of course, the area where they dumped the truck didn't have any security cameras or traffic cams I could tap into."

"When will Jon and Eli be cut loose from the cops?"

"Not for a while. They were able to talk to the boss for a minute. He's waiting for you in his office."

When they arrived at his outer office, Brent's assistant waved them on without announcing them. Ben knocked on the door and guided Ruth inside.

The Fortress CEO waved them to the chairs in front of his desk while he wrapped up a phone call. When he replaced the handset on the cradle, Brent studied Ruth a moment. Seeming satisfied with what he saw, he glanced at Ben. "I talked to Wolfe and Smith. You have a problem."

A snort. "Only one? Must be a slow day in the terrorist business."

"This problem is an old one."

He froze. "How old?"

"Twenty years."

Ben grimaced and turned to Ruth. "I'm sorry, sunshine."

Something was seriously wrong. Fear for Ben sent her heart rate into the stratosphere. "Why?"

Instead of answering her question, he glanced at Brent. "You know what needs to be done."

"Is that what you want?"

"No, but it's what is best for Ruth. I don't have a choice, do I?"

She laid her hand on his arm. "What is it? What's wrong?"

He cupped her cheek with his palm, regret and simmering rage in his eyes. "My worst nightmare has risen from the dead."

One look at his face and she knew this rage was connected in some way to what he'd promised to tell her when they were alone. She also knew protection was bound in his DNA. If he thought his past was a danger to her, he'd remove himself from the equation to protect her. "What do you plan to do?"

"The only thing I can do to protect you. Resign as your bodyguard."

CHAPTER FIFTEEN

Ben's heart hurt at the thought of handing over responsibility for Ruth's safety to another operative, even one he trusted implicitly. He didn't trust anyone with her life as much as he did himself. But that privilege was slipping through his fingers.

Ruth thought he was a good man. He was so far from her ideal that Ruth would be horrified if she realized the truth. Her belief in Ben made him want to be better than he was. But he knew better. He was dark and deadly, meant to live the shadows, not in the sunshine. Looked like the dream to have Ruth Monihan in his life was just that, an unattainable dream.

He fought down the bitter anger threatening to overwhelm him until he was alone and had time to deal with the specter from his past. Would his past never die? Didn't matter that the cascade of events wasn't a result of anything he'd done. He'd had no choice in the matter. He was just a kid at the time, unable to understand the repercussions of a decision that changed his life and dragged him into the ugliest pit imaginable until he'd escaped and taken back his freedom at an unimaginable cost.

Ruth's hand dropped from his arm and she took a step away from him. The small distance she put between them broke something inside him. He tried to seal up the breach, but it was impossible. Somehow in the past few months, Ruth had burrowed her way into his heart and taken up residence.

She raised her chin as she stared at Ben a moment, then turned to Brent. "Thank you for your help. Send me your bill. I will no longer be requiring the services of Fortress Security."

Ben scowled and caught Ruth's arm as she moved toward the door. "What are you doing?"

"I told you." Her voice was even. "The only bodyguard I'll accept is you. If you won't do the job, I'll go without protection."

He tightened his grip. "I can't do the job."

"What's the difference?"

"I'm trying to protect you."

"By abandoning me?"

"I'll choose your new bodyguard myself."

Brent stood. "I need some coffee and a short walk to clear my head. I'll return in fifteen minutes." He closed the door.

Ruth shook her head, her gaze locked with Ben's. "It's you or no one."

"The stalker or a potential rival for your jobs isn't your biggest threat right now. I am."

"You're also my best protection."

He hauled her close, deliberately got into her personal space. "Do you think I'd hand off your security to another operative, especially another man, if I didn't think it was necessary?" Ben bent his head until his mouth was next to her ear. "You should know me better than that. I protect what's mine."

Ruth stilled. "Who said I'm yours?"

"You did. You gave me that gift. I'm not letting you take it back."

"Maybe not, but you'll give me to another operative."

That brought a scowl. "Your security, not you." The thought of another man being responsible for her safety was eating him up inside.

"No."

"Ruth..."

"Forget it, Ben. We started the media machine this afternoon. By now, news of my new boyfriend is all over the Internet. If you won't go with me to Mexico, I'll go without a security detail and spread the word that my boyfriend couldn't make the trip with me this time due to work conflicts."

He hissed out a breath, furious at the situation hurting both of them. "Why are you being so stubborn?"

"Because I need you. Only you make me feel safe." She buried her face against his chest as though embarrassed at her admission.

Another arrow shot into his heart at a new possibility. "Is that why you want to be with me? Safety?" The possibility hadn't occurred to him before now, a foolish mistake. Why would any good woman want him? Was she like all the others, wanting him for something he could provide rather than wanting Ben for himself?

That brought her head up in a hurry. "Safety is a nice benefit, but that's not the main reason."

"What is?"

"You. Your confidence, your heart, your courage and loyalty. You, Ben Martin. You're right. Another operative could keep me safe, but he's not you."

Ben drew in a ragged breath. "I'm not who you think I am."

She gave a soft laugh. "Who is? I thought I knew who I was until Hugo kidnapped me. Now, I don't know myself."

What did that mean? He had nothing to compare the Ruth before Torino to the Ruth after. He had known of her. Anyone who hadn't heard of Roxanne had to be a hermit living in a cave.

The woman standing in front of him had been strong before Torino got his hands on her. Otherwise, she wouldn't have survived the worst that life could throw at her and come out the other side of the storm as strong as steel. He'd be honored to have her at his back any time.

When Shadow had snatched her from Torino, Ruth hadn't panicked or held them back. Despite the trauma she'd suffered, Ruth had been feisty and protective of her sister. She'd even gone so far as to question whether or not Trace was good enough for Bridget. No, that woman wasn't missing any pieces from her time with the gunrunner.

So, what was he going to do? He couldn't let her go to Mexico without protection. Someone, maybe more than one person, had placed a target on her back. But if Ben was with her, his past would be a danger to her as well.

Ben released her and stepped away to pace the office. "Don't ask me to do this." Yeah, he was begging, but what choice did he have? He wanted her safe. Having him at her side made her more vulnerable than ever.

"Too late."

"You don't know the truth about me."

"You promised to tell me."

"We don't have the time or the privacy for that discussion. I'm sure not doing it in here where Maddox's office is wired for video and sound."

Ruth's mouth gaped. "Brent records what's said and done in his office?"

"We're a security firm, and Maddox has access to secrets that men would steal and kill for." He inclined his head toward the small camera in the ceiling at the right-hand corner of the room. "That's the obvious camera. There are two others that are well hidden. If anyone enters the office, the boss knows about it."

She glanced uneasily at the camera and shifted closer to Ben. Voice low, Ruth said, "Is he watching and listening to us now?"

"Why would he? He'll know in a few minutes what I've decided to do."

That brought a frown. "We. This isn't a monarchy, Martin. We'll decide what to do."

"Right. We'll decide as long as it's what you want. If not, you'll fire the lot of us." He was trying everything he knew to protect her and yet Ruth was forcing his hand. He didn't have any doubt that she'd do as she threatened and go to her photoshoot without protection.

"Does Brent know about your past?"

"Some. Not all." No one knew everything. He wasn't sure he could tell Ruth all the sordid details. Some things shouldn't be in her head and Ben had no intention of adding to the nightmares she already fought each night.

Her gaze searched his for a moment. "What's your decision? Do I book alternate transportation for myself to Mexico or are we catching the Fortress jet with your team?"

Ben drew her close with a gentle tug despite the violence of his churning emotions. He stared into her beloved face and knew he was lost. He gave her one more chance to back away from this, from him and his world. "You don't know what you're asking."

"Are you going with me or am I going alone?"

He bent his head until his mouth was a hairsbreadth from hers. "Be sure, Ruth," he murmured, his lips brushing hers with every word he spoke. "If we do this, there's no going back for either of us. If you give yourself into my keeping, I'll do anything necessary to keep you safe whether you approve of my tactics or not."

"Am I only a job to you?" she whispered.

His grip on her shoulders tightened. "You already know the answer to that. From the first moment I saw you, you've haunted my dreams and occupied my thoughts when I should have been focused on my job. Right now, I can let you walk away." Maybe. At this moment, he wasn't sure he was being honest with Ruth. "If we make this relationship real, I will fight to keep you. Be sure, baby." Tension twisted his gut and held his body immobile as he waited for the verdict from the woman of his dreams. If she rejected him, the sliver of humanity still left in his soul would shatter.

Ruth wrapped her arms around his neck and closed the distance between them. Her mouth cruised over his in a series of butterfly kisses that drove him crazy. Unable to withstand the feather-light teasing, Ben crushed his mouth to hers and took control of the kiss.

He shuddered at the heat and sunshine that flooded his veins. This was what he needed to fight the darkness. Ruth's touch and trust. Her care. As battered as he was internally, Ben didn't think she would ever be able to love him. If this was all he could have, he'd count himself blessed for the rest of his life.

Slowly, he pulled himself out of the haze enough to realize he'd backed Ruth against Maddox's desk and was seconds away from crossing a line neither were ready for. Ben broke the kiss, dragged in a few ragged breaths, and whispered, "Last chance, sunshine. Is this what you want?" Is he what she wanted?

Ruth laid her hand on his chest right over his pounding heart. "I'm sure."

So be it. She'd made her choice. There was no going back. "Let's go. We have a plane to catch." And he had plans to make.

Ben escorted her from Maddox's office, praying he hadn't made a mistake that would cost both of them their lives.

CHAPTER SIXTEEN

Once the jet leveled out, Ruth unlatched her seatbelt and glanced at her companion. Ben had been quiet since he'd informed Brent that he and his team would be accompanying her to Mexico.

The Fortress CEO didn't seem to be surprised. He'd nodded and handed Ben a small envelope with instructions to give Ruth the contents when it was time.

She flicked another glance Ben's direction. If he didn't talk soon, she'd resort to underhanded tactics to break his silence. She had a feeling the rest of Shadow would razz the silent man beside her when she announced to the passengers on the private jet that she and Ben were a real couple now and that she'd blackmailed him into giving her a real chance.

Ruth should have felt guilty for the way she forced the issue with Ben in his boss's office. That she didn't was a good indication of how far gone she was over the operative.

He'd worked for several years with Nico, Joe, Sam, and Trace yet they didn't know about his past. How was that possible? They cared about him. Why hadn't they unearthed his secret? His teammates had to know that his past haunted him.

As she observed the others, Ruth noted the concerned glances sent Ben's direction. They knew something was wrong, but chose to respect his privacy. Guilt assailed her. Should she have backed off and followed their example?

If she had, she'd be on her way to Mexico without a security detail. Although she didn't believe the stalker wouldn't strike while she was on this photoshoot, gambling on her gut instinct was foolish. Her experience with Hugo should be proof enough that her judgment of men was suspect.

Except where Ben was concerned. With Hugo, she'd been lonely and swept away by his charm. His lavish spending had lulled Ruth into lowering her guard since she didn't have to worry that he courted her for her bank account. She'd been naive and the cost had been steep.

Enough. She couldn't undo the past, only move forward. Ruth refocused her attention. Uneasiness had her hands fisting. What if Ben was right and she had more than a stalker to worry about? What if the danger to her came from a colleague?

She found it hard to believe the models would actively try to harm her, prime gig or not. If a co-worker was responsible for threats and attempted harm to Ruth, he or she would be blackballed in the modeling community. How would that help a fellow model attain the supermodel goal?

Nico stood, drawing everyone's attention. "Take the next hour to finish your research on your assigned models. Let's see what we can piece together. We'll meet around the conference table and compare notes. After that, we rest until we're wheels down in Mexico. We're on duty the minute we step foot off this jet."

The other operatives grabbed laptops and got to work. Ruth turned to Ben. He was still lost in thought. She laid her hand on top of his. When he glanced at her, Ruth almost flinched at the intense, fierce look in his eyes. What had caused that reaction? Ben would never hurt her. No doubt in her mind. No matter what he thought of himself, he wasn't a monster. That title belonged to the Hugo Torino's of the world. What had he been thinking to cause that reaction? "Ready to get to work?"

He watched her a moment, then retrieved his laptop from the overhead bin. "What do you know about Lindsey Collette?"

"Lindsey is a newcomer. She's only been in modeling for a couple of years."

A frown. "Why is she on this assignment with you if she's green?"

"She's talented and has the looks the fashion house wanted. A plus for the photographer is that she's easy to work with."

"But you mentioned that she was one of those models who would scratch your eyes out to get ahead."

"Oh, she is. She's easy for the photographer to work with, not the other models. When she's on site, things happen."

"What kind of things?"

"Wardrobe mishaps. Clothes go missing. Makeup is misplaced. Accidents involving other models."

Ben scowled. "She's hurt you on the job?"

"Not me, but some of the other models." She didn't admit that Lindsey had tried several times to cause Ruth harm and failed. Anger already simmered in his gaze without her adding fuel to the fire.

"Would she hurt you given the chance?"

She hesitated. Man, she didn't want to lie to him. That wasn't the way to build a relationship.

"Ruth?"

Dancing around the fact wouldn't help and might hinder their investigation. "Lindsey has already tried and failed. I'm sure this job won't be any different."

"Are you kidding me?" Ben's voice rose, anger sharpening his tone. The rest of his teammates paused in their work to look at them. Trace scowled. Ben ignored them all, his focus on Ruth. He did, however, drop his voice. "Why didn't you tell me this was going on?"

"You don't tell me when a terrorist mistreats you."

"That's different. My job is dangerous. I do my best to dodge bullets, knives, and fists, but it's inevitable that I'll return home with an injury or two on occasion. You, on the other hand, should never have to actively avoid being injured on the job."

"What about when another operative tries to push you around?" she asked although she couldn't imagine a colleague trying such a thing with Ben.

"No one has been stupid enough to try. Again, why didn't you tell me this was going on?"

Ruth understood the reluctance of other operatives to engage Ben in a dominance battle. Hands down, he'd win every challenge. He'd never stop fighting until he came out on top. "My job is standing in front of a camera. I don't dodge bullets for a living. I'm not going to whine to you about another model pulling a few dirty tricks while we're on a photoshoot. Besides, you've been gone more than you've been home since I met you."

"That won't change any time soon. I'm a long way from retiring."

Unlike her. Ruth understood his concern. She knew what she was getting with Ben. How could she complain about his absences when her work schedule had only allowed her to be home for two or three days a month for the past 10 years?

"Communication between us has to be open and honest. Otherwise, we aren't going to make it." He leaned closer. "This is my life, Ruth. If you can't accept this part of me, walk away now before we get in too deep and end up hurting each other."

She was already past that point. "I'm not asking you to change your job for me. It's part of who you are." Time to chance the subject. This was too personal to discuss in a plane full of people more interested in them than their work. She motioned toward the laptop. "We'd better get busy."

"We will finish this discussion later."

Ben booted up his laptop and soon they were deep into Lindsey's life. On the surface, she appeared to be an ambitious model, climbing the ranks in the modeling world. She'd managed to snag a few prime assignments over the past year. The look of an innocent girl next door had garnered Lindsey the type of modeling jobs that Ruth had used as building blocks for her own career. Unless something happened to stop her rise to the top, Lindsey Collette was on her way to the top of the industry in a couple years. Maybe sooner if Ruth stepped away from the camera permanently.

She glanced at Ben. What would he think of her decision to change her life? Knowing how security conscious he was, she suspected the operative would be more than happy to have her remain in the US and out of the public eye.

"Did you see this?" Ben pointed toward the screen.

Ruth scanned the article, frowning. "Is this from a magazine?"

"Hometown newspaper."

"Her best friend died under suspicious circumstances during their senior year." She looked at the operative. "Do you think Lindsey was responsible for her friend's death?"

"Can't tell from this. It's an interesting coincidence."

"And you don't believe in coincidences, do you?" Trace and Bridget had mentioned something similar several times over the past few months in relation to their work.

He shook his head. Another click of the mouse brought up another article, this one from a gossip magazine. "Check this out."

Again, she read the article he'd indicated, growing more troubled the further she read. "Another accident with a model this time." The accident had occurred at the beginning of Lindsey's career. The model tripped and fell into a glass table, shattering the glass. The result was multiple cuts to the model's face, some very deep. The other woman recovered but never modeled again. According to the writer, the other woman refused to point a finger at anyone for her accident.

Chill bumps surged up Ruth's spine. The accident was eerily similar to what could have happened to her three months ago at a different photo shoot. She'd tripped and almost fell into a glass table. Fortunately, Ruth twisted, shifting her momentum enough to land beside the table instead of on it, thanks to Ben and Trace's sessions with her in self-defense. Lindsey had been near her along with several other models.

All the models had acted horrified at the close call. Now, Ruth wasn't so sure it had been an accident. Was it possible that Lindsey was targeting her? Was she using stalker tactics to scare her away from the Mexico job? If so, would Lindsey continue her terror campaign until Ruth was injured or dead?

CHAPTER SEVENTEEN

When the Shadow unit and Ruth gathered around the conference table, Nico looked at Trace. "What did you find on your assigned model?"

"Jade Conroy has been in the business for five years and is popular with the fashion houses and designers. Photographers love to work with her. Rumors abound about her being less popular with her fellow models."

Nico glanced at Ruth. "What do you know about her?"

"She grew up on a Wisconsin dairy farm and is desperate to make it big so she won't have to go back. Jade is a dream to work with if you're a designer or photographer. In other words, she works hard for those who are important in the industry. The rest of us know to stay out of her way. The camera loves her. Fellow models, not so much. Her agent is a shark in a suit. Monty Benson offers Jade's modeling services for a little less than the models under consideration for various contracts, undercutting the competition."

Sam frowned. "Does that tactic work? I would have thought the best strategy is to jack up her price."

"That's usually the way it works. Fortunately for her, Jade is gorgeous and willing to do anything asked of her on a job without complaint. Because of that, she's making a good living and gaining more exposure than the top models who are more temperamental and difficult to work with."

Ben's eyebrows rose. The description of a temperamental model didn't fit Ruth.

Nico motioned for Trace to continue.

"Jade began modeling at age eighteen. She's now 24. As Ruth mentioned, she's doing well financially. No hiccups in her background that I found on the first pass. I can dig deeper once we're in Mexico if you think it's warranted."

"Married?"

"Divorced twice. She's engaged to Lance Coltraine, the defensive coordinator for the Tennessee Titans. The couple is planning a wedding in March."

Nico shifted his gaze to the newlyweds.

Joe glanced at his laptop. "Autumn Wesley is 26, never married, but currently dating Tito Monterro, the star pitcher for the Dodgers. She's been in the modeling business for eight years and is rumored to be retiring at the end of the year."

Ruth straightened. "Retiring? Why? She still has the look fashion designers are after and she's growing in popularity. Why would she quit now?"

"Her relationship with Monterro is becoming serious."

She looked puzzled. "That doesn't mean she couldn't have a meaningful relationship with Tito and still work."

"A dating relationship would be a challenge, but doable. Marriage, though?" Ben shook his head. "That would be difficult. I can see why she's considering ending her career." Building a rock-solid marriage was hard enough without adding the stress of a spouse being away from home ninety-five percent of the time like Ruth.

He blinked. What was he doing even thinking about Ruth and marriage in the same sentence? Who was he to judge Autumn and Tito's relationship and possible pitfalls?

Those problems were exactly why he hadn't considered pursuing anything with Ruth before now. That, and the price on his head.

He scowled, knowing his past would always be an albatross around his neck. If he was smart, he'd stay far away from Ruth. He suspected protecting his heart from Ruth was impossible now. Ben was already in too deep to back away with his heart and soul intact when she decided he wasn't worth the risk.

"The rumor mill is circulating the news of an impending engagement," Joe said. "A couple of sources I checked mentioned that Monterro wants to start a family right away, something difficult to do if they're not on the same continent." When Sam elbowed him, Joe grinned and winked at his wife.

The other operatives chuckled. Ruth, however, looked wistful. Ben watched her, wondering. Did she want a family of her own? She obviously loved kids and would be a great mother. In his mind, he could see her rocking a baby with a look of adoration on her face as she gazed down at their child.

Ben's hands fisted. What was he doing fantasizing about having a family with Ruth?

"He also wants her to travel with him during baseball season. Monterro is crazy about Autumn and hates being away from her for any length of time," Joe continued.

"Financial background?" Nico asked.

"She's doing okay, but her earnings have slipped in the past two years."

"Ruth?"

Ruth's lips curved. "When we're on photoshoots during baseball season, she spends every spare minute on the phone with Tito. Autumn works hard and doesn't complain on site or off. She stays out of trouble, preferring to be in her hotel room talking to her boyfriend than partying with some of the wilder models. Of all the models I've worked with over the past few years, I'm always glad to know she's on an assignment with me. Autumn has been losing contracts to Jade." She wrinkled her nose. "All of us have."

"Any problems in Autumn's background that you know about?"

"Not really. I think an old boyfriend was stalking her a while back, but that's been resolved. Tito confronted him when he found out about the harassment. When that didn't work and the stalking continued, he and Autumn contacted the police with security camera footage of her ex breaking into Autumn's apartment and taking personal items from her home. The police went to his home and found the stolen items plus many more that he'd taken over several months and a bedroom with the walls covered with pictures of Autumn. Most of them were obviously taken without her consent, especially the ones with her undressing and in the shower." Ruth swallowed hard. "The ex had planted cameras throughout her house, recording hours of video footage. The police arrested him and he's serving time now for stalking and breaking and entering. Other than that, I don't know of any problems."

Trace frowned. "Autumn doesn't sound like a threat."

"Nico asked for the names of models I work with most often and the ones who compete for my jobs. Autumn is part of the list. I don't believe she wants to harm me. We're not close, but I consider her a friend."

Ben laid his hand on hers. "But someone who has access to you on photoshoots is threatening you. If these models aren't involved, they might have seen something that would help us catch the culprit. We can't afford to blow this off. I don't like the strawberry incident. Figuring out that you avoid strawberries and why wouldn't be hard."

"But why would Ruth be foolish enough to eat a strawberry if she's allergic to it?" Sam asked.

"She wouldn't. It's the threat of harm. What worries me is the possibility they do know about the allergy and plan to use it to cause Ruth to go into anaphylactic shock."

"We'll be vigilant," Sam promised. "I'm prepared in case Ruth has a problem."

He was prepared as well and so was Ruth. But would it be enough to keep her safe?

Nico looked at his own laptop. "I checked into Sapphire Willis. And before you ask, yes, Sapphire is her birth name. She's from Dallas, Texas and is engaged to Tom Hatcher who is also a model. The two of them are considered a power couple in the world of modeling and have been contracted for this assignment, too. No trouble in Sapphire's background. Her financial standing is solid and has grown exponentially in the past two years. Ruth?"

"Sapphire is driven and aggressive as is Tom. They work hard."

Ben's eyes narrowed. "You know more than you want to say. We need to know everything, rumors or facts included." Together, he and his team would figure out what was fact or fiction.

She sighed, reluctance in her eyes. "They're antagonistic on photoshoots, always stealing shots from other models. They frequently work together and complain about the other models on their jobs, running them down when talking to the photographers and fashion designers. The camera loves Sapphire and Tom, but they're both troublemakers. If I have a choice, I prefer not to work with them."

He stiffened. "Have either of them physically threatened you?"

She shook her head. "It's all verbal, Ben. While they don't mind badmouthing others, I've never seen them do anyone bodily harm."

"But one or both of them have been on site when other accidents have occurred?"

"It's just a coincidence." Ruth held up her hands in mock surrender. "Don't say it. I know. There are no coincidences in your line of work. In my world, coincidences do happen."

"Any other insights to add about Sapphire and her boyfriend?" Nico asked. At her head shake, he pointed at Ben. "What do you and Ruth have on Lindsey Collette?"

"Lindsey looks like the girl next door, but she was questioned in the death of her best friend in high school and was on site when several accidents that injured other models occurred on photoshoots. She's ambitious and doesn't mind stepping on other models on her way to the top. She's only been in the business for two years, but she's made the most of them. Financial background is good. She's making bank on her modeling gigs. She'd love to see Ruth out of the business altogether."

Nico's eyebrows rose as he turned his attention to Ruth. "Is that true?"

"Unfortunately. Everyone loves working with her except her fellow models. She's even becoming the media darling." Color stained her cheeks. "I hate to say it because this might not be true, but rumors are flying hot and heavy around the modeling community that Lindsey is sleeping her way to the top of the modeling profession. I hope the rumors are wrong, but they might have some merit. Her rise to the top has been meteoric. I don't want to know if that part's true and I won't repeat that outside of this setting. You can look into the rumors if you want, but I'm not going there."

Trace scowled. "Did Lindsey try to hurt you?"

"Yes, although I can't prove it."

"What did she do?" Sam asked.

"There were several incidents, one of which stands out. Although I'm usually sure-footed, I tripped and nearly fell face-first into a glass table while I was on a photoshoot in Morocco with Lindsey and a few other models. No one saw the push even though I felt a hand shove me. Lindsey was directly behind me."

"That could have been an accident if Lindsey or someone else behind you tripped and fell into you, then didn't want to admit it," Sam said.

"I would believe that if Lindsey hadn't been on site when another model fell into a glass table and sustained serious, deep cuts to her face. That model never worked in the industry again. A year after that incident, the injured model committed suicide."

Silence greeted her statement as the operatives exchanged glances. Finally, Joe rubbed his jaw and said, "Good grief. Who would have thought the world's most beautiful people were that dangerous?"

"Money and power." Trace shook his head. "That's what it boils down to. These models want top billing as a supermodel and Ruth is standing in their way."

"All right," Nico said. "Dig deeper into your assigned models when we're at Casa del Mar. Instead of having too few suspects, we have too many. Whoever is threatening Ruth is good enough to evade detection. We'll have to be in top form to catch them and stop the campaign of terror before they lay a hand on Ruth. Between now and the time we land in Mexico, catch some sleep."

Ben's jaw clenched. Even then, the danger wouldn't be over for Ruth, not if he kept her in his life as he intended to do. Not for the first time, Ben wished he could go back in time and persuade his mother to turn away from the prophet and his demented followers. Ben paid the price for her gullibility. He refused to lose Ruth to a crazy cult leader.

The operatives rose from the conference table. Ben wrapped his arm around Ruth's waist to steady her when turbulence caused her to stumble into him.

"Sorry," she murmured.

"I'm not going to complain when a beautiful woman falls for me," he teased. At her soft laughter, his hold tightened around her waist, already falling harder for her, admitting to himself he was already too far gone to recover if their relationship didn't work out.

Ben guided her toward their seats at the back of the jet. He reached into the overhead bin for blankets and took his place beside her. He raised the armrest and shoved it out of the way, not wanting even that much separation between them despite the fact Ruth was safe in the jet with his teammates.

"Want water or herbal tea?" He already knew she wouldn't drink anything with calories although he believed she needed to gain some weight. That wouldn't happen as long as she modeled.

How long would she keep working? As a supermodel, she would be in the media spotlight, a place too dangerous for him because of his past and his work with Fortress, but he couldn't walk away from her.

Ruth shook her head, her gaze dropping to her hands.

Ben leaned closer, his voice barely above a whisper. "Something wrong?"

"I shouldn't sleep on the plane."

Not what he'd expected to hear. She looked exhausted and needed rest. "Why not?"

"It's not important. I'll just read the book I brought."

He cupped her chin and gently turned her face toward his. "Talk to me, sunshine. Why shouldn't you sleep?"

Color flooded her cheeks. "You know I still have nightmares. I don't want to wake everyone with my screams."

He understood. Man, did he get it. The nightmares were the reason he bought a house outside of Nashville instead of renting an apartment. "Rest. I'll wake you before you reach that point."

"How? You'll be asleep."

He didn't sleep on the jet for the same reason. His teammates would understand if he admitted the truth.

Didn't mean he wanted to subject them to remnants of his past. "I'm a light sleeper." True enough although it wouldn't matter in this case. He'd be honored to watch over her while she rested. "I'll hear the change in your breathing."

She looked skeptical.

"Trust me."

After another moment, the stiffness left Ruth's shoulders and she gave a short nod.

Excellent. Ben shook out one of the blankets and draped it over her, then helped Ruth recline her seat. He did the same, closed his eyes, and willed himself to stillness.

Like always, he was aware of everything and everyone around him, especially the woman by his side. As his teammates settled in, the noises gradually faded to soft breathing. Ruth, however, remained awake, her body practically vibrating with tension as she struggled and failed to fall asleep.

"Come here," he murmured. When Ruth turned toward him, Ben wrapped his arm around her shoulders and settled her against his chest. Hopefully, his presence and body warmth would help.

"I'll be all right," she whispered. "You can't be comfortable like this."

"Close your eyes, sunshine. Holding you is a gift. Let me enjoy it." He kissed the top of her head and settled back in his seat again.

Within minutes, Ruth was out. Ben relaxed and soaked in the privilege of holding her in his arms. On this flight, he'd enjoy the hours before landing and taking on the next assignment.

Twice during the flight, Ruth moaned in her sleep and shuddered. Each time Ben held her tighter and whispered reassurances in her ear. The second time she moaned, Trace glanced at them, concern in his gaze. Ben used a hand signal to tell Ruth's brother-in-law that she was fine. Although Trace didn't look convinced, he settled down to sleep again. Thankful he didn't have to deflect an inquiry from Trace at the moment, that was coming in the near future. His best friend wouldn't let this slide for long.

When the Fortress jet was ten minutes from landing, Ben coasted his hand up and down Ruth's back, easing her back to full consciousness. Her breathing changed as she snuggled closer. His heart skipped a beat. He could get used to this. "We'll be landing soon," he murmured.

Ruth tilted her head back to look at him, surprise in her eyes. "Already?"

He chuckled. "You've been asleep for hours."

"Did I wake anyone?"

"No, ma'am."

She pushed her hair from her eyes. "You couldn't have rested with me using you for a pillow."

Ben shrugged. "I told you. Holding you is a privilege and I'm not feeling the least bit guilty over enjoying it."

Ruth's laughter was soft. "You'll spoil me."

He trailed the backs of his fingers down her cheek, reveling in the softness of her skin. "That's my goal." Maybe spoiling her would make up for the danger she'd live with as long as Ruth was involved with him.

Her eyes darkened. "We need to talk."

Ben drew in a slow breath, knowing she was right and yet dreading the necessity all the same. "Soon."

Up and down the aisle, his teammates raised their seats and stowed blankets and pillows in the bins in preparation for landing. "Are you hungry?" Ben asked Ruth.

She nodded. "I doubt the kitchen will be open at the hotel, though."

"We'll figure out something." If he had to, he'd send one of his teammates to a store to pick up fruit and yogurt, one of Ruth's preferred snacks.

Minutes later, the Fortress jet taxied to a stop on the tarmac. The operatives gathered their gear while Ben retrieved his bags and Ruth's suitcase. As they exited the cabin, Nico hoisted Ben's equipment bag over his shoulder, leaving him free to handle Ruth's suitcase and keep her close to his side in case of trouble.

At the edge of the tarmac, two men waited beside SUVs. Ben slowed his approach to the vehicles and allowed his teammates to move ahead of him and Ruth. If trouble broke out, the rest of Shadow was their first line of defense.

Nico and Trace greeted the men while Sam and Joe positioned themselves in front of Ben and Ruth. Hand resting on the grip of his weapon, Ben watched the men's body language. When nothing set off warning alarms, he scanned the area. This late at night, the private airstrip was quiet, just the way he liked it. Soon, the two men left the airstrip by taxi.

Tension eased from Ben's muscles. When he urged Ruth forward, Nico motioned for Ben and Ruth to ride in the first SUV with him. Trace, Joe, and Sam loaded their gear into the second vehicle.

After seating Ruth inside the SUV and storing their bags in the cargo area, Ben joined Ruth in the back while Nico cranked the engine. A moment later, the SUVs headed for Casa del Mar. On the journey, Ben stayed vigilant, his gaze quartering the areas they passed. The route had a decent amount of lighting. Only a few places gave him pause as they drove by.

Although he'd seen pictures of the hotel, they didn't do the place justice. The architecture reminded him of Old World Spain, beautiful with its sweeping curves and arches and stone facade, a beautiful backdrop for a photoshoot. Even though they had arrived well after midnight, the hotel was well lit, and patrons came and went from the front entrance. The structure appeared to be a hotspot for tourists and area residents alike.

As he exited the vehicle, the scent and sounds of the nearby ocean enveloped him in warmth and peace. He'd always loved the ocean, one of the reasons he'd chosen to serve as a Navy SEAL.

The balmy night was one made for romance. Too bad this wasn't a vacation where he could pull out all the stops and court Ruth the way she deserved. Ben held out his hand and assisted her from the vehicle. He guided her toward the entrance, scanning the doorman for weapons.

"What about our bags?" Ruth asked.

"Nico and the others will get them. I want you in a more secure location."

"I won't be inside during the photoshoot."

A fact that made his gut knot. "Believe me, I haven't forgotten. Let's get you settled in the suite." As they approached the registration desk, a swarthy-skinned, dark-haired man looked up.

He smiled and asked in accented English, "May I help you?"

"We have a reservation. Ben Slocum."

Ruth's eyes widened but she remained silent as Ben produced the necessary identification.

"Ah, yes, Mr. Slocum. We have a suite ready for you, your wife, and the Whitsons." After entering data into his computer, the desk clerk slid over two key cards. "If you need anything, please let us know." He motioned for the bellhop.

Ben held up his hand and shook his head at the bellhop. "We don't need assistance with our luggage." He turned back to the clerk. "Is the kitchen still open?"

"Yes, sir. You may order room service at any time, day or night. Our menu offerings are quite extensive."

"Excellent. Thanks." He wrapped his arm around Ruth's shoulders and met Joe and Sam away from the clerk's hearing. He handed one of the key cards to Joe. "Fourth floor. Oceanside view."

"Nice." Joe handed Ben his bags and Ruth's. "Second honeymoon, Sparky?"

Sam smiled. "Every day is a honeymoon with you."

Oh, boy. Having the two lovebirds in the suite might prove awkward. Ben was also a little envious of their relationship. Would he ever have that life with the woman he adored?

They exited the elevator on the fourth floor and turned left. At the end of the hall, a set of double doors identified their suite. Ben nudged Ruth to the side and used his key card to unlock the door. He slipped into the suite and scanned the dimly lit living area, weapon in hand. After completing a sweep of the rest of the suite, he slid his Sig into his holster.

His attention shifted to the fruit basket on the coffee table. Ben checked the card attached and read the welcome greetings from Casa del Mar's management.

Returning to the hallway, he held the door to the suite. "Management sent a fruit basket, but I'd prefer you not eat anything from it, Ruth. The basket may be a kind gesture, but I don't want to take any chances. After you choose a bedroom, we'll order food. I could do with a meal."

"Me, too." Joe rubbed his stomach. "I'd love a cheeseburger and fries."

Ruth walked to the bedroom on the right, rolling her suitcase behind her, and stepped inside. She returned a moment later. "This suite is amazing, Ben, but it only has two bedrooms. Where will you sleep?"

"On the couch. I want to be on hand if someone breaks into the suite."

"We're not safe here?"

"No one will touch you." Anyone who tried would have to go through him first.

CHAPTER EIGHTEEN

Ruth set her empty plate on the serving cart and looked at Ben. "Is it safe for me to be on the balcony?" After being cooped up for hours in the plane, she wanted some fresh air.

She also needed a few minutes of listening to the waves crash against the shore. She didn't want to admit to the tough Navy SEAL that she feared the person out to hurt her would injure or kill Ben. She'd never forgive herself if something happened to him. Maybe Ruth should have fired them all and come to Mexico alone anyway. Not that the action would have done her any good. Ben would have followed her to provide protection whether she wanted him to or not and he wouldn't have had his teammates as backup. At least this way, Shadow would watch his back as well as help with her security.

She should go to bed, but needed a breather before wrestling night terrors or squashing the fear that something bad would happen to the man she was fast falling in love with. Call her a fool, but something about the dark, deadly, and mysterious SEAL had caught her and wouldn't let go, no matter how often she told herself to walk away to protect herself and her wounded warrior. No, he hadn't told her his story, but Ruth recognized the symptoms in the stalwart man she adored.

"For tonight, you should be safe enough. Give me a minute and I'll go with you."

Of course he'd insist on going with her. Ruth vowed to keep her sojourn on the balcony short. Ben needed to rest. Although he hadn't admitted as much, Ben hadn't slept at all on the plane. She could see the lines of fatigue around his eyes and in the way he carried himself.

He sent a text, received a response, then slid his phone away. After a quiet conversation with Sam and Joe, he walked to her side and opened the French door to the balcony.

Immediately, a warm ocean breeze blew strands of her hair across her face. She walked to the railing and gazed at the waves, the rhythm soothing her heart and easing her worry for a heartbeat of time.

For this moment, nothing mattered except the silvery moonlight glittering on the darkened surface of the ocean and the salty breeze caressing her face. Ruth set aside the nagging worry about stalkers and unnamed danger from Ben's past, shutting out everything else.

A moment later, the French door closed and Ben moved to stand beside her at the railing. He didn't say anything for long minutes, his body still.

She envied him the ability to remain utterly motionless. Her work required minutes where she did nothing except smile for the camera until she thought her mouth would freeze in that position.

"Sam and Joe went to bed," he murmured without looking at her. "We won't be interrupted if you want to talk about what's happening between us and the ugliness of my past."

"When you're ready, Ben. I'll wait until you are."

He remained silent for so long, Ruth was sure the operative had accepted her offer of an easy out. Then he shook his head. "No. It's time for truth between us." Ben slanted a glance her direction. "You need to know everything so you can make an informed decision about where you want this relationship to go. I won't have secrets between us that aren't necessary for my work."

Sensing he wouldn't be comfortable disclosing his secret with her watching every emotion bared to her gaze, Ruth nudged him back a step from the railing and moved in front of him, her back to his chest. Immediately, his arms circled her waist as though needing the comfort of holding her while he divulged something horrific. Nothing else would have made Ben so reluctant to tell her the truth.

Ruth kept her gaze on the peaceful vista while she cradled his arms against her stomach and waited for her warrior to find a starting place for his story. Five minutes passed. Ten.

Ben sighed and tightened his hold on her. "My father was a beat cop in Miami, Florida. He and my mother were sweethearts from their first day of middle school and married the day after they graduated from high school. Eighteen years old and so in love that they thought nothing bad could ever happen to them."

Her heart hurt for them and their son. What tragedy had torn them apart and left a jagged hole inside their strong, brave son?

"Dad worked two jobs while he attended community college. After two years, he graduated with a degree in criminal justice. The next fall he started training at the police academy. Within six months, Dad graduated and hit the streets. Man, he loved his job and my mother was so proud of him for doing his part to keep our city safe. Two years after he graduated from the academy, I came along."

He kissed her temple. "According to my mom, Dad was so proud of his new son that his co-workers knew when he came to work each night, he'd bring more pictures of me to show off. Mom stayed home with me and Dad didn't think anything of working extra shifts to provide for his family. Life was good until the summer I turned eight and everything changed."

When he fell silent again, Ruth covered his hands with hers, offering wordless support. If he stopped now, she'd suck it up and deal with the disappointment. That Ben Martin, stoic man of mystery, had opened up to her this much was a miracle and a blessing that she would treasure.

Ben tugged her closer. "On August 7, my father pulled over a car that he'd clocked going ninety miles an hour in a residential neighborhood. When he approached the car, the driver shot him in the face, killing him instantly."

Tears streaked down Ruth's cheeks, pain for him and his mother shredding her heart.

"The cops never found the driver. Mom was so devastated at the loss of her mate that she drifted around the house for months, aimless, barely able to function enough to be sure I went to school and had food to eat and clean clothes to wear. Dad had made sure we were taken care of financially if something happened to him, but money didn't fill the void in our lives. Things continued that way for about three months. One day in November, I came home from school, and Mom was different."

Another kiss to her temple. "She was dressed in jeans and a pretty blouse instead of the torn, dingy sweats she'd taken to wearing the day after Dad's funeral. She'd taken a bath, fixed her hair, and put makeup on her face. She looked like my mom for the first time in months. I couldn't believe the difference."

"She met someone?" Ruth asked, voice soft.

He snorted. "Oh, yeah. Jeremiah Davidson, better known as the prophet, the leader of the Eden commune. At first, I didn't care what caused the change as long as I had my mother back. Losing my dad was hard enough, but I knew I couldn't raise myself."

"What happened?"

"Mom started talking about selling the house and moving to Tennessee. I couldn't understand it. One day, I couldn't get her to respond to me at all. The next thing I knew, she was planning to sell the house and move us away from our friends. I was supposed to start spring training for the baseball season at school. The last thing I wanted to do was move. I didn't want to go and let her know about it. She told me I was being selfish. Everything in our house reminded her of Dad and made her sad. She couldn't stand it anymore. Mom insisted this was a chance to start over somewhere new, a place that didn't have reminders of Dad or people who looked at her with pity in their eyes because she was a cop's widow."

Ben's voice thickened. "I didn't have the heart to fight her further and agreed to try it. If I didn't like the new place, she promised we would leave and find somewhere else that would welcome both of us. We left Miami the day after the school year ended for the semester with a suitcase for each of us. The rest of our belongings were put in storage until we knew what our living arrangements would be."

Ruth frowned. "Wait. Are you telling me your mother moved the two of you to a place she'd never seen based on the word of this stranger?"

"That's right. He sold her on the whole peace, love, and joy of the commune with people who accepted you exactly as you were. Davidson said it was a place for her to heal and become the woman she'd always been meant to be and a chance for me to grow into a real man."

"Did he try to sell you the same pipe dream?"

"I never saw him until we were inside the gates of the commune and there was no way out. Once we arrived, Mom and I were escorted to Davidson's office where he greeted her with a kiss to her hand. I didn't like the way he looked at her."

A protector, even at the age of eight. Ruth wasn't a bit surprised.

His hold tightened. "We were separated immediately. Mom went with Davidson to what I later learned was his house. I was taken to the building where the boys slept. The girls were housed in a building across the compound. I was assigned a room and given a list of tasks to complete before I would be allowed to eat or sleep. If it took all night, that was too bad for me because everyone was required to be up by five o'clock every morning. That list of chores was a long one, so I didn't finish everything until nearly midnight. One of the women was still awake. She felt sorry for me and fed me, then I was taken back to my room and locked in for the night."

Ruth had to push aside her anger for that long-ago boy so lost and alone in a strange place in order to speak. "When was the next time you saw your mother?"

"The next morning at sunrise service and breakfast. Davidson made everyone listen to one of his sermons at 5:30 every morning, rain or shine. Anyway, Mom was radiant, her attention riveted by the prophet. She barely acknowledged me. Before I could tell her about all the chores I'd been forced to do, the boys were rounded up and sent to work."

"Doing what?"

"Working the garden and mowing grass when spring came. Since it was winter when we arrived, I helped with maintenance around the property, chopping wood, building pens for animals, cleaning up after them and feeding them, all tasks that were necessary to keep the commune running and earning income and feeding its members."

She thought about that a moment. "Gardening and raising animals for slaughter couldn't be the only way they earned money. It wouldn't have been enough, especially during winter."

"They had a side business that brought in a lot more cash all year long. I'll get to that. The girls were taught domestic chores. Cooking, cleaning, quilting and sewing, and catering to the men of the commune, especially the prophet." Bitterness filled his voice.

"Except for catering to the men, life for the girls doesn't sound too bad," she murmured, wondering what she was missing.

"It reminded me of life around the time of Laura Ingalls Wilder," he admitted. "Mom was a big fan of the television series based on Wilder's books."

"But something was wrong in that commune."

"Oh, yeah. Took me a while to figure out what it was." Ben shuddered. "Within two months of us arriving at the commune, Mom was pregnant with Davidson's baby. My half-sister was born seven months later. They named her Lydia. The prophet was very pleased, and word spread through the commune that Mom was to stay secluded in his house until Lydia was healthy and strong. The only problem was that Lydia was given to one of the other women to take care of not long after she was born. If Davidson was so concerned with Lydia's health and wellbeing, why would he send her to another woman to raise as her own?"

Ruth's stomach tightened into a knot, memories of her own captivity at the hands of Hugo flooding her mind. "He kept your mother a prisoner."

"She became pregnant again two months after Lydia's birth when she was allowed to leave Davidson's house for short periods of time with a male escort. I did what I could to keep an eye on both Mom and Lydia, but it wasn't easy. The men of the commune kept me away from them. I found ways to visit for a few minutes every few days without a guard discovering my presence.

"The next summer, the commune held a coming-of-age celebration for the boys and girls who turned ten during the year. To me, it was like a big party and a day away from the field which I enjoyed. I didn't think anything of it until the year I turned ten."

When Ben fell silent again, Ruth couldn't stand it anymore. She had to comfort him however she could. In her heart, she knew the hardest, ugliest part of the story was yet to come.

Turning, Ruth wrapped her arms around his waist and held him tight. "Finish it," she whispered with her head resting against his chest.

Ben's hold on her tightened. When he resumed speaking, his voice had roughened. "At age ten, the children are either given to the men of the inner circle to train for their own use or as sex slaves for the benefit of the commune coffers."

Fury like nothing she'd ever felt in her life swamped Ruth. Her hands fisted in Ben's shirt. "Did that include the boys?"

"Yes."

"Please tell me one of the inner circle chose you for a laborer."

"Sorry, sunshine. I can't. The prophet's sick son, Silas, chose me, all right, but not only for a worker."

She growled. "Let me guess. He preferred boys to girls?"

"You got it. Punishment was harsh for not finishing work on time or according to Silas's exacting standards. He always found fault with my work and the work of the others. The guy was a degenerate and took pleasure in hurting me and the other boys. Because he was the prophet's son, his word was law as much as his father's in the commune. You didn't cross him without conscquences."

She kissed his throat, shaking in her outrage for the helpless boy he'd once been. "That's why you said you understood about my time with Hugo. You really do understand."

"I told you the truth, babe. I know exactly how helpless and violated you felt."

"Did you tell your mother what was happening?"

"Of course. It took me four months to sneak off without detection to talk to her. She didn't believe me. According to her, Silas was a good man who treated her with honor and respect as his father's first wife. He'd never do something as despicable as what I accused him of. She told me if I said something so horrible again, she would tell him and the prophet, and let them punish me as I deserved."

"She'd been fully indoctrinated by that point."

"Mom bought into it all, hook, line, and sinker."

"When did you escape?"

He stilled. "Why are you so sure that I did?"

Ruth's laughter was quiet. "Even at ten, you wouldn't have allowed an adult to abuse you if you could find a way to stop it. How long did it take you?"

"Two years. I plotted, planned, and waited for my chance, all the while finding ways to increase my strength. Silas was over six feet tall and weighed a good 250 pounds. I knew I would only have one chance. If I failed to escape, he would either punish me until I broke or kill me. The boys in his care were nothing to him. There would always be a new crop the next year if the current ones didn't make it. Of all the boys in his home, I was the one he disliked the most. Because of Mom's favored status with his father, Silas made sure the bruises and whip marks didn't show and he was careful to keep me alive and functional."

Another kiss to his throat to make herself feel better. "And no one in the commune questioned what was happening to you and the other boys?"

"No one dared. In the meantime, I endured whatever he dished out, knowing one day I would be big enough and strong enough to escape him and the commune."

"What about your mother? Did you have any interaction with her?"

"I kept an eye on her and my sister to make sure they were safe, but didn't try to contact either of them again. Silas didn't allow his boys enough freedom to be out of his sight for long. To escape, I had to remain as free from injury as possible. My chance came the night of another coming-of-age party when I was twelve. Silas chose three more boys and planned to start their training that night. First, though, he decided I hadn't completed some task to his liking and started with me."

"He didn't..."

"No. I was prepared. I had stolen a sharp knife from the kitchen earlier in the evening. When Silas came to my room, I fought him off and ended up slicing his jugular vein. By the time I gathered what little belongings I owned in my backpack, Silas was dead."

CHAPTER NINETEEN

Ben refused to look down at Ruth after his revelation, not wanting to see the condemnation in her eyes or, worse, disgust that the man who held her had killed a man at the age of twelve. He tightened his hold, storing the feel of her wrapped in his arms in case she wised up and kicked him to the curb, knowing what was left of his heart would shatter when she did.

"You're sure Silas is dead?" Ruth asked.

"Oh, yeah. I'm positive." No one could have survived that much blood loss and lived.

"Good."

Stunned, Ben eased her back to look into her eyes. "Good?"

"He was a sick man who hurt children. I'm glad you escaped from his tyranny and abuse. There's no telling how many boys you saved from him by your selfless act of courage."

He had to make sure she understood. "Baby, I'm no hero. I killed a man when I was twelve to save my own life."

"To escape an abuser," she corrected.

"I've killed several men over the years."

"In defense of others and to protect our country. I know, Ben."

"The fact that I'm a killer doesn't bother you?"

"You're a protector and I'm honored to be yours."

His heart skipped a beat. She was incredible and he desperately wanted to keep her, but she had to know everything. "There's more to my story."

"Tell me the rest."

"There's a contract out on me."

"Who wants you dead?"

"Jeremiah Davidson. He wants revenge for the death of his son and for me dropping anonymous tips to the cops whenever I discover the location of the Eden commune."

"How does he know you're the one sending the police after them?"

"I'm a loose end. I know what's going on inside that snake pit and I share insider details to entice the police to go after them."

"Why is Davidson still free? He should be in prison."

"He's wily and has a high-priced attorney on call who always knows the right thing to say to convince the police that Davidson is as pure as snow. While the gate thugs hold off the police, the Eden community's children are hustled into well-hidden underground bunkers. No kids for the cops to question about abuse. All the adults in the compound swear that Eden is an adults-only community and it's clear they're happy and healthy. When law enforcement leaves, the community packs up and moves to another location and the process of soliciting new sex-trafficking clients starts all over again."

"I'm surprised you haven't gone after Davidson yourself."

He gave a rough laugh. "I'd love to, but I'd be outnumbered. I don't want to risk my teammates' lives on a personal vendetta."

"You haven't told them the details of your past."

"No." Heat bloomed in his cheeks, making him doubly glad their balcony was wreathed in darkness. "If Shadow knew, they'd go after Davidson and his cronies, no matter the odds of us surviving the encounter."

"You wrenched the decision out of their hands. They won't be happy when they learn the truth. Why didn't you go to the police and tell them what was happening in the commune when you first escaped?"

His lips curved. "I was twelve years old and afraid of being arrested for murder. I hitched a ride to the nearest city, then across the country, out of Davidson's reach. When I felt I was safe from discovery, I turned myself in to child services in Phoenix and told my assigned social worker that my parents were dead from a fire and I didn't have any relatives. I also told her my mother gave birth to me at home and didn't report a live birth or apply for a social security number. All I wanted was a roof over my head, food in my stomach, and a chance to go to school. Saving myself meant having the ability to get a job when I was old enough. That required schooling."

"And she believed you?"

"I gave her a fake name. She couldn't check my story and connect me to the Eden commune. From that moment on, I became Ben Martin."

"What was your birth name?" She held up a hand. "If you'd rather not tell me, I'll understand. No pressure."

Ben bent his head and brushed a soft kiss over her sweet pink lips. He would never get enough of her. Ruth had already become as necessary to him as air. "My birth name is Cameron Barrett."

Ruth smiled. "Nice to meet you, Cameron."

"You can't use the name in public."

"I won't use the name at all. To me, you'll always be Ben Martin."

Ben captured her mouth with his and soaked in her care and comfort to heal some of the fissures in his soul.

When he came up for air, he rested his forehead against Ruth's. "I'm crazy about you, Ruth Monihan."

"I'm crazy about you, too."

"I don't want to let you go but I should for your own safety. Davidson will never stop coming after me until I'm dead. If he sees my picture with you and recognizes me, you'll be a target as well."

"That's why you kept distance between us except for the phone calls and training sessions, isn't it?"

"I've been trying to protect you from Davidson and his cronies. I also can't be in the spotlight because of my job with Fortress. I work in covert operations. Notoriety isn't safe for me or my teammates. We work in the shadows for a reason. It's the safest place for us and it's where we belong."

"My popularity will endanger you," she whispered.

He didn't say a word. She was right. As long as she was in the media spotlight and he was in her life, his chances of being spotted and recognized by Davidson or one of the other enemies with his name on their hit list remained high.

"Can I tell you a secret?"

Ben tilted his head. "Anything." After all, she couldn't tell him anything that was worse than him being a murderer at an early age.

"I won't be a model for much longer."

He froze. "Why do you say that? You're at the top of your profession and more in demand every day."

"Autumn isn't the only one retiring soon. This job is the first of my last three contracts."

He studied her beloved face for a moment. "Don't do this for me, Ruth. I won't hold you back from doing the job you love."

"I'm retiring for me. I've made enough money to support myself and a huge family for life plus buy a small country and keep its budget in the black for the next one hundred years. I'll never be able to spend all the money I've earned."

"What do you want to do?"

"Start a charitable foundation to benefit children suffering from serious illness."

He wasn't surprised that her first thought was to aid sick children. "It's a worthy endeavor. You could start the foundation without retiring from modeling, though. Don't give up your career to protect me. I'll take precautions if you want to continue." He refused to admit the idea of her traveling the world without him for modeling jobs made him break out into a cold sweat. So many things could go wrong. He could lose her in a heartbeat if the security around her wasn't the best. What he'd seen of the security measures surrounding Ruth before Shadow took over was a joke.

Ruth shook her head. "I was thinking about retiring before Hugo kidnapped me. My time as his prisoner simply moved up the timeline."

"Have you talked to Marcus about this?"

"He told me to wait until I'd been in counseling for six months before making a decision I might regret. I broached the subject with him again last month and told him my feelings hadn't changed."

"What did he say?"

"To trust myself to make the right choice. Retiring is the right choice for me. I don't have the heart to be in the spotlight anymore, Ben. I accomplished my goal of reaching the top of my profession. I've enjoyed the ride and now it's time to walk away and really live."

He cupped the side of her neck with his palm. "What is it you want to do aside from establishing the foundation?"

"I want to eat pizza and go to movies."

Ben smiled. "A plan I heartily endorse. What else?"

"I don't want to work out two or three hours a day or watch every morsel of food that passes my lips. I don't want to worry about gaining a pound or crash dieting to lose weight before a photoshoot so I can fit into a certain outfit or look a certain way on camera.

"I want to walk on the beach in the moonlight with you, spend time getting to know my sister again, and find out who my brother-in-law is and what makes him so special to Bridget. I'd love to watch television without English subtitles to tell me what's going on. I want to walk down the street and not worry about someone recognizing me and hounding me with questions and requests for autographs or money." Ruth wrapped her arms around his neck. "More than anything, I want to become an expert on all things pertaining to Ben Martin, the man who steals my breath and makes my heart race."

"Even knowing you'll have to be alert for trouble as long as we're together? You can't ever forget the price on my head."

"Even knowing all that, I still choose to be with you." She stopped, uncertainty filling her eyes. "If you want me."

He bent his head and took her mouth in a long, blistering kiss that sent his heart rate into the stratosphere. When he had to grab a much-needed breath, he looked into her beautiful eyes. "Never doubt that I want you in my life, Ruth. I know I'm not good enough for you, but I swear I will do everything in my power to make you happy."

"We'll make each other happy, starting with me finishing my last three contracts and walking away from a career that has consumed my life for ten years. I'm ready to move on with my life and I want to do it with you. Will you let me?"

"Are you sure, sunshine? If you accept all of me into your life, I won't be able to let you go. I'm almost in too deep to release you." Who was he kidding? He was in over his head already. No question about it. He was falling in love with Ruth and the prospect scared the living daylights out of him.

"I'm sure," she whispered. "I don't have any doubts."

Hoping she understood the ramifications of her decision, he lowered his head again until his mouth brushed against hers and prayed they hadn't made a fatal mistake.

CHAPTER TWENTY

After another a few minutes of indulging his need to hold Ruth, Ben said, "You need to sleep. The photoshoot starts in a few hours." He walked her inside the suite to the door of her room.

Following another kiss, this one as sweet and gentle as he could make it, Ben nudged her inside the room. "Rest. I'll be on the couch if you need me. No one will get past me to hurt you."

"I know." She took two steps into the room, paused, and looked over her shoulder. "Even though I won't regret my decision to make this relationship real, you might."

"Why?"

"I have...issues from my time with Hugo. I'm working on them, but it will take time."

The tension eased from Ben's muscles. "I have lingering issues from my time with Silas. I'm not in a hurry, Ruth. You're mine now. We'll take the next steps when we're ready on our timetable, no one else's. Even when we think we've overcome a hurdle, something may trigger a setback for either of us. It's part of the process. We'll deal with each setback and move ahead. How we deal with it is no one's business but our own. Just know that my feelings for you run deep and strong. You gave yourself to me. I'm in this for as long as you'll allow me in your life."

When she turned and made a move toward him, Ben stepped back, hands raised to ward her off. "Don't. My control is gone. If I touch you again, I can't guarantee I'll be able to stop."

Although he feared his confession would send her into a panic, the truth of his words made her smile, a look of smug satisfaction in her eyes. "I'll see you in a few hours, Ben." With a lingering look, she closed the door to her room.

Ben closed his eyes and mentally dismantled the most complicated bomb he'd ever worked on. By the time the mental process was complete long minutes later, he'd regained control. Man, the chemistry between him and Ruth was a powder keg waiting to explode. Neither one of them was ready for that.

Time to get his mind back on the job of protecting her from his past and the person trying to scare her away from this photoshoot.

He glanced at his watch. Joe would be on duty in three hours. That left Ben time to do research into the backgrounds of Ruth's photographer and her agent.

Two hours later, he wasn't any closer to narrowing down the pool of suspects. He was, however, convinced both men wanted more than a professional relationship with the supermodel, even the happily-married agent.

He examined the side-by-side pictures he'd selected and displayed on his computer screen. One was of Ruth with her photographer, the second with her agent. In both pictures, she was smiling for the camera. The men were looking at her. The proprietary look on each of their faces set off Ben's temper, stoking his already fierce possessiveness.

Was one of these men behind the threats? If she'd been afraid and didn't have him in her life, would Ruth turn to one of those men for protection and comfort?

Ben's hands fisted. Never going to happen. After tomorrow, both men would know beyond a doubt that she belonged to him and he protected what was his. She might accuse him of being a Neanderthal, and Ruth wouldn't be far off the mark.

When he was unable to find more information, Ben set aside his laptop and walked to the French doors to scan the deserted beach. The view was peaceful yet in a few short hours, his woman would be on that beach, vulnerable to long-range attack. The thought made him nearly sick with worry. How could he protect her from a sniper's bullet?

The only thing that gave him a measure of peace was that no one had threated her with a rifle. A handgun didn't have the same range and he wouldn't be far from her during the photo shoot no matter what her agent or photographer wanted. He trusted his teammates. If anyone could spot a long-range shooter, it was Trace and Joe.

He kept vigil at the French doors until Joe and Sam's bedroom door opened and his teammate stepped out. Joe looked toward the small kitchen. "Do we have coffee?"

"In the carafe. We have enough supplies to make three more pots. If we need more, we can order from room service."

"Awesome." Shadow's spotter poured himself a mug of coffee and joined Ben. He sipped his steaming drink. "Any problems?"

"Not so far."

"Hope it stays quiet for Ruth's sake."

"Me, too."

They stood in silence for a while until Joe glanced at Ben. "Want to tell me about it?"

"About what?"

"You and Ruth. Are you a real couple or not?"

"Why do you ask?"

"Come on, Ben. You practically vibrate with tension whenever an unattached male is within a few feet of her. When you look at her, I don't see friendship. I see a man warning off any potential rivals for her heart."

Should have known he wouldn't be able to fool Joe. The man was wicked smart and observant. Denying the obvious wouldn't matter now. The only thing fake about this situation was listing Ruth as his wife when he registered for the suite. "She's mine."

A slow smile curved Joe's mouth. "I knew it. You two have been dancing around each other for months."

"Yeah, yeah."

Joe chuckled and clapped Ben on the shoulder. "Good job, buddy. I was afraid you'd let her slip through your fingers."

"It's too late for that."

The spotter's eyes widened. "Whoa. That's kind of sudden, isn't it?"

"Not really. She started working her way inside my armor the night we snatched her from Torino. Now, I need her."

Joe remained silent a moment as he studied Ben's face. "You're in love with her."

He shot a look at the second bedroom to be sure Ruth's door remained closed. "From the first moment I saw her," he said, voice soft. "It's not just her face and body, although she's perfect. Her courage, strength, and soft heart combined with her beauty just does it for me." Ben turned to his friend. "There will never be anyone else for me but Ruth."

"Does she know how you feel?"

"Some, not all." No need to scare the woman to death. She'd deal with it when it was time.

A soft whistle. "Good luck, Ben." Joe's lips curved. "Now, if you'd just shut up long enough, you'd have time to catch some sleep before your lady rises for the day."

He snorted as he walked to the couch. Joe was right. Ben needed to sleep a few hours to be alert. Stretching out on the cushions with his weapon close at hand, he closed his eyes, hoped he wouldn't embarrass himself by waking the entire suite with his nightmares, and dropped off to sleep in less than a minute.

Three hours later, Ben woke when Sam joined Joe at the French doors for a morning kiss.

His lips curved, glad to have an excuse to razz Joe and Sam. "Get a room," he murmured.

Joe chuckled. "We have one. You're just jealous."

If Joe had made that comment two weeks ago, Ben would have agreed. Instead, now he looked forward to seeing Ruth again even though they'd only separated a few hours earlier.

Ben walked to the kitchen and started another pot of coffee, then called room service to place a large breakfast order, including more supplies for coffee and packets of herbal tea for Ruth.

As he hung up the phone, Ruth's bedroom door opened and she walked out dressed in a pair of white capris and a blue tank top. Her face was clear of makeup. Her face lit when she saw him, a smile curving her lips.

His heart turned over in his chest. Wow. She was even more beautiful this morning than she was last night. Knowing they had an avid audience, Ben closed the gap between himself and Ruth.

He cupped her nape and drew her in for a long, deep kiss, claiming her mouth because he couldn't resist her, grateful for the right to touch her at last. "Good morning, sunshine."

"Hi, handsome. Did you sleep?"

"Long enough to be alert. Don't worry. The military trained me to recharge on four hours. I'm fine."

She studied him a moment and must have been satisfied with what she saw. "I have to be on the beach in an hour. The photographer wants some early-morning shots."

"We'll be there. Room service will deliver breakfast in fifteen minutes. I ordered something light for you, but you're going to eat."

He turned her toward the couch he'd just vacated and noticed the broad smiles on Joe and Sam's faces. "Shut up," he muttered. "And keep your thoughts to yourself."

"No way," Sam crowed. "When did this happen?"

"Last night. Lay off, Sam."

She laughed, a wicked light in her eyes.

Ben scowled at Joe. "Control your wife."

"Not going to happen, my friend. Besides, once Nico and Trace see you and Ruth are together for real, they'll weigh in as well, especially Trace. Better face the truth. You're doomed to be ragged on, Ben, and most likely due for some hard questions about your intentions toward his sister-in-law."

Deciding the best course of action was to ignore the newlyweds, he sat on the couch beside Ruth and sent a text to his team leader on the breakfast delivery time. That done, he looked at Ruth. "Anything from Bridget?"

"She's still tracing the email threats, but not making much progress."

"Figured as much. Will your agent also be here this week?"

She nodded. "He always comes to my photoshoots. He's very protective."

Yeah, Ben just bet he was. Old Rich was in for an unhappy surprise today.

Ten minutes later, a knock sounded on the door. Ben surged to his feet, weapon in hand as he checked the peephole. Nico and Trace. Unlocking the door, he stepped back to admit his teammates.

With Ruth also on her feet, Trace gave her a one-armed hug. "How are you doing, Stretch?"

She wrinkled her nose. "You're taller than I am."

"My legs aren't as pretty as yours or my gorgeous wife's. You appear to be all legs, honey."

"They're just legs," she muttered.

"Not yours and not in this lifetime."

Since Ruth appeared to be uncomfortable with the attention focused on her, Ben looked at Nico. "Any news from Fortress?"

"Maddox called a few minutes ago. The price on your head has gone up."

Ben scowled. That wasn't the news he wanted to hear. "How much?"

"Another million. The boss said twenty years hasn't tamped down the fire." Nico's eyes narrowed. "You want to explain that?"

Not really. Thankfully, another knock sounded on the door. Perfect timing. Trace shifted to stand in front of Ruth as Ben checked the peephole again. Room service this time.

A minute later, Nico and Ben pushed two serving carts into the suite. While the rest of Shadow and Ruth browsed the selections, Nico motioned for Ben to follow him out to the balcony.

Reluctantly, he trailed his team leader outside, closing the door behind him.

"Tell me."

"There isn't enough time."

"Holding back isn't doing you any favors and might cost one of our lives. I'm responsible for all of Shadow, including you. Whatever went on in your past is playing an important role in the present. I need to know, Ben, otherwise I wouldn't invade your privacy. If you want me to make it an order, I will."

He stared hard at the waves rolling onto the shoreline, knowing what he needed to do and reluctant to bare his soul to a man he respected more than almost any other.

The French door opened again, and Ben knew without turning around that Ruth had followed them. Seconds later, she appeared at his side and wrapped her hand around one of his in wordless support.

Some of the balls of ice in his stomach melted at her touch. Man, how had he gotten so lucky to have this special woman in his life? With a past like his, she should have run from him. That she hadn't reiterated how strong she was.

Nico braced his hands against the railing, gaze locked on the vast ocean. "Talk to me," he murmured.

Ruth squeezed Ben's hand. When he glanced at her, she gave a small nod, encouraging him to break his silence. All right, then. Nico was one of his best friends. He just prayed that wouldn't change after his revelations.

He began to talk, starting with his father's death, continuing through his mother's transformation, and his training at Silas's hands. When he finished, Ben waited for Nico's reaction.

When his team leader was silent for too long, Ben chanced a glance his direction. His heart sank at the disgust and raw fury on Nico's face. Would he have to ask Maddox for a team reassignment? The possibility made him want to puke. He loved working with Shadow. Losing them would be akin to losing his family all over again.

Nico turned and clamped a hand over Ben's shoulder. "When we smoke out Ruth's stalker, we're going after that viper and destroying his nest. We're going to finish this, Ben."

"They don't have a website and keep a low profile," he choked out. "They're like that Whack-A-Mole game. You beat them down with a hammer and they'll pop back up again in a different place."

"Davidson and his cronies won't be able to hide from Fortress or us. They don't know it yet, buddy, but they're days are numbered. They won't be able to hurt any more kids when we're finished with them."

Ben shook his head. "I can't ask you to do this. It's my problem, my nightmare. I won't risk any of you."

"You're not asking. We're a team, a family. What hurts you hurts us, too. We'll do recon to find out what we're up against. If we need more teams, Maddox will be glad to assign them. Shadow is going to take Eden down."

"Not all the men of the commune are evil. Some of them didn't know what was going on because they weren't part of the power structure. Only those in the inner circle or leaders were given children to train. By the time they finished with the kids, they were too afraid or beaten down to tell anyone what had been going on."

"Are all the men of the commune armed?"

Ben frowned and thought back to his time in the compound. He blinked as the truth dawned on him. "No, only the leaders and those in power along with the guards. They're tasked with protecting the commune if we come under attack. Why didn't I remember that before now?"

"The only reference you have is the child's memories," Ruth said. "The child didn't think in terms of weapons and guard rotations like you would now as a military-trained adult."

"I'm a Navy SEAL as well as black ops. That should have been my first consideration. Instead, my boyhood fears came to the front."

"Learned response," Nico said. "You did what you could to get law enforcement on the task of shutting down Eden. Unfortunately, the police have to follow the rules. We don't. However, I think it might be worth our while to get the feds involved."

Ben flinched. "Seriously? They always screw things up."

"Yeah, I know. Davidson has taken his commune of horrors on the road across state lines several times over the years that you've been trying to nail them. The feds aren't a fan of human traffickers and that's exactly what Davidson and his buddies are. Trust me, the feds will want in on this and chances are pretty good that they'll be happy to have a big coup like this one to crow about to the media. I want to broach the subject with Maddox and possibly Rafe Torres. He's the best fed I know, especially since he's now one of us. Is that acceptable to you?"

Ben stared at the ocean for a minute, running through every other possible scenario. In the end, he realized he didn't have any other options. He'd tried working with local law enforcement and they had failed. Now, his future with Ruth was on the line. He wanted the freedom to love her without being afraid to leave her alone when he was on assignment for fear that Davidson or one of his flock would kidnap Ruth and subject her to the same treatment that he'd suffered.

He gripped Ruth's hand and turned to Nico. "Do it."

CHAPTER TWENTY-ONE

Sandwiched between Ben and Joe with Sam standing in front of her, Ruth's level of worry grew as the Casa del Mar elevator descended to the lobby.

Ben's hand tightened around hers. "We've got this, sunshine. Concentrate on your job and let us handle the rest." He kissed her fingers as the silver doors slid open. "We're good at what we do." They walked through the lobby and out a side door to the beach.

Ruth paused at the end of the boardwalk and removed her shoes. Her bodyguards, however, did not.

"You'll get sand in your shoes," Ruth murmured to Ben.

"Bare feet are a drawback in a fight." Ben wrapped his arm around Ruth's waist as they crossed the sand.

"Do you expect trouble?"

"Always."

No wonder he stayed alert when they were in public. Thinking back through the past few days, Ruth realized she was alive because Ben prepared for the worst. Nothing caught him by surprise.

Her lips curved. Except her. She surprised him when she wouldn't walk away from Ben after he revealed his past. But he didn't know that she'd been falling in love with him from his first grouchy comment when Shadow snatched her from Hugo's lair. Instead of treating her as a fragile, helpless woman, Ben demanded she fight back and help in her rescue. To her surprise, she had responded and discovered more inner strength than she ever imagined.

While she healed, she wanted to help Ben heal, too. He needed someone in his life who accepted every part of him, his past included, and loved him anyway. She wanted to be the person Ben turned to, knowing that he could trust her with his heart.

As Ruth walked toward a large air-conditioned tent and milling people, two men watched her progress across the sand. Both looked surprised, then frowned at Ben's proprietary hold.

She sighed. Great. A rocky start to the day. Scott Barber, the photographer, strode toward her while her agent, Rich Eisenhower, remained in place, glowering at Ben.

"You're late," Scott snapped. "We're losing the dawn light."

"My fault," Ben said. He held out his hand. "I'm Ben."

"Scott Barber. I'm Roxanne's photographer."

Ruth's mouth gaped at his blatant attempt to claim her for himself. Even before her imprisonment in Mexico, she didn't have a personal interest in the photographer. After meeting Ben, no one else interested her, including Scott.

A nod from Ben. "Roxanne told me how talented you are. Your pictures of her are impressive."

Scott's lip curled. "She's kept you a secret." The photographer's gaze shifted to Ruth. "Come. You need to dress for the shoot before we lose the light. We have a full slate today." He frowned at Ben. "Wait here."

"Not happening." Ben's gaze locked on Scott. "Where she goes, I go."

"Don't be ridiculous. I'm escorting her to the tent for a wardrobe change and makeup. You aren't allowed in there."

Ben turned to her, a silent warning in his eyes.

"I'll work it out." She tugged on his hand. "Come on."

"Wait a minute," Scott protested. "Who is this guy?"

"Hers," Ben said.

"What does that mean?"

"We're dating," Ruth clarified. Ignoring the shocked expression on Scott's face, she led Ben to the tent where Xena, the makeup artist, and Delayne, the wardrobe mistress, waited.

"There you are." Xena waved Ruth into a chair in front of a long table with mirrors attached. "We have to hurry. Scott's been ranting about your tardiness."

"Who is this handsome guy?" Delayne asked, eyes gleaming.

"Ben, the man I'm dating."

The two women exchanged glances. "Do Scott and Rich know about him?" Delayne asked as she selected an outfit from the rack of clothes marked off for Ruth.

"They know," Ben said, tone mild. The expression in his eyes, however, was anything but mild. That look said he'd staked a claim on her and would fight to keep her.

Ruth submitted to Xena's ministrations while Ben watched both women. Ruth wanted to assure him Xena and Delayne weren't a threat to her safety, but he trusted no one except his teammates, his Fortress co-workers, and her.

When Xena finished working her magic, Ruth turned to Delayne. "Will you set up the divider, please?" The screen would allow her to change clothes while Ben remained in the tent.

Delayne's gaze shifted to Ben. A cat-like smile curved her lips. "Of course. I'll be happy to entertain your boyfriend while he waits."

Of course she would. Delayne was always prowling for a new man. She'd be disappointed. Ben wouldn't look twice at the wardrobe mistress except to assess if she threatened Ruth's safety.

While Ruth changed clothes, Delayne attempted to have a conversation with Ben. His muffled answers were succinct and frustrated the other woman, evidenced by her glittering eyes and flushed cheeks when Ruth emerged dressed for her first camera session.

Ben held out his hand to her. "Ready?" he asked, cutting off Delayne's latest comment.

Ruth nodded.

As they walked toward her photographer and agent, Ben murmured, "You look beautiful, but I prefer how you looked before Xena and Delayne's handiwork."

She stopped and stared at him. "Are you serious?"

"Dressed like this, you're Roxanne. I prefer Ruth, the beautiful woman with a heart of gold." He bent his head and brushed a light kiss over her lips.

"Any day now," Scott snapped.

Ben squeezed her hand. "Go to work, sunshine. I'll be close."

"The other models will arrive soon," Rich growled.

Ruth dashed across the sand. While she worked, changing poses at Scott's direction, she noticed that Sam, Joe, and Ben formed a loose triangle around the job site and divided their attention between scanning the beach and watching Scott and Rich.

When Scott requested a wardrobe change, Rich caught her arm and dragged her close. "What's going on?" he hissed. "Who are these people?"

At his touch, a wave of revulsion washed over Ruth to the point that she feared she'd be sick. "Let go."

Instead of complying, her agent tightened his grip. "Answer me. I have a right to know."

In the next instant, she was free, Ben holding Rich's wrist with a white-knuckled grip. Her agent gasped and sank to his knees.

"The lady asked you to release her," Ben said without loosening his grip. He maintained his hold a few more seconds before releasing Rich and gathering Ruth against his side. He walked with her across the sand. "Are you okay?"

She nodded. "I'm sorry. I wasn't prepared for him to touch me."

"No apologies between us. You don't have to explain what his touch did to you, the memories he triggered. I know."

"A touch on my arm shouldn't have been a big deal." Was she that fragile? Maybe she wasn't strong enough to be with Ben.

"The hold on your arm was only part of the problem." He stopped several feet from the tent. "You felt threatened by Rich like you did with Torino. Your instincts are on target. Don't second guess yourself."

How did this tough operative know the right words to bolster her confidence? "Thanks."

He winked and escorted her into the tent.

"Wardrobe change," Ruth told Delayne.

The wardrobe mistress checked her master list and grabbed the outfit assigned for the next round of photos. "Do you need water?"

Ruth shook her head and stepped behind the screen. Five minutes later, she and Ben walked to the site. "Where is Nico?" she asked.

"Ahead of us."

She looked beyond Rich and Scott. Ruth smiled at the sight of Nico lounging on a beach chair under a wide umbrella, dark sunglasses on his face, a large cooler at his side. "Are you sure he's not sleeping on the job?"

"Positive. He's been scanning the area with his binoculars. His rifle is in the cooler. Trace is to your right."

She glanced that direction to see her brother-in-law with a pair of binoculars to his eyes.

"Roxanne, hurry up," Scott called. "Time is money."

Although irritated with his attitude, he was correct. Also, the heat would climb throughout the day. The faster Scott got what he wanted, the quicker she'd be finished for the day.

"I'd like to punch him," Joe groused. "How do you stand to work with him?"

"He's usually not so bad-tempered."

Sam grinned. "I think Ben has a lot to do with Scott's attitude."

When Ruth posed again, Sam and Joe rented beach chairs like tourists and set up a short distance away. Although they didn't have coolers like Nico and Trace, she knew they were armed and ready.

Within 30 minutes, the other models arrived and swarmed into the changing tent. As Ruth had expected, Autumn, Jade, Lindsey, Sapphire, and Tom were part of this shoot. The security guys also arrived to keep the public away from the models and crew.

Between wardrobe changes, Ruth introduced the Fortress operative at her side to the security guys and explained the need for own team. "Please don't say anything to anyone aside from your men," she asked Alan, the head of the security team. "Ben wants to catch the stalker by surprise."

"You sure this guy is any good?" Alan asked, arms folded over his massive chest.

She grinned. "I'm sure."

"We'll keep an eye on you anyway. Can't be too careful with celebrities like you."

"I appreciate it. Thanks, Alan."

"Roxanne," Scott shouted. "Quit gabbing and change."

Ben took a step toward Scott.

Ruth grabbed his hand. "He's not worth the trouble he'll cause."

He watched the photographer until Scott turned away with a muttered curse and returned to his task, ordering the other models into different positions.

In the air-conditioned tent, Xena touched up Ruth's makeup, then she slipped behind the screen for another wardrobe change. On her way out of the tent, Delayne pressed a bottle of cold water into her hands and tossed one to Ben. "You need to stay hydrated."

"Thanks." Ruth opened the bottle and drank a quarter of the liquid before handing the bottle to Ben. "This is the last set before we break for lunch."

A few minutes into the photo session, a wave of dizziness hit Ruth and her heart began to race. She frowned. What was wrong? Was she dehydrated?

"Roxanne, pay attention," Scott snapped.

Ruth tried to focus on his direction, but couldn't. She struggled to breathe. In a panic, she started toward Ben and sank to her knees.

CHAPTER TWENTY-TWO

Ben raced toward Ruth as she sank to her knees. He reached her side in time to catch her before she keeled over onto the sand. Ruth wheezed in a breath, eyes wide with panic as she struggled to breathe.

"Back off," he snapped to the crowd gathering. "Sam!" Ben grabbed an epinephrine pen from his pocket. Had someone poisoned her? He hadn't seen suspicious behavior and he'd been watching her. Some bodyguard he was.

The medic shoved aside people blocking her way and dropped beside Ruth. After a quick assessment, she looked at the injector in Ben's hand. "Do it."

He placed the tip against the middle of Ruth's outer thigh. Ben pushed the auto-injector into her thigh until it clicked and held the injector firmly in place for three seconds, praying the medicine did its job.

"What's going on?" Rich demanded, scowling at Ben and Ruth.

"Get back, Eisenhower." Joe clamped a hand on his shoulder and forced him to comply.

"Take your hands off me. Who are you?"

"A friend of Roxanne's."

"She needs to get back to work before Scott pitches a fit. We can't afford for him to go off the rails and refuse to complete the contract."

"Not happening." Sam glared at the red-faced agent. "Roxanne is going to the hospital."

"Why? She looks fine to me."

"She had an allergic reaction, and the epinephrine Ben administered will wear off in 20 minutes. She'll need more medical help. Scott will have to take shots of the other models while she recovers because Roxanne won't be back on the beach today." Sam grabbed her mike bag and hoisted it over her shoulder. "Let's go, Ben. The clock's ticking."

He shoved the empty injector into a different pocket and scooped Ruth into his arms as Sam sent Trace for one of the SUVs.

"Ben," Ruth whispered and nuzzled her face against his neck, her breathing easier. "I'm okay."

Not by a long shot. How had someone poisoned her with him and the others watching? "Just hold on, baby."

"Hate hospitals."

"You can handle a few hours while the doctors monitor you."

"Ben," she moaned.

"No arguments. Sam says you need to go. You're going." He glanced down at her. "Do it for me."

"Not playing fair."

"I play to win, sunshine. Keep that in mind." When Ruth pressed a kiss to his neck, Ben tightened his grip. If he or Sam hadn't brought the epinephrine, he shuddered to think what would have happened to Ruth. No matter what she said, he wouldn't be convinced Ruth was all right until a doctor confirmed it.

At the front of the hotel, Trace waited in an SUV, address of the closest hospital in the navigation system. Sam motioned for Ben to climb into the backseat with

Ruth. She tucked a blanket around the shivering model and got in beside them while Joe sat in the shotgun seat.

"Go," Ben ordered Trace.

"What happened?" his friend asked.

"Severe allergic reaction. Someone got to Ruth."

Trace glared in the rearview mirror. "How? She didn't eat anything after we left the suite."

Joe twisted in his seat. "She drank bottled water. Someone could have spiked it with strawberry. Would it take much to hurt Ruth, Sparky?"

"Not with a severe allergy."

"Text Nico," Ben said. "Tell him to grab our water bottles. I want the outside tested as well as the water. Also, have him to talk to Delayne. She's the one who gave us the water."

Joe grabbed his phone.

Never again. Ben's jaw clenched. Ruth wasn't taking food or drink from anyone connected with the photoshoot. He hoped his team leader got some answers from Delayne. If he didn't, Ben would have a private, unpleasant conversation with the lady. Someone tried to kill his woman. Whoever targeted her would regret the attempt.

As Trace stopped at the emergency room entrance, Joe's phone signaled an incoming text. "Nico has the water bottles and arranged for a courier to transport them to a private lab for testing." He opened the back door to assist Ben.

He strode into the hospital with Ruth in his arms. While the medical personnel rushed her into an examination room, he filled out paperwork for Ruth Slocum. When Zane provided background for an undercover operation, he planned for every contingency. He also had a fake marriage license on record.

Ben hoped registering Ruth under a fake name would keep her location a secret from the media and give her a chance to rest before returning to the photoshoot. No matter how much she protested, Ben wasn't letting her back on the beach until tomorrow even if the doctor released her from the hospital in a few hours.

When Ben completed the paperwork, he stationed himself outside Ruth's exam room. After parking the SUV, Trace joined him. "Nothing yet," he told his friend.

"If Delayne did this, Nico will find out," Trace murmured.

Ben's fists clenched, gaze locked on the closed door in front of him. What was taking so long? Even though Sam assured him that Ruth would recover, Ben wanted to see her. He'd never been more afraid in his life with the woman he loved gasping for air. Thank God he'd had the medicine she needed.

"This assignment isn't just a job to you, is it? You're in love with Ruth." Trace stared at Ben.

"Yes." Why hide the truth from his best friend? Trace knew him better than anyone on Shadow.

"Does she know what she's getting into?"

Ben stiffened, his gaze locking with Trace's. "What do you mean?"

"Come on, man." He shifted closer and dropped his voice. "Of all of us, you have the darkest past. Ruth's been through enough trauma. She's not strong enough to deal with whatever baggage you're carrying around plus her own."

"You don't have a clue how strong she is. You and everyone around Ruth insist on treating her as though she's a hothouse flower that wilts at the first sign of trouble. She's stronger than all of us put together. Before you push the issue and wind up with my fist in your face, Ruth knows everything. I'm not hiding anything from her. I wouldn't do that to her although obviously you don't think much of me or my moral compass." And that hurt. He and Trace had been through tough situations and firefights together and come out the other side bloody but triumphant.

Of all his teammates, Ben had believed Trace trusted him the most. Guess he was wrong.

Trace glared at him. "Knock it off. She's my sister-in-law. Bridget would have my hide if I let anything or anyone hurt her, including you. Yeah, I'm protective of a woman who's been through the wringer and deserves better. I won't apologize for caring about Ruth. Does she know you love her?"

"No, and you aren't going to tell her. When we're both ready, I'll tell her how I feel. She's mine, Trace. I will never hurt her. I'd sooner slit my own throat than cause her one moment of pain. In the end, she may wise up and wash her hands of me, but I'll do everything in my power to keep her happy and safe. No one matters more to me than Ruth."

"Are you going to ask her to marry you?"

He snorted. "What do you think?"

Trace chuckled. "I think you'll slip a ring on her finger as fast as you can find a jewelry store."

"That would be my first choice, but I don't want to scare her. Agreeing to date me is a huge step." But, man, he wanted his ring on her finger to declare her off limits to the rest of the men on the planet.

"Don't push her too fast. She needs to heal."

Ben tore his gaze from the door to look at his friend. "No need for the warning. I know what she went through."

Surprise widened Trace's eyes. "She told you?"

"Enough for me to put the pieces together. Like I said, she's mine. I'm content with that. We'll move forward on our own timetable."

The exam room door opened and a man in a white coat with a stethoscope draped around his neck walked out. He pulled up short when he saw Ben and Trace. He frowned. "You are here for Mrs. Slocum?"

Glad that she'd remembered her cover name, Ben nodded. "I'm Ruth's husband, Ben. How is she?"

"I'm Dr. Garcia. Mrs. Slocum is very lucky that you had epinephrine. She will be fine. I want to admit her for observation until tomorrow. I will release her in the morning if all goes well."

Relief weakened Ben's knees. Thank God. "Will she have long-term repercussions?"

Garcia shook his head. "She'll fully recover. Be vigilant about her food allergy and keep epinephrine handy. You need two doses with you at all times. Something may go wrong while you try to administer the first dose, or you may be far enough from medical help that a second dose will be necessary."

He'd have to get another dose from Sam. Shadow's medic had packed several doses in her mike bag in case there was a problem. "We'll have what we need by the time we leave tomorrow."

"Good. She'll be moved to a room soon. Her body has been through a trauma. She needs as much rest as possible."

"I'm staying with her. I don't care what your hospital policy is."

The doctor smiled. "I understand. I'll make sure you receive no trouble from the medical staff."

"Clear my friends, too. One of them will sit outside the door at all times."

Garcia's eyebrows rose. "Why? She's safe here."

"Ruth has a stalker and the allergic reaction may be linked. I won't take chances with her life."

"No one will protest as long as corridor access is clear."

"Thanks. I want to see Ruth."

"Of course. The orderly will soon take your wife to her room."

"Thank you, Dr. Garcia."

With a nod, the physician strode to the next exam room and walked inside.

Trace clapped Ben on the shoulder. "I'll keep watch."

He walked into the exam room. Ruth lay on a bed clad in a hospital gown with an identification band around her wrist. Even though a blanket was draped over her, she was shivering. "Ruth." Ben wrapped his hand around hers.

She opened her eyes and smiled. "Hi."

"How do you feel?"

"Jittery from the epinephrine, but I can breathe. When can I leave?"

"You're a guest of the hospital until tomorrow morning. The doctor wants to make sure you don't have complications."

Her smile faded. "I'm staying overnight?" Dismay filled her voice.

"It's for your own safety."

"When do you have to leave?"

"I'm not. I'll be by your side every minute. Your doctor is clearing it with hospital personnel."

"I can't stay, Ben. What if I wake up screaming in the middle of the night?"

"I'll wake you before that happens." He squeezed her hand. "Another member of Shadow will be on guard at your door until we leave. No one will slip past us."

"I don't understand how this could have happened. I didn't eat anything once we reached the beach."

"Nico sent off our water bottles for testing at a private lab."

A soft tap on the door brought his free hand to the weapon hidden under his shirt. Ben moved to block Ruth from the view of the person on the other side of the door.

Trace peered inside. "The orderly is here to take Ruth to her room. He's clear. No weapons."

He could imagine how well that search went down. Ben motioned for Trace to allow the man to enter.

A linebacker-sized man pushed a wheelchair into the room with a glower on his face. "I'm Emilio. I'm here to transport Mrs. Slocum to her room." Emilio pushed the chair to the side of the bed, locked the wheels, and reached to assist Ruth from the bed.

Ben inserted himself between the orderly and Ruth. "I'll get her. No offense, buddy, but we're newlyweds. I don't want any man touching her but me."

The orderly backed off with his hands raised in surrender. "I have to push your wife to her room. Hospital rules."

"No problem." He turned to Ruth. "Ready?"

She nodded and wrapped her arms around his neck as he lifted her into his arms.

"I've got you," he whispered against her ear. "No one will touch you unless you want them to."

He set her in the wheelchair and wrapped his hand around hers. Ben walked beside the wheelchair as Emilio transported Ruth to the elevator and then into her assigned room while Trace trailed behind them. When Ben lifted Ruth into his arms, the orderly raised the head of the bed, then pulled back the sheet and blanket for her.

After settling her on the bed, Ben nodded his thanks to the orderly. Once Emilio left, Ruth relaxed.

"Thank you."

He bent and brushed his mouth over hers. "I'm happy to be seen as a possessive jerk who doesn't trust any man around his wife." Another kiss. "Rest now. I'll be here."

She closed her eyes as Ben sat in a chair by her bedside, her hand clasped in his.

Nurses checked on Ruth every two hours. By late afternoon, Dr. Garcia returned and pronounced her improved yet refused to release her until the following morning.

Nico took over the watch from Trace, sending Ruth's brother-in-law to the hotel to rest. Sam and Joe would take the watch at midnight.

By the time the sun set, Ruth's eyes were heavy. Ben brushed strands of hair away from her forehead. "Go to sleep. I'll watch over you."

"You'll be so tired, Ben," she murmured.

"With my teammates in the hall, I'll nap between nurse visits."

She looked at him, an unspoken question in her eyes.

He straightened, alert. "What is it?"

"Would you hold me for a few minutes?"

His heart turned over in his chest. "I'd love to."

She scooted over to make room for him. Ben tugged her blanket higher, eased onto the bed, and wrapped his arm around Ruth's shoulders. He tucked her against his side so her head rested on his chest. Within minutes, she was asleep.

Ben kissed the top of her head and relaxed against the pillow, his weapon within easy reach. He doubted anyone would make it past his teammates, but he never took anything for granted, especially when Ruth's life was at stake. He'd screwed up today. That wouldn't happen again. He'd kill anyone who tried to take her from him.

CHAPTER TWENTY-THREE

Ben woke when Ruth jerked in his arms and moaned. He tightened his hold. "You're safe, baby. I've got you."

"No," she murmured, fighting to free herself. "Please, don't."

"Ruth, wake up."

She jerked awake with a gasp, eyes wide and unfocused in the dim light of the room. "Ben?"

"I'm right here." Ben kissed her forehead. "Bad dream?"

"Bad memory."

Her anguish made him wish he'd taken out Torino when he'd had the chance. Ben had held himself back, not wanting Ruth to see him for the killer that he was.

"Need water?" When Ruth nodded, Ben opened one of the bottles of water Sam had given him.

After she drank her fill, he set the bottle aside and settled Ruth against his chest again. "We have a few hours before the doctor makes his rounds."

"You should go back to the hotel and rest."

"I'm not leaving you. This is the most sleep I've had in a long time." Although Ruth looked skeptical, Ben had told her the truth. "I love holding you."

He loved her. The words wanted to pour from his mouth. Ruth wasn't ready. Soon, he hoped. He'd worked undercover ops and could lie if necessary. He didn't like it, though, especially now. Withholding a truth this monumental from the woman he loved bothered him.

She snuggled closer. "If you're exhausted tomorrow, I won't be happy with you."

Ben smiled. Yeah, he loved this amazing woman. "Yes, ma'am."

The rest of the night passed with two more visits from nurses but no nightmares. Ruth stirred as the sun rose. She smiled at Ben. "Good morning."

"Good morning, beautiful. You ready to tackle this day?"

Determination shone on her face. "If that includes tracking down the jerk who tried to kill me, I'm more than ready."

"Sam brought a change of clothes for you if you want to freshen up before the doctor arrives."

"That's perfect. I wasn't looking forward to walking out of the hospital in a swimsuit covered in a thin wrap."

"Need an assist to the bathroom?"

Color flooded her cheeks. "I feel fine."

Ben kissed her lightly and stood. "I'll wait in the hallway. If you need anything, call out." Another kiss and he walked out.

In the hall, he glanced at Sam. "She's in the bathroom. Do you mind waiting inside the room in case Ruth needs help?"

"Of course not." The medic slipped into the room and closed the door.

Ben turned to Joe. "Need a break?"

"I wouldn't mind a cup of coffee. Want me to bring you a cup?"

"I'd appreciate it."

"Food?"

"I'll wait until we leave here. I want to make sure Ruth eats before she steps in front of the camera again."

With a nod, the spotter strode to the stairwell. He returned minutes later, four to-go cups of steaming liquid in a cardboard carrier. "I brought herbal tea for Ruth. If you think she'd rather have coffee, I'll go back and get her a cup."

"She doesn't mainline coffee like we do, and I think hot tea will settle better on her stomach."

"How did she do overnight?"

"Not bad. She's one tough lady."

A slow smile curved his friend's mouth. "You looked comfortable the times I looked in on you."

Ben didn't deny it. He loved holding her while she slept and knowing that she was safe in his arms. He'd be the same if he convinced her to marry him. One of the Fortress shrinks would tell him he feared losing someone else he loved like he'd lost his parents within months of each other since he considered his mother choosing Davidson over him as a loss.

Maybe after he and Ruth had been married one hundred years, the feeling would dissipate. Probably not, though. If Ruth agreed to marry him, she'd have to live with his fear until he conquered it.

Twenty minutes later, Dr. Garcia strode toward Ruth's room. "Mr. Slocum, how was your wife overnight?"

Soft and warm, but not what Garcia wanted to know. "She rested comfortably." In his arms. Man, he was in so much trouble. He'd promised to be patient and wait for Ruth to be ready for marriage. Ben hadn't counted on his falling in love with her starting an unquenchable fire inside him.

"Good. I'll check her, then we'll take care of the paperwork to release her."

"She's changing clothes. Let me see if she's ready."

The physician motioned for Ben to proceed.

He tapped on the door and opened it a crack without looking inside. "Sam, the doctor's here."

"She's ready."

Ben opened the door for Garcia and waited in the hall with Joe, pacing as the minutes crawled by. When he was ready to walk inside to demand an update, Garcia opened the door and stepped out.

"Good news, Mr. Slocum. Your wife is ready to leave. Do you have two epinephrine pens in your possession?"

He nodded, glad that Sam had packed several. She'd slipped him a second one last night when she and Joe took over the watch. "I have her covered."

"Excellent. Be vigilant about her allergy. We wouldn't want a repeat."

"I'll be careful," he promised.

"The nurse will arrive soon with your wife's release papers. Enjoy the rest of your stay in Mexico." After shaking Ben's hand and nodding at Joe, he left.

Minutes later, Joe drove them away from the hospital.

"I have to be on the beach in less than an hour," Ruth said.

Ben's hand tightened around hers. "Breakfast first."

She wrinkled her nose. "I'll gain weight if you keep insisting I eat."

"You could stand to gain several pounds."

Ruth smiled. "You're the first man in over ten years to tell me I was too skinny."

"Then the rest of the males of your acquaintance are idiots."

That brought a laugh from Sam and Joe as well as Ruth.

"Our first real date out of public scrutiny will include pizza and a movie complete with popcorn and a soft drink. No diet stuff."

She beamed at him. "You remembered."

"Of course. I'm trying to win your heart."

Ruth's stunned gaze locked with his. His statement was a hard push. Ben needed to nudge her further along the path as soon as possible. He wouldn't be able to hide how he felt much longer.

Joe laughed and glanced at Ben in the rearview mirror. "Pizza and popcorn? What happened to a steak dinner with all the trimmings as a way to woo the lady?"

"This lady has been living on rabbit food for ten years. It's time for her to enjoy life."

Sam's eyebrows rose. "She can't eat that way often because of her job."

"Once in a while won't hurt me." Ruth squeezed Ben's hand.

Guess she didn't want to tell Sam and Joe about her retirement yet. "Anything new from Fortress?"

Joe and Sam exchanged glances.

Eyes narrowed, Ben said, "Spill it."

"Maddox contacted Nico two hours ago," Joe said. "Zane is close to locating Davidson's latest compound."

The Fortress tech wizard should have contacted him with the news. That he hadn't wasn't a good sign. "Tell me."

Joe flicked a glance at Ruth.

"She can handle it," Ben insisted. She'd have to if they were going to make this relationship work, something he wanted more than he'd wanted anything in his life.

"Zane tapped favors from people who owe Fortress. The intel indicates that Davidson and his commune have relocated to Mexico."

He froze. As far as he knew, the prophet had never moved his commune out of the US. "Is Zane sure? Davidson has always stayed inside US borders."

"I contacted Z while I was in the cafeteria. A DEA agent contacted Veronica Walker about a group of Americans who set up a compound two hours from here. The agent didn't know specifics about the location, but even that much information will help Zane narrow his search."

Two hours away. Ben gritted his teeth. Too close for his peace of mind. Ruth had to stay at Casa del Mar for another two or three days, depending on how fast the photographer got the shots necessary for the fashion designer's needs. As much as he longed to rush Ruth to safety, she had obligations.

News of Roxanne being at Casa del Mar would hit the news media soon. When a picture of her on the beach with Ben at her side leaked, a media firestorm would ignite and make the woman he loved a target of Jeremiah Davidson.

Resolve hardened in Ben. Let the prophet come. If he made a move against Ruth, Davidson regret the decision for what remained of his short life.

CHAPTER TWENTY-FOUR

Ruth walked toward the job site chosen for the day's photoshoot, her hand wrapped around Ben's. The operative at her side remained watchful, his gaze scanning the beach for trouble. "Everything will be fine," she murmured.

But the odds weren't good. Nothing new to Ben and his teammates. When they'd rescued her before, the odds for success had been against them yet they still freed her, captured her kidnapper, and dismantled most of the Torino organization. Shadow would get the job done. And Ben? He was flat out amazing.

Ben shook his head. "Davidson is too close. Two hours away is nothing. Once the news media gets wind of Roxanne being at Casa del Mar with her new boyfriend, pictures of us will flood the airwaves and Internet."

"Rumors are flying already because of the fundraiser pictures. You haven't been part of the commune since you were twelve. You've changed since then."

"Not enough. I look like my father's twin. If no one else recognizes me, my mother will."

Ruth longed to say that his mother wouldn't turn on him. She couldn't. Mrs. Barrett had already proved disloyal to her son, a concept Ruth was at a loss to accept or explain. If she was blessed with children, they wouldn't wonder if she loved them. "What do you want to do?"

"Whisk you away from here now and hide you where Davidson and his fanatic cronies can't find you. Once you were secure, I'd go hunting."

"You're going to kill him?"

He slid her a glance, his eyes impossible to read behind his dark sunglasses. "If a credible law enforcement agency can't put him in prison, what choice do I have? The longer he's free, more children will be abused and turned into sex slaves. I won't allow my past to threaten you."

"This won't be the last time we're threatened. Will you kill everyone who is a danger to me?"

"If it's necessary to keep you safe, I'll use deadly force. I told you the truth about me. I'm not a nice man, Ruth. I'm an operative. I abide by the law when I can. When I can't?" He shrugged. "I do what has to be done."

Ruth swung around to face him, her hand cupping his jaw with a gentle touch. "I know who and what you are. I saw you in action against Hugo and his organization. I haven't turned a blind eye to the truth. I see you, Ben, the real you. You're a protector. Because you are, I'm asking you to work within the law if you can."

"And if I can't?" He held himself still, tension evident in the lines of his body.

She pressed a soft kiss to his mouth. "I trust you to use your best judgment for what's necessary in the moment. I'll never condemn you for protecting me."

Ben gripped her upper arms and kissed her, long and deep. When he drew back, he drew her into his embrace. "I know I don't deserve you, but I swear I'll do everything in my power to be a man you'll be proud of."

"I'm already proud of you and especially proud to be yours."

With Scott yelling at her to get a move on, Ruth eased out of Ben's embrace and threaded her fingers through his.

"Come on. We should go before Scott and Rich have a meltdown."

He squeezed her fingers and started them toward the scowling men. "Take breaks when you need them, sunshine. Don't let your agent and photographer set back your progress. If they won't cooperate, I'll force them to back off."

Oh, yeah. Ben Martin was in protection mode.

When they paused near Scott and Rich, Ruth's agent reached out to touch her. Ben shifted to cut off Rich's access to her.

Rich scowled. "Isn't that overkill? I'd never hurt Roxanne."

"She was just released from the hospital. You can't blame me for being protective."

"What happened yesterday?" Scott scanned Ruth from head to foot. "You look healthy."

"I had an allergic reaction."

Ben's phone chimed with an incoming text message. He glanced at the screen, frowning.

Rich and Scott exchanged glances, puzzled looks on their faces. "To what?" Rich demanded. "I didn't know you had allergies."

"Strawberries. Somehow, I was exposed to the fruit or juice although I'm not sure how."

Ben slid his phone into a pocket. "The water in our bottles was contaminated with strawberry juice. The lab found a hole the size of a pinprick in each bottle. Someone jabbed a syringe through the plastic and added strawberry juice to the water."

"If that's true, why didn't she taste it?" Scott asked.

"Wouldn't take much to spark a reaction when your sensitivity is high."

Rich snorted. "You're insane if you think someone deliberately hurt Roxanne."

"Evidence doesn't lie. This wasn't an accident."

The photographer sighed. "This isn't getting us anywhere. I worked up a new schedule last night. We're tight on time today, Roxanne. Go change. The other models will arrive soon, and we have a lot of work to make up because of you."

Ruth hoped Ben would be patient as the day progressed. Photoshoots were grueling with multiple wardrobe changes and backgrounds. Not only would this be difficult on her, the other models were now under the same time crunch. Everyone would be tired and cranky by the time the last shot was taken.

While Joe and Sam set up nearby with their umbrella, beach chairs, and small cooler, Ben escorted Ruth to the tent. As soon as she entered the air-conditioned space, Xena and Delayne hurried to her, talking over each other to ask questions and express their concern.

"I'll answer your questions as soon as I change. Scott's in a hurry to get started."

Delayne consulted her list and snatched an outfit from the rack of clothes. "Here. Put this on, then we'll talk." Her frosty gaze darted to Ben. "I guess you'll be sticking around."

He inclined his head, arms folded across his chest.

Ruth quickly changed clothes. At least this time, she wasn't wearing a swimsuit. She much preferred wearing capris and a tank top.

Soon, she sat in the makeup chair and patiently answered questions thrown at her from the two women.

"Are you kidding me?" Delayne scowled. "That's why the drop-dead Latino peppered me with questions yesterday about the water. You can't believe I would try to hurt you. We all know you're the big money-maker here."

Ruth blinked at the bitterness she heard in the wardrobe mistress's voice. "This is a team effort. I just model clothes for designers. Everyone else takes care of the important details. Without you and Xena, Scott and his assistants, and even Rich, I wouldn't be able to do the job at all."

"Then why did that man think I hurt you?"

"Nico asked questions to find out if the allergic reaction was an accident or a deliberate attempt to hurt me."

"Why would someone do that?" Xena powdered Ruth's face. "No one can take your place."

"I don't know about that, but I have a contract to fulfill."

"Roxanne has a stalker," Ben said. "This isn't the first attempt to harm her."

"Roxanne!" Scott yelled from outside the tent. "Let's go."

"Well, I'm not the one who did it." Delayne glared at him.

"Then you have nothing to worry about."

Xena removed the protective cape from Ruth. "Better go."

The morning passed with a dizzying array of wardrobe changes. As the morning wore on, tempers flared, especially those of Rich and Scott when Ben insisted they give her a break every hour for five minutes to rest and hydrate.

When they broke for lunch, Scott yelled for everyone to take 90 minutes for lunch and be ready for a new session at the outdoor pool when they resumed.

Autumn walked with Ruth and Ben toward the hotel. She smiled at Ben. "I'm Autumn."

"Ben."

"It's good to meet you. Roxanne has been keeping you a well-guarded secret."

"I'm in private security. She's been protecting me from public scrutiny."

The other model's eyebrows rose. "You're a bodyguard?"

"Among other things."

"How did you meet him, Roxanne?"

Ruth glanced at Ben. When he gave a slight nod, she turned her to Autumn. "Ben was part of the team who rescued me when I was kidnapped."

"What? When did that happen?"

"A few months ago."

Eyes wide, Autumn said, "I'm glad he and his team were able to find you." A slow smile curved her mouth. "It's romantic, too. This would make a great novel."

"Ben is definitely hero material," Ruth agreed.

He snorted although his grip on her hand tightened.

"How is Tito?"

Autumn's face lit up. "Fantastic. He's flying in later this afternoon."

They ate lunch at one of the hotel's restaurants. Autumn and Ruth both laughed when Ben's hamburger with all the trimmings arrived along with their small salads and fruit. "I'm looking forward to eating like a real person," Autumn said when she'd caught her breath. "A few more months and I'm finished with this part of my life."

"I heard you were retiring soon," Ruth said. "What will you do?"

"I've been taking online classes and will graduate in December with a degree in graphic art design. I've already been designing websites on the side for more than a year."

"That's great, Autumn. Congratulations. I know you'll be a success." And she might be the perfect person to design the website for Ruth's foundation for children. "What does Tito think about your plan?"

"He loves the idea." Joy flooded the other woman's face. "It's the perfect job for me to be able to travel with him when it's baseball season. It's also a win for me. I hate being away from him."

"Should I expect a wedding invitation soon?"

"If you're not on assignment, we'd love for you to come."

"Send me an invitation. I'll work it out."

"Awesome! You're welcome to come as well, Ben."

When they finished their meals, Ben escorted the women back to the changing tent where they donned new swimsuits. After changing, they went to the pool deck where the rest of Shadow stationed themselves around the fenced perimeter.

As Ruth followed Scott's directions for various poses, she noticed a dark-haired, dark-complected man watching from inside the hotel. At first, she didn't think much about it. Every time she was on a photoshoot, she and the other models attracted attention.

The man made her uneasy. She did her best to ignore him and focus on the job. The sooner Scott got his shots, the quicker she and the other models would be able to call it quits for the day.

In between poses, she checked to see if the man was in the same place and perhaps why he made her uncomfortable. Thirty minutes into the session, she figured out what caused the alarm. The man didn't watch the proceedings as a whole. His gaze never deviated from her.

CHAPTER TWENTY-FIVE

Ben's nape felt as though spiders crawled on it. He slowly scanned the pool area. Wall-to-wall people crowded around the exterior of the wrought-iron fence and beyond to the lobby doors of Casa del Mar. Although no one acted suspicious, someone set off his alarm. He couldn't shake the feeling he was missing someone focused on him or Ruth.

Nico caught his eye, eyebrow raised in silent question. Ben sent him a hand signal and his team leader surveyed of the area, his movement casual and easy.

Ben shifted a few feet to the right and leaned against the fence to change in his field of vision. Although concentrating on the milling crowd of excited onlookers, he noticed when Ruth missed a cue and earned a sharp verbal reprimand from the photographer. That wasn't her first slip in the past few minutes. Was she feeling the same thing he was?

He glanced at her and caught the subtle tension of her body. Despite doing her best to follow Scott's instructions, Ruth was distracted. Was she feeling the residual effects of the allergic reaction or did she see something that alarmed her?

A movement on the other side of a lobby window caught Ben's attention. As soon as he focused on the man, the stranger turned away and left, disappearing into the crowd of people pressing close to the windows to watch the activity around the pool.

When he looked back at Ruth, she seemed more at ease. That was enough for Ben. Whoever that guy was, he'd been the source of Ruth's uneasiness. Signaling his teammates to watch over his woman, Ben hurried into the hotel and weaved through the crowd. Since the watcher had a big head start, Ben doubted he'd catch the man. He wanted a better look at his target to give Zane a decent description to narrow the suspect pool.

This man didn't have access to Ruth's job sites, though. Perhaps he was a nosy guy watching beautiful women. If so, he was one of many lingering near the pool to watch the models.

Ben's gut said that wasn't the case, either. No, this was probably connected to Davidson and his cronies. The knowledge sat heavy in his gut. Instead of being a protective shield for Ruth, he'd become a danger magnet.

He pushed free from the crowd and hurried through the lobby to the front of the hotel. He made it onto the sidewalk in time to see a black four door luxury sedan pull away from the hotel at a high rate of speed. He committed the license plate to memory and grabbed his phone.

"Yeah, Murphy."

"It's Ben. I need you to run a license plate."

"Go."

He rattled off the plate number and description of the car and driver. "I don't know if this guy is connected to our situation or not. Could have been interested in watching a bunch of beautiful women modeling swimsuits like about a thousand other men near the pool."

"But you don't think so."

"Nope."

"I'll see what I can find out."

"I need a picture of the driver. I didn't get a good look at him." He gave the time frame and camera locations in and around the hotel as well as the direction the man had driven when he left.

"I'll ask Bridget to run the plates. She's still learning the fine art of hacking. By the time I'm through with her, she'll be as versatile as I am on the Net."

That brought a smile. "You're turning her into a white-hat criminal. You're a bad influence, my friend."

A snort. "Tell that to the boss. He's pushing me to train her faster."

"She must be doing well."

"Bridget is the most talented researcher we've had, but her talents are wasted keeping her on the right side of the law and Maddox is itching to expand her responsibilities." After promising to get back to Ben soon, Zane ended the call.

When another careful scan of the activity in front of the hotel yielded nothing of concern, Ben returned to the pool deck. The models posed for one last series of shots before Scott sent them for another wardrobe change.

Instead of following her co-workers to the tent, Ruth approached Ben. "Is everything okay?" Concern filled her eyes.

He reeled her in for a gentle kiss. "Just checking things out," he murmured.

"You followed the man who was watching me?"

Ben nodded. "He got into his car and left before I was close enough to talk with him."

"It's probably nothing. I'm sorry to raise an unnecessary alarm."

He brushed her cheek gently with the pad of his thumb. "Always listen to your gut. I agree with your instinct. Something was off about the watcher. Bridget is running his license plate. We'll see what happens."

The car could have been stolen or the plate swapped with one that belonged to another vehicle. Ben hoped Zane's hacking skills led to a clear photograph to run through the Fortress facial recognition program. If this man had a record anywhere, Z's database would find him.

"Roxanne!" Rich yelled. "Make out with your boyfriend off the clock."

Cheeks flaring with color, Ruth sent a dark look toward her agent, pivoted, and walked toward the changing tent with Sam close behind.

Ben stared at the belligerent agent until the man's cheeks reddened and he turned away to consult with the photographer. Both men shot angry glares his direction.

Rich and Scott were becoming a problem. For men who were supposed to have Ruth's best interests at heart, neither was concerned about her welfare or her wishes. From the looks thrown his direction, the dynamic duo would gladly drop Ben off in the deepest part of the ocean and leave him for the sharks to eat.

Nico moved to Ben's side. "Find out anything from Mystery Man?"

"The guy moved through the crowd like a greased pig. When I reached the front of the hotel, he took off. I called in the plate to Z. Bridget's running that down while Z checks the camera feeds for a picture."

"Did you recognize him?"

A head shake. "I hope our facial recognition software will help." When Nico remained silent, Ben glanced at his friend, "I know. You don't have to tell me. This is probably related to me rather than Ruth. I can't do anything different at the moment." No matter how much he wanted to.

"Send her to a safe house."

"I wish. She has a contract to fulfill and places everyone in a lurch if she goes off the grid. She'd see it as turning tail and running like a coward." He couldn't blame her for that. She didn't want to see herself as a victim. Ruth wouldn't leave and cede the victory to the creep terrorizing her. His woman was amazing although for once he wished she didn't have that steel spine. Protecting her would be simpler if Ruth was out of sight.

"Being seen as a coward is better than being dead."

"Would you go into hiding if danger threatened you?"

Nico sent him a cool glance.

"Exactly. Ruth had all choices taken from her by that psycho who kidnapped her. I won't do the same. It's my job to keep her safe no matter what her choice is."

"Our job," Nico corrected mildly. He sighed. "All right. I don't like it, but I understand. Mercy wouldn't dodge danger either when I first met her. Strong women, like my wife and Ruth, dig in their heels and stand their ground. We have your back, Ben. Yours and Ruth's. Let's just hope we're able to see and head off the danger before something else happens to her."

"Keep an eye on the agent and photographer. Both of them would like nothing better than to see me buried six feet underground."

"What else is new? You aren't the warm and cuddly type, buddy."

He chuckled. "Ruth wouldn't agree with you."

"Shows what she knows."

Although his team leader was yanking his chain to get a rise out of him, Ben couldn't help but consider the truth of Nico's statement. Of all the people in his life, Ruth did know him better than anyone else. She got him. He used a rock-hard exterior to keep people at bay while inside, he had scars and wounds that hadn't healed from his father's death and his mother's abandonment. She knew the truth and still wanted him. If he was lucky, he'd coax her into falling in love with him before she bailed.

Soon, the models returned, and the photoshoot resumed. By early in the evening, the models were exhausted, and Scott was frustrated at the bad positioning of the sun. The photographer called a halt to the day's work.

"Be on the beach tomorrow morning. By some miracle, we're back on our original schedule." He glared at the models. "No excuses for being late or not in top form. You can't stay up all night and expect to look refreshed and perfect in front of the camera. If everything goes according to plan, we'll be finished with this job by tomorrow evening." With that, he dismissed the models, turned to his assistants, and told them to pack up their equipment for the day.

Before Ruth had taken more than a few steps toward Ben, Rich cut her off and, with a firm grip on her arm, herded her away from the others and Ben.

Ben's blood heated when she attempted to free herself and her agent hauled her in closer, bending until he was in her personal space, creating a false sense of intimacy that Ben knew Ruth wouldn't appreciate. He covered the space separating him from Ruth quickly, Trace moving in from the opposite direction with a grim expression on his face.

Rich glanced over his shoulder to see Ben bearing down on him. He scowled. "Back off. This is a business discussion that doesn't concern you."

Ben grabbed Rich's wrist with a strong grip and forced him to release Ruth. "Business discussions don't require you to touch Roxanne or restrain her when she's not comfortable with your touch."

"Don't be ridiculous," her agent scoffed. "We're friends. She knows I'd never hurt her. In fact, I've been in her life for years. How long have you known her?"

"Long enough." Ben eased Ruth behind him, retaining his hold on her hand. "I'm not warning you a third time. If you touch her again without her consent, you won't like the consequences."

"You're threatening me?"

"I'm explaining the facts to you. Keep your hands to yourself. Talk all you want, but not today. She's wiped out from the work and her allergic reaction, and needs to rest."

Rich rounded on Ruth. "We need to talk without him interfering. This is private business between us. You know I wouldn't hurt you, baby. I don't have any reason to."

Her hand wrapped tighter around Ben's. "You have more reason than anyone," she said, voice soft. "If I'm not working, your paycheck drops. We've already talked about this more than once over the past few months. I haven't changed my mind. If anything, the way this job has gone, I'm more convinced than ever that this is the right decision for me."

The agent moved closer, dropping his voice. "You have more to offer the world. You're beautiful, sweetheart, and we need you and your beauty to make the world a better place. You aren't going to let this Neanderthal force you to retire, are you?"

Trace's eyes widened as he stared at Ruth.

Oh, boy. Her brother-in-law would have a lot of questions once they were free to talk without an audience.

Ruth shook her head. "I'm doing this for me. My interest is shifting to other areas, and my window of opportunity is closing in this industry. I'm okay with that. I want a life, Rich, one out of the spotlight of the media and public. While I'm grateful for the opportunities you helped me secure over the years, I'm finished with this part of my life. We're not discussing my decision again. Once my two remaining contracts are fulfilled, I'm walking into a different future."

"With him?" Contempt filled his gaze as he glowered at Ben. "A glorified rent-a-cop? Come on. You can do better than him. You deserve more than what he can offer you."

"That isn't your business." Ruth turned to Ben. "I'm ready to go."

Although Rich continued to protest, swearing viciously, Ben escorted Ruth from the pool deck with his teammates surrounding them.

Trace turned to Ruth as soon as the elevator doors slid shut. "What was that all about?" he demanded, eyes narrowed.

"Later," Nico murmured, his gaze flicking to the camera in the corner.

The sniper subsided and spun to face the sleek silver doors.

Exiting on their floor, Ben pressed his hand to Ruth's lower back as they walked to the suite. Once inside, he held up his hand to hold off all questions as he checked the rooms for hidden cameras or listening devices. Getting a green light from his electronic signal tracker, Ben slid the device back into his pocket. "We're clear."

"What's going on, Ruth?" Trace folded his arms across his chest. "Did I understand correctly? You're planning to retire from modeling?"

"I have two more contracts, then I'm walking away from this life."

"Why? You love this job."

"At one point, I did. I don't want this life anymore, Trace. I want a real life where I can help people instead of being on display all the time. I just want to be normal."

Ben drew her against his side, offering her his silent support as she faced his teammates. He sent a pointed glance at Trace. "Decision's been made, Trace. Let it go."

His best friend's eyes narrowed. "Is her agent right? Is she quitting because you're insisting on it for your own safety?"

"That's not fair," Ruth protested. "I was considering retirement before Hugo kidnapped me. Now that Ben and I are together, I'll do anything I can to keep him safe, including retiring."

"Don't give up a job you love for a new relationship that might not be permanent. Ben's not good relationship material, honey. What will you do if your relationship fails?"

Great. Nice to know his best friend thought he was a bad bet for a woman.

"My decision stands. I want to do something different with my life, Trace. It's time I branched out and lived the life I've dreamed about for a decade."

"What will you do?" Sam asked.

"I'm establishing a charitable foundation to help sick children, a cause I'm passionate about. I have the name and facial recognition to solicit funds."

"You've researched this, haven't you?" Joe said.

She nodded. "Except for fundraisers, I'll work behind the scenes. I've already begun assimilating a team to help me establish and run the foundation. This has been my dream for years. My agent, family, and friends won't derail my plans."

Trace frowned. "Hey, I wanted to know the decision was yours without prompting from Ben. Our team is years away from retiring, Ruth. If you leave modeling, you may not be able to return if things don't work out."

"I'm aware of the consequences."

When his teammates began to pepper Ruth with questions, Ben held up his hand. "Enough questions for now. Ruth needs to change clothes and rest for a few minutes."

Trace pinned Ruth with his gaze. "You need to tell Bridget before word leaks to the media. Your agent will blame your new boyfriend."

"I'll call her tonight."

"If retiring makes you happy, she'll support you." A smile curved his lips. "Bridget misses spending time with you."

Ben nudged Ruth toward her bedroom. "Go change. Take your time."

Ruth squeezed his hand, then went to her room and closed the door.

"You better not be playing her," Trace said as soon as the door shut, voice barely above a growl. "You promised me you wouldn't hurt her."

"I haven't broken my word. In fact, Ruth has all the power in this relationship." She had the power to completely destroy him.

"Take a break and head to your separate corners," Nico said. "We all need a breather. Are you eating dinner in the suite or taking Ruth out?"

"I'll ask her preference when she returns."

"We'll back you up if she wants to enjoy a meal out before leaving Mexico."

Joe rolled his eyes. "Not much to enjoy when you're only allowed to eat rabbit food."

"That's the best reason of all to ditch the modeling gig," Sam said.

"She loves Mexican food," Trace said. "Because of her job, she can't eat what she wants and spends hours each day working out to maintain her figure."

Joe scowled. "That's ridiculous. What man wants a pencil-thin woman a good gust of wind could blow over when he could have one with natural curves he can hold on to?"

"Tell that to the modeling world." Ben's phone signaled an incoming call. He glanced at the screen. "It's Zane."

"On speaker," Nico said.

With a nod, Ben answered the call. "It's Ben. You're on speaker with Shadow."

"Enjoying the weather in sunny Mexico?"

"Sure, if you call roasting in the sun while listening to a photographer with an ego the size of New York yell and scream at models fun," Trace drawled.

The tech wizard chuckled.

"What do you have, Z?" Nico asked.

"Bridget ran the plates Ben gave us. The car is a late-model Lexus registered to Maria Gutierrez."

Ben frowned. "That's equivalent to Jane Smith in the US. There must be thousands of women by that name."

"This Ms. Gutierrez is 80 years old with no family. Never married, either."

His heart sank. "Let me guess. The lady reported her car as stolen?"

"You got it. She lives outside Juarez."

Nico's expression grew grim. "Juarez is three hours from here."

Ben's hand fisted. "Is Juarez in the area where you're looking for Davidson?"

"I'm afraid so."

"No question, then?" Nico asked Zane.

"None."

"What about the driver?" Standing by the French door, Joe glanced over his shoulder. "Were you able to ID him, Zane?"

"His name is Ernest Gorman. Goes by Ernie."

"He's American?" Trace frowned.

"From Texas."

"What's he doing in Mexico?" Nico folded his arms across his chest.

"The last anyone knew, Ernie was still in Texas. He went off the grid six months ago when he hooked up with a religious cult."

Would his past never die? Davidson and his cronies were honing in on Ruth, looking for a way to use her to hurt him.

CHAPTER TWENTY-SIX

Ruth glanced at her reflection in the mirror. A shower and fresh clothes couldn't eliminate her obvious fatigue. Great way to impress the man you loved. She needed several hours of uninterrupted sleep, but first came food. Her lunch salad was long gone. As many calories as Ben and the others burned on a regular basis, they must be starving.

She grabbed her purse, opened the door and walked into the living room. Members of Shadow turned with smiles or nods, but she didn't see Ben. Did he leave?

"Feel better?" Trace asked.

"I do. Where's Ben?"

He inclined his head toward the balcony.

Ben stood at the railing, staring into the darkening twilight with his hands braced on the flat surface. His body language indicated distress. "What happened?"

"Zane called." Nico pinned her with his gaze. "His news wasn't what Ben wanted to hear."

She waited a beat but Shadow's leader remained silent. "What did he say?"

"Ben will want to tell you himself," Joe said. "Before you talk to him, we've been discussing dinner. Do you want to eat out or order room service?"

"Eat out if security won't be a problem." Her attention shifted to Ben. "Excuse me."

Ruth dropped her purse on the couch and walked out on the balcony, closing the door behind her. Ben shifted slightly but didn't turn. She wrapped her arms around him from behind and held him. Ben was a good man who carried a heavy weight on his shoulders.

Their balcony was wreathed in shadows, the weather perfect for a night out. She loved warm nights with a gentle breeze from the ocean. Darkness brought a sense of anonymity. With the crowds in and around Casa del Mar, perhaps she would blend in with other American tourists. Hopefully, the locals would ignore the American models.

Ben turned and gathered her against him. "Thanks," he murmured after a few moments of silence. "I needed that hug."

"I'm happy to distribute hugs for the right price."

His lips edged up. "Yeah? What's your price? I'm not sure I can afford to pay."

"You won't have a problem meeting my price. Kisses. Lots of kisses."

"I'm in."

She kissed his jaw. "Trace said Zane called."

"He tracked down the owner of the vehicle I saw and the person driving the car."

"They weren't the same person?"

"The owner is an elderly lady named Maria Gutierrez. The driver is Ernie Gorman from Texas. The last anyone heard, he'd hooked up with a religious cult."

That explained Ben's reaction. "He's associated with Davidson. This doesn't change anything."

He frowned. "I'm drawing Davidson and his crew to you."

"They would have targeted me sooner or later, Ben. The public relations machine is already at work."

"It's my job to protect you."

"You saved my life yesterday, protected me when bullets flew, and prevented me from being hit by a car. You're doing a great job."

"I should have you stashed in a safe house while I ferreted out the stalker and Davidson."

"That's not an option." She steeled herself. Ben wouldn't like her next words. "I have a suggestion."

Ben looked at her. "Let's hear it."

"Since we know the media will play up our romance, let's use them to spread the news and draw out both the stalker and Davidson."

He scowled. "I'm not using you as bait."

"It's time to put Davidson out of business permanently. We have the perfect opportunity to stop him. He wants you dead because of Silas. He won't be able to resist using me to draw you out."

"It's too dangerous. Baby, you don't know what he's capable of. Sleeping with any woman he wants is standard procedure for him. If Davidson gets his hands on you...."

The thought of the prophet touching her made Ruth's stomach lurch in revulsion. This plan had to work. Ben wouldn't be able to focus on his missions if Davidson was still a threat the next time he deployed. She could lose him in a heartbeat. No. Just no. "You won't let him."

"No matter how well we plan, missions go wrong." His hold on her tightened. "If we do this, I can't guarantee your safety. I'm not willing to gamble on those odds."

"I am. I don't want the shadow of this man hanging over us."

"Someone will always be a threat to us."

"We'll eliminate those threats as they appear. Right now, Davidson is at the front of the line. We're already making a splash in the media. Davidson will send his people to kill you or take me. Let's set a trap and end this threat." Ruth wanted Ben safe. He wouldn't be with Davidson's contract on his head. As long as the reward for killing Ben was on the table, assassins would keep coming until one of them succeeded.

"What if Davidson doesn't want to kidnap you?" Ben's voice grew rough.

She blinked. "Why wouldn't he?"

"With Shadow guarding you, he'll have a hard time getting to you. If he wants me to suffer, all he has to do is kill you."

Tears stung her eyes.

"Don't ask me to do this. I can't lose you, Ruth. I wouldn't survive."

What did that mean? Although her heart longed to believe he loved her, she didn't dare assume anything, not with a man so good at concealing his thoughts.

He cupped her cheek with his rough palm. "I love you. I know it's too soon to tell you, but you have to understand what you're asking of me with this plan. Losing you would shatter me into a million pieces and complete the work that Davidson and his son started."

Ruth wrapped her arms around his neck and drew him to her for a long, tender kiss, conveying without words how much he meant to her. Equal parts joy and trepidation filled her at the knowledge that Ben Martin, her own personal guardian, loved her.

When she broke the kiss, she held his gaze with her own. "I love you, Ben. I started falling in love with you the moment you grabbed my hand, snapped out a grumpy order, and dragged me out of the stairwell in Hugo's compound."

He closed his eyes a moment, relief on his face. "Thank God. I was sure I'd have to beg you to let me stay in your life after this mission was finished."

"Why would you think that?"

"Once we uncover the stalker, you won't need me anymore."

"I'll always need you. Never doubt that." Her smile faded. "I still have issues to work through."

"No pressure. We have a lifetime to look forward to."

"I don't know of another man who would give me the room I need to be ready to heal without pressing for more."

"Good thing you won't have the chance to find out. I'm smart enough not to let you go." Ben glanced into the suite. "We should go in." But he watched her a moment. "You're going through with this plan, aren't you?"

"We've been on borrowed time. We won't be reckless or foolish, but we aren't running. We have a future to plan. Although I'll take whatever precautions you want and follow your instructions, now is the time to end Davidson's ugly enterprise. Instead of chasing him, we're going to lead him into a trap and take him down for good."

The corners of Ben's mouth tipped up. "Listen to you, tough girl."

Ruth grinned. "I learned from the best. Come on. I'm starving."

When they entered the suite, Ben said, "Before we go out for dinner, we should call Bridget. We have news she'll want to hear."

Trace's eyebrows winged upward. He pulled out his phone and hit speed dial. A moment later, Bridget said, "Hello, handsome."

"Hi, beautiful. You're on speaker with the rest of Shadow and Ruth."

"Hi, guys. How are you, Ruth?"

"Fantastic. I have something to tell you."

A pause, then, "Let's hear it."

"Ben and I are an official couple, and we love each other."

"Good job," Joe said to Ben. "She's the best thing that ever happened to you, buddy."

"Congratulations," Nico murmured.

"Wait a minute," Bridget said, voice sharp. "You just left Nashville with a pretend relationship for cover. You don't really know him."

"Ben and I have been spending time together for months."

"Since when? You're always gone for modeling jobs, Ruth. You can't build a relationship on one or two days a month in the same city."

"We can if we spend two or three hours each night on the phone. I thought you'd be happy for me, Bridget."

"I'm just worried. You're...."

"Don't you dare say I'm fragile. I know my own heart. I love Ben. I've been falling in love with him for months."

A sigh came over the phone's speaker. "I don't want to see you hurt."

"Ben would never hurt me. Be happy for me instead of worried."

"While you have Bridget on the phone, you should tell her your other news," Ben murmured.

Right. She wondered if this news would go over any better. "After I complete two more modeling contracts, I'm retiring from modeling."

Bridget gasped. "Are you serious?"

"I've been thinking about it for months. It's time, Bridget. I'm tired of traveling all the time, I miss you like crazy, and I'm ready for a real life out of the limelight."

"Fantastic! I can't wait to spend more time with you. What's your plan?" When Ruth told her about the charitable foundation, Bridget said, "I'm happy for you, Ruth." Her sister laughed. "I'm especially happy for me. I can't wait to spend more time with you."

"Same. I love you, sis."

"Love you, too. Now, any other bombshells before I get back to work?"

Trace chuckled. "I think we're at our limits."

"All right. I love you, Trace. Be safe, all of you."

"I'll call you later tonight," Trace said and ended the call.

"Ruth said she wanted dinner out," Nico said. "We have two suggestions. You choose, Ruth." He told her the restaurants' names and the type of food they served. "Both have excellent reviews and aren't far from the hotel."

"I've heard good things about Cinco de Mayo."

"Trace and I will bring around the SUVs. The restaurant's close enough to walk, but we'd would prefer to have you inside a vehicle for safety."

She glanced at the man by her side. He gave a slight nod. Good enough for her. "All right. Thank you, Nico."

"Yes, ma'am." He glanced at Trace and the two men left the suite.

"You don't mess around when you have a goal, do you?" Sam said to Ben.

"I didn't intend to tell Ruth how I felt this soon."

Joe frowned. "What changed your mind?"

"Not what. Who. Ruth wants to set herself up as bait to draw Davidson out of his cave and into a trap. I wanted her to know what it would cost me if I lost her."

A soft whistle. "You've got the courage of a lion, lady. It's not a good idea, though."

Ruth's lips curved. "Ben made that clear. It's only a matter of time before news of our relationship goes viral. Ernie Gorman's presence at the pool today indicates Davidson already suspects. Why not set a trap for him?"

"Plans never work like you anticipate."

"So I hear."

Ben released Ruth and went into her bedroom where his bags were stashed. When he returned, he held a small envelope in his hand. Opening the flap, he poured jewelry into his palm. "These might not go with your outfit, but put them on anyway."

"Is this the jewelry with GPS trackers?" Bridget had a set Trace insisted she wear every time she left the house.

He nodded. "With Davidson and his cronies sniffing around, I want extra security in case something goes wrong."

Ruth changed her earrings, then added the bracelet and necklace. "The lilies are beautiful, Ben. Thank you for choosing this design for me."

He shrugged. "They reminded me of sunshine and you."

Joe clapped Ben on the shoulder. "Enough mush, buddy. I'm starving. Let's go."

CHAPTER TWENTY-SEVEN

Ben nudged Ruth's plate closer to her. "You haven't eaten much." She hadn't eaten much all day. At least he'd insisted on frequent breaks throughout the day for Ruth to drink water. Scott wasn't concerned with her health or that of the other models.

He hadn't thought much about Ruth's job aside from hating the media spotlight. Now that he'd seen how taxing the job was, he admired the effort she gave to her work.

She smiled. "I ate more than I should have."

What she'd eaten throughout the day wouldn't add up to the calorie count for one of his meals. "The contract wraps up tomorrow. Eat what you want, Ruth. I doubt the camera will show you consumed a few extra calories for one night."

"Put him out of his misery," Sam said.

Ruth picked up her fork again. "Now I know why the other models raved about this place. The food is excellent."

"It is good," Nico agreed, his gaze scanning the room. "If I come back to this area with my wife, I'll bring Mercy here."

A commotion near the front of the restaurant drew attention to the entrance. The other models arrived with

Scott and Rich in tow. Fantastic. Ben had hoped to give Ruth one dinner out without feeling as though the dynamic duo watched her like a hawk. Rich and Scott scowled when they saw Ruth with the Shadow unit.

"What is their problem?" Joe muttered.

"They're convinced I'm a controlling jerk who is dictating Ruth's life and interfering with their plans for her."

"I can talk to them," Ruth offered. "Tell them to back off."

"Those two are spoiling for a fight with Ben," Sam said. "If they upset you again, you'll play right into their hands. Ben won't stand on the sidelines while those two jerks rail at you."

"We don't want to attract the attention of law enforcement," Trace murmured. "Fortress doesn't have many friends down here. We need to keep a low profile."

Ruth looked stricken. "I'm sorry. I forgot about that problem."

The models, Scott, and Rich were seated at a table a few feet from the Fortress group. Autumn and her boyfriend sat with the others but didn't look happy. Based on the glances tossed his direction from the other members of their party, the topic of conversation was him.

He shifted his focus to Ruth. She appeared poised and at ease if you didn't notice her hand trembling. Ben captured her hand with his and lifted it to his lips. "What's wrong?"

"I want to curl up somewhere safe and go to sleep."

Trace straightened. "I'll get the check if you want to head back to the hotel."

"Excellent idea." Nico stood. "Meet in the suite to work out details for tomorrow."

Ben helped Ruth to her feet and wrapped his hand around hers. When they passed the table with the models, Autumn caught Ruth's hand and introduced her and Ben to her boyfriend. After making plans to eat lunch together the next day, Ben escorted Ruth from the restaurant in Nico's wake.

Inside the safety of the suite, Ben checked for bugs and cameras and found nothing. Excellent. "We're clear. Would you like some herbal tea, Ruth?"

"I'll brew my tea while the rest of you plan for tomorrow." She placed her purse on the breakfast bar and rummaged through the complimentary basket of tea bags.

As the microwave signaled the end of the heating cycle, the rest of Shadow returned to the suite. Once the watch shifts had been assigned for the night, Nico and Trace left, and Sam and Joe retreated to their room.

"I guess you drew the short straw for the first guard shift." Ruth wrapped both hands around her tea mug.

"Nothing I do to protect you is a problem." Ben led Ruth to the couch and wrapped his arm around her shoulders. After grabbing the remote, he channel surfed until he found a baseball game and turned the volume down low. When Ruth finished her tea, he tucked her close to his side, her head resting on his chest. "Relax for a few minutes while we watch the game."

"I'll probably fall asleep," she murmured.

"If you do, I'll carry you to your bedroom." After he had a chance to hold her for a while. He craved the feel of her in his arms.

"You love showing off those amazing muscles."

He chuckled. "Caught me. Push everything else out of your mind and be in this moment with me."

Ben focused on the game, banking on his body heat to lull Ruth to sleep. Within minutes, Ruth was limp in his arms. He settled deeper into the couch as he watched the Rangers trounce the Dodgers.

An hour later, he lifted Ruth into his arms and carried her to her bed. After tucking her in with a light kiss to her forehead, he left, leaving the door cracked in case she had another nightmare.

Taking up his watch at the French doors, he listened to the progression of the game while he scanned for trouble and considered what was likely to come. Davidson would come if he wasn't already circling.

By the time Trace arrived for his shift, Ben still didn't like the odds. Him facing danger was one thing. He didn't want Ruth in the line of fire. She meant too much to him.

"Ruth's been okay?" Trace asked softly.

"So far."

"Good. Rest, Ben. I've got this."

He stretched out on the couch, closed his eyes, and dropped off to sleep.

Some time later, an alarm blared in the hallway. Ben frowned and swung his feet to the floor. "The fire alarm."

"I'll check it out," Trace said, heading to the door as Sam and Joe entered the living room, weapons in their hands. Sam had her mike bag slung over her shoulder. "Stay here."

Ben knocked on Ruth's door and eased it open. "Ruth, wake up."

"What's wrong?"

"The fire alarm is going off."

She gasped. "The hotel's on fire?"

"Trace is checking. We stay in place until he tells us if this is legitimate."

"I'll be right there."

By the time she walked into the living room, Trace was back, his expression grim. "Looks legit. Smoke's pouring from the laundry room on the ground floor on the east side of the building. Hotel guests are evacuating and the fire department is en route."

Joe frowned. "I still don't like it. Could be a trap."

A knock sounded on the door.

Trace peered through the peephole and opened the door for Nico.

"Sit rep." He scowled when Trace told him what he'd learned. "We'll evacuate, but stay alert for trouble."

In the hallway, Ben steered Ruth toward the back stairwell, away from guests streaming toward the front stairwell.

"Why aren't we following everyone else?" she whispered.

"If this is a setup, we'll be expected to follow the crowd. We don't want to make the trap easier to spring." He stepped into the stairwell first to check for threats. Satisfied for the moment, Ben tugged Ruth into the dimly lit interior.

In the stairwell, Trace and Nico took the lead while Joe and Sam brought up the rear. They made their way to the bottom floor where Nico led them toward the back entrance of the hotel.

Smoke hung heavy in the air. Shouted orders to evacuate and fear-filled voices of guests heading outside added to the cacophony. Several guests abandoned their attempt to leave the hotel from the front entrance and pushed in front of the Fortress group with more falling in behind Joe and Sam. The hallway quickly filled with people determined to leave the premises as fast as possible.

Ben tightened his grip on Ruth's hand, uneasiness twisting his gut into a knot. So many things could go wrong. Was this a trap?

At that moment, the lights went out and the corridor leading to the exit plunged into darkness. Panic swept through the crowd surrounding the Fortress group. Women screamed and men shouted, many shoving past Joe and Sam to make a fevered plunge toward the exit.

Acting on instinct, Ben wrapped his arm around Ruth's waist and thrust her on the right side of his body where he served as a buffer between her and the panicked crowd.

People jostled him as they shoved aside anyone in their path.

After one hard shove, a streak of fire raced down Ben's side. He hissed as pain exploded from his ribcage down to his lower back.

"Ben?" Ruth's hand clamped over his. "What is it?"

"Later." He gritted his teeth as hot liquid spilled down his side and slid under the waistband of his cargo pants. Grim realization struck. Ben needed to get Ruth to safety before blood loss made him ineffective. One of the people in the hallway had cut him with a knife.

Finally, Nico and Trace plunged into the night, forming a protective barrier as Ben hurried Ruth into the alley behind the hotel. Sam and Joe rushed out behind them.

"Go," Ben said, tightening his hold on Ruth. He scanned the people nearby. No one seemed interested in the Fortress group. Whoever cut him could be any one of the people milling around in the confusion.

Nico led the group away from the hotel through a series of winding alleys and back streets until he reached a wooded greenway.

Ben stumbled to a halt, blinking to clear the fuzziness of his vision. Not good. Although he fought to stay on his feet, he sank to his knees and collapsed on his uninjured side.

"Ben!"

The darkness closed in.

CHAPTER TWENTY-EIGHT

Ruth dropped to her knees beside Ben. She gripped his side and frowned. Why was her hand wet? She held it up to the light as Sam crouched beside the fallen operative. She gasped. "He's bleeding, Sam." How had he gotten hurt? He'd been beside her from the moment they left the hotel suite.

The medic slid her bag off her shoulder and turned on a small flashlight. The beam illuminated Ben's back and side to reveal a shirt soaked with blood and a long slice in the material.

Sam covered her hands with thin rubber gloves and ripped the material of Ben's shirt to expose the wound. "Someone cut him. He's losing a lot of blood."

Ruth's stomach knotted. "In the hotel hallway, Ben made a noise like he was in pain. When I asked about it, he said he'd explain later." Who would do this and why?

Nico crouched beside her. "Can you handle his injury, Sam, or do we take him to the hospital?"

"I can handle it, but I need a safe place to work and time to do the job right."

"Trace, get one of the SUVs. I'll find a place to hide out for a few hours. Patch him up for now, Sam."

"Yes, sir."

Patch him up? Ruth stared at Nico in disbelief as she gripped Ben's hand. Although Sam was the best medic according to Ben and would know if an injury was life threatening, Ruth's first instinct was to take the man she loved to the nearest emergency room. Shadow, however, had utmost confidence in the medic's ability to treat wounds. She'd have to accept their word.

Nico squeezed Ruth's shoulder briefly and moved a short distance away to make a call while Trace sprinted back toward the hotel.

"What can I do?" Ruth asked Sam.

"You squeamish?"

"Under normal circumstances, yes. But I'll do whatever I have to do for Ben. If I need to barf, I'll do it later."

A quick smile from the medic. "Joe will keep the enemy off our backs while we work." Sam opened her bag and pulled out several white packets and another pair of gloves. "Put these on. Hold the flashlight and open the bandage packets for me. We'll close the wound with butterfly bandages and hope they hold when one of the guys carts Ben out of here."

Ruth frowned. "Butterfly bandages aren't meant for a wound like this." Her stomach churned at the sight of the gaping wound down Ben's side and back. How had he stayed on his feet as long as he did?

"The adhesive is stronger than what you can buy over the counter. I use them in the field when we're on the run from the enemy. In a pinch, I've even used duct tape."

She blinked. Right. Every field medic's kit wouldn't be complete without a supply of all-purpose duct tape. Ripping open a package, Ruth handed the medic one of the bandages. "Sorry. I'm worried about him."

"So am I." Sam flicked her a glance and held out her hand for another bandage. "Your man is tough as nails,

Ruth. We'll get him through this, and he'll be as good as new once he heals."

Perhaps. In the meantime, however, her invincible SEAL would be the walking wounded. Yet again, Ruth wished she'd insisted on Ben and the others standing down from this assignment. Impossible, she knew. Ben would no more duck and run from danger than any Fortress operative.

Ruth shoved her guilt aside and focused on her task.

"Fair warning, though." Joe glanced over his shoulder with a quick grin. "Ben will be grumpy while he heals. He's a terrible patient."

"True," Sam agreed. "He hates being laid up and refuses to take pain meds unless it's necessary." She smiled at Ruth. "All of the operatives refuse pain meds unless the pain is unbearable."

Ben was tough, all right. No wonder she was crazy about this man. As she continued handing bandages to the medic, Ruth's fear settled to a manageable level. Sam worked fast, but she wasn't in a panic which gave Ruth more confidence that Ben would survive.

Nico returned, sliding his phone into his pocket. "Found a safe house thirty minutes out. Will Ben hold?"

"He'll make it." Sam applied another bandage and held out her hand for another. "The sooner we go, the better."

"I agree," Joe muttered, scanning the area with his weapon held by his side. "We're too exposed out here."

Two minutes later, Nico's phone signaled an incoming text message. "Trace is parked one block from here, waiting for us. Can we move Ben?"

"Thirty more seconds," Sam said. She applied two more bandages. "Go. Be careful."

Ruth scrambled back as the medic scooped the medical detritus and dumped it into her bag, then moved aside.

Between the two of them, Joe and Nico maneuvered Ben to his feet, and Shadow's leader hoisted him over his shoulder. Nico signaled for Joe to take the lead. When he fell in behind Joe, Sam urged Ruth to walk in front of her.

She hurried to keep up with the operatives who'd set a fast pace, on alert for distress from Ben or someone who intended to harm him further. She might not be a trained operative, but she would alert Shadow if she spotted trouble before they did.

Two minutes later, Joe held up his fist when he reached the edge of the tree line. Nico stopped. After a few seconds, Joe used another hand signal and moved toward the black SUV idling at the curb.

"Sit on the floorboard in the back," Sam murmured. "They'll lay Ben on the backseat. If Ben wakes, he has to know you're safe or he'll undo my handiwork to get to you."

Ruth watched as Nico and Joe maneuvered Ben onto the backseat where Sam could work on their injured teammate if necessary while Trace drove them to safety.

When Nico motioned to her, Ruth sprinted for the vehicle and leaped into the back. She scrambled to the far side as Sam got in behind her. Joe climbed into the cargo area and Nico claimed the shotgun seat.

Trace sped away from the curb as sirens grew louder. Sam pressed several packets of alcohol wipes into Ruth's hands. "Take off your gloves and clean your hands."

After complying with the medic's orders, she dropped the trash into a bag from Sam. Ruth concentrated on keeping her balance as Trace took corners too fast in the race toward the safe house. Did Bridget know about Trace's mad driving skills?

Ten minutes later, Ben groaned. "Ruth?" he murmured.

Thank God. "I'm here. Don't move. You have a bad cut on your back."

He stirred. "You hurt?"

Sam sent her a sharp look, reminding her without words to keep Ben from moving.

"I'm fine. Be still. Sam only had time to slap on a few bandages. Don't make more work for her than necessary."

His lips curved. "Yes, ma'am." He raised his voice. "Anyone get a look at the joker who knifed me?"

No one had. Ruth wasn't surprised. The hallway was pitch black after the lights went out.

"Two of the models were ten yards behind us in the hall," Joe said.

Ruth frowned. "Who?"

"Sapphire Willis and Tom Hatcher. When the lights went out and the crowd panicked, I lost track of them."

Sapphire and Tom? Ruth couldn't see them stooping to cutting someone to get ahead. Besides, why attack Ben? He wasn't a professional rival.

Her breath caught. Unless one of them meant to hurt her in the chaos. When the lights had gone out, Ben moved her to his right side so she was cocooned between his body and the wall. Did one of them mean to cut her and cut Ben by mistake? "Your injury is my fault."

"Won't be the last injury I have on the job."

She kissed his temple. "I'm sorry, sweetheart."

"I'm not, especially if you call me sweetheart again. My job is to protect you from everything, including knife wounds. I'm just sorry I didn't move fast enough to get both of us out of danger." He sounded disgusted as well as weak.

"Stop talking, Ben," Sam said. "Rest while you can. As soon as we reach the safe house, I'll break out my suture kit." She grinned and wiggled her still gloved fingers where he could see them.

Ben groaned again. "You enjoy working on me way too much."

"Don't present me with injuries to suture so often," she tossed back. "Shut up and conserve your strength."

"Brat," he grumbled.

"Watch it," Joe said, his tone mild.

Ruth wrapped her hand around Ben's and held on tight as his eyes closed and he lapsed into silence.

A few minutes later, Sam applied another bandage, then grabbed a vial of medicine and a syringe. After wiping his arm with an alcohol wipe, she murmured to Ben, "A little stick. This is an antibiotic. I'll save the good stuff for suturing." Ben growled. Sam stowed the needle in a hard plastic case and dropped it into her bag.

The journey to the safe house seemed to take forever. Finally, though, Trace turned into a driveway and drove around the back of a darkened house.

When Ruth reached for the door handle, Ben squeezed her hand. "Wait," he whispered. "Let someone check first."

Ruth remained in place while Nico and Joe bailed from the SUV and scouted the surroundings. A moment later, a light came on inside the house and a white-haired man opened the back door. He motioned for them to come inside.

Nico approached the elderly man with caution, weapon in hand. After a short conversation, Shadow's leader signaled the rest of them.

"It's safe," Trace said, turned off the engine, and opened his door.

Ruth scrambled from the SUV and moved out of the way as Nico and Trace assisted Ben from the vehicle and draped his arms across their shoulders. They carried him inside the house while Joe watched their host.

"Last room on the right," Nico said when they were inside. "Mr. Lopez has a room ready."

"Why is he helping us?" Trace asked, voice soft.

"He owes Maddox a big favor and isn't a friend of the cartels or human traffickers. Lopez knows not to ask questions or talk to anyone about us. We're safe for the moment."

The operatives laid Ben on a bed with a thin covering of plastic over the comforter.

Mr. Lopez came into the room with a stack of clean towels, multiple cloths, and a large bowl of steaming water. He spoke to Nico a moment and left.

"What did he say?" Sam asked.

"He's leaving for the rest of the night, staying with a friend who won't ask questions. We're free to use anything in the house, but we have to leave before noon before his son arrives."

"Joe, wash your hands. I might need your help." Sam set her bag on the floor beside the bed and grabbed a fresh pair of gloves. "I'll work as fast as I can, Nico."

"Do what you need to do. Trace and I will set up a perimeter watch. I don't think anyone followed us, but if they did, we'll keep them off your back long enough to work on Ben."

Sam glanced at Ruth. "Sit on the bed beside Ben. Distract him while I work."

"I'm right here," Ben grumbled.

Joe grinned at Ruth, mischief dancing in his eyes.

Right. Grumpy patient. She sat beside Ben. "You're proving your teammates right. They told me you're a terrible patient."

He scowled. "My back's on fire."

"Quit being a baby," Sam said as she pulled more alcohol swabs from her bag. "I'm going to clean your wound and numb your back."

"Yeah, yeah." Ben's gaze locked with Ruth's as Joe helped Sam roll Ben to his uninjured side. "You sure you're okay?"

"I'm fine except I need a nap." Side effects of adrenaline dump.

Sam used swab after swab to clean and sanitize Ben's back, then injected medicine. Throughout the process, Ben didn't flinch. Tough guy, indeed. "As soon as the lidocaine kicks in, I'll close the wound."

"How bad is it?" he asked, not taking his gaze from Ruth's.

"Your modeling career is over."

Ben snorted. "Another scratch, huh?"

"More than a scratch this time. You'll have an impressive scar to add to your collection."

The light was good enough for Ruth to see scars from previous injuries to his chest, a road map pointing to his hard life and dangerous career.

"One more among dozens means nothing. Will I be mobile?"

"Yes, although you won't be happy about it."

"I'll deal."

A few minutes later, Sam pinched various places on Ben's back. "Feel anything?"

"Pressure."

"Excellent. Time for me to go to work."

Sam grabbed a kit from her bag and opened it. The contents made Ruth flinch. Oh, boy. This might be more than her stomach could handle.

"Eyes on mine," Ben murmured. "This is better than our standard operating procedure, you know."

"Why do you say that?"

"Normally, we're evading detection or under fire. This is a walk in the park in comparison."

That surprised a laugh from Ruth. "If you say so."

"Have you been to the Nashville Zoo?"

"No, why?"

Ben smiled. "Our next date will be ogling a bunch of furry creatures."

"What happened to the movie with popcorn and soft drink you promised me?"

"The zoo is world class and has popcorn and soft drinks. I'm sure to earn a few extra kisses at the movie that night after seeing those cute and cuddly animals in natural surroundings."

Joe snorted. "Remind me to send you a list of never-fail date ideas, Ben. We don't want Ruth to wise up and dump you for a man with better ideas to woo his woman."

"I've already wooed her and captured her heart. Now, I'm introducing her to the concept of fun."

Ruth smiled. "You mean I shouldn't consider running from bullets, surviving anaphylactic shock, and escaping from a fire fun?"

"Only if you're loony," Sam said. "You should take a page from Joe's date ideas. He's creative."

Joe beamed at his wife. "Thanks, Sparky."

"I don't need your lame ideas," Ben groused. "I can handle this on my own."

"Yeah, sure. Don't come crying to me when Ruth decides you're hopeless in the romance department."

"Never going to happen." He winked at Ruth. "She loves me."

Indeed, she did.

Thirty minutes later, Sam sat back. "That should do it. Are you feeling anything, Ben?"

"Nope."

"That will change soon. You need pain meds."

Another scowl from Ben. "No."

"You don't have a choice this time. Suck it up and deal, Martin."

"I have to be functional to protect Ruth."

"I'll make sure you can do your job, but this is non-negotiable. Otherwise, you won't be able to rest."

Ruth squeezed his hand. "Ben, please do as Sam recommends."

He sighed. "All right, but not before I talk to Nico about security."

Joe rose. "I'll get him."

Minutes later, Nico walked in. "How is he?" he asked Sam.

"Thirty-nine stitches and cranky. He won't take pain meds until he talks to you."

Shadow's leader came to the side of the bed. "Perimeter is secure. No indication that we were followed. We have eight hours before we have to vacate the premises. Take the meds."

"Ruth has to be on the beach in five hours. She needs to finish the contract on time so I can get her out of here."

"Understood. Sam, give Ben enough pain medicine to take the edge off. We'll stay for the next four hours, then return to the hotel."

"Yes, sir." After she administered the pain medicine and set up an IV, the medic rose. "Ruth, stay with him. That's the only way he'll agree to rest. I'll be back to check on him in an hour. If he needs anything, call out."

Relief swept over her. Four hours wasn't enough, but it was better than Ben returning to duty immediately. "Thanks, Sam."

Nico followed Sam from the room, leaving Ben and Ruth alone.

"Come here," Ben murmured, stretching out his arm. "I need to hold you for a few minutes."

She scooted closer. "Won't that hurt you?"

"I'm not feeling anything right now. Let me enjoy it. The lidocaine will wear off soon and I'll feel everything."

Ruth settled her head on his arm. "Sleep. Your team is on watch and we're safe for the moment."

His eyes closed. Between one heartbeat and the next, he was asleep.

She stared in amazement. Incredible. She wished she could do that. Although she was determined to stay awake and watch over Ben, she grew sleepy. Ruth drifted until Sam returned. "How is Ben?"

"Running a fever. Not unexpected. That's why I gave him the antibiotic." The medic glanced over her shoulder at her husband who leaned one shoulder against the door jamb. "Ice packs."

"You got it." He left and returned with ice in plastic bags and two hand towels.

"Thanks, babe." Sam settled one against Ben's neck and draped the second over his forehead.

He shivered and groaned. "Off."

"Nope. You have a fever."

"You're enjoying this."

"I live to make you suffer."

"Knew it."

Sam patted his shoulder. "I'll be back soon. Ruth, make sure he leaves the ice packs in place."

After she left, Ben reached for the ice pack on his neck. Ruth grabbed his hand and brought it back to her waist. "You heard the lady. I don't want to be on her bad side."

"Wuss."

"Yep, that's me. I might be a foot taller than Sam, but she could take me down. I don't want to tick her off. I'll leave that honor to you."

His lips curved as he drifted back to sleep.

Throughout the hours they rested, the medic checked on Ben in intervals. Finally, a few minutes after eight, Ben opened his eyes and cupped Ruth's cheek. "Hi, beautiful."

"How do you feel?"

"Like a truck ran over me. You?"

"Same."

"Great way to end this contract. How much trouble will you get into with Scott and Rich if you're late again?"

"Don't know or care. Will you stay in the suite and rest today?"

"Not a chance. Sam will watch me while I watch you. With the exception of Autumn and maybe her boyfriend, I don't trust your co-workers."

Sam returned. "How do you feel, Ben?"

He frowned at her over his shoulder. "Like Dr. Frankenstein used me for a pin cushion. How about you?"

The medic grinned as she checked his vitals. "I need a nap. Some of us didn't get our beauty rest like you did."

"Well?" he said a moment later.

"My professional diagnosis is that you'll live. Fever's down and the wound isn't showing signs of infection."

"Great. I need a shirt. Any chance I can take a shower with these stitches?"

"I'll rig up something for you."

"Thanks, Sam. For everything."

"Yep. Let's get you on your feet." Sam removed the IV and called for her husband. When he entered the room, the two of them assisted Ben to his feet.

Face draining of blood, Ben's knees gave out.

"Whoa there, buddy." Joe eased him back down to the side of the bed. "Give yourself a minute."

"Don't have it. We need to go."

"You can sit for five minutes. We're not that far from the hotel."

Sam glanced at Ruth. "See if Mr. Lopez has a bottle of water in the kitchen."

"Sure." She pressed a light kiss to Ben's bare shoulder and scrambled off the bed. In the kitchen, she checked the refrigerator. Nothing. After a fruitless search in the pantry, she turned to the laundry room.

Ruth peered inside and breathed a sigh of relief. Mr. Lopez had several cases of water stacked against the far wall. Grabbing two bottles, she returned to the bedroom and handed them to Sam.

"Perfect." The medic dumped powder into the bottles and shook them. She pressed one into Ben's hand. "Drink. Let's see if this will do the trick. You'll still be weak," she warned. "You should stay in bed today."

The operative shook his head as he guzzled half the contents of one bottle.

"Stubborn much?" When Sam judged he'd consumed enough, she set aside the drink and nodded at Joe. "Let's try again." They maneuvered Ben to his feet a second time.

He swayed but his legs didn't fold. After a few seconds, he straightened away from his teammates. "I'm good. Find me a shirt and we'll get out of here."

CHAPTER TWENTY-NINE

Ben shifted on the beach chair to find a more comfortable position. The effort proved futile. All he wanted was a long nap in the air-conditioned suite.

At this rate, he'd soon sound like the cranky toddler his teammates accused him of imitating. He tried not to show his discomfort since Ruth and Sam watched him closely. More than once, Scott yelled at Ruth when she missed a positioning cue because she focused on him instead of the photographer.

Shadow's medic handed him another bottle of water spiked with electrolytes and two capsules. "Mild pain meds," she murmured. "Take them for Ruth if not for yourself."

Ben swallowed the pills. "No one has shown interest in my health," he murmured. "I'm disappointed."

"Maybe the models aren't guilty."

He hadn't ruled them out. When he returned to the suite, he planned to call Zane. The tech wizard might locate security footage of the hallway where he'd been knifed before the lights went out. "What did Joe learn from the hotel manager?"

"Someone set hotel linens and towels on fire in the laundry room. Two dryers were damaged in the blaze, but no one was hurt."

"Except me."

"The police don't know that since we didn't report the incident."

He refocused his gaze on Ruth. "Anything else?"

"A party Ruth is expected to attend is planned for tonight. It's a fundraiser for a local charity and a photo op for the designer's new line of clothes."

Fantastic. Another event where Ben and his teammates would be stretched thin to protect Ruth. "When and where?"

"Hotel ballroom on the second floor at 7:00. Thankfully, it's not a black-tie event. The models are to wear beach casual clothing donated by the designer."

"We need to come up with a security plan."

"The rest of us will cover security. You stick close to Ruth."

A lot of good that did earlier. He'd ended up with a boatload of stitches in his back and side.

"Drink the water, Ben. The photoshoot should finish in two more hours."

Those minutes tested his patience. Ben restrained himself when Rich and Scott continually berated the models, Ruth in particular. What was their problem? All the models did their best to follow orders and smile on command.

Good thing Ben wasn't one of the models. He'd have plowed his fist into the faces of the dynamic duo several times over by the time the photographer declared the job a wrap.

Ben rose as Ruth hurried toward him. "I'm fine," he said, voice soft when she reached his side. "Sam's been pushing fluids and pain meds on me." He tapped her nose gently. "You aren't supposed to let on that I'm hurt, remember? I'm your invincible jerk of a boyfriend."

She kissed him, a sweet, gentle touch that wrapped whispers of love around his heart. "I can't help worrying. I love you."

Ben brought her against him for a longer kiss, confident that his teammates had his back and would watch for trouble. "I love you, too." He threaded his fingers through hers. "Let's go. I've had my fill of sun and sand for a while."

Starting them toward the suite, he said, "I understand you have a charity event tonight."

"How did you find out?"

He winked at her. "I discover many things I'm not supposed to know. When were you going to tell me?" Later, he and Ruth would talk about the length of time needed to plan security for events such as this one.

"I wasn't. I knew the party would be a security nightmare with too many people, entrances, and exits."

He stared at her, eyebrows raised in surprise.

"Trace points out security risks when I spend time with him and Bridget in public." She edged closer. "Even if I wanted to go, you're not up to it. We can enjoy a quiet night in the suite with a late-night walk on the beach."

He watched her a moment. "Who benefits from the charity?"

"A local children's hospital. The money goes into a fund for patients unable to pay for medical care."

A cause close to her heart. "We have two hours before the party. We'll go for an hour or so, then slip out and go for a moonlit walk along the shore. What do you think?"

Her eyes lit. "We don't have to go. I planned to donate money whether I attended or not."

"We'll work it out."

Ruth's smile conveyed her delight. "Thank you, Ben."

"You'll stay by my side the whole time we're in the ballroom."

"Absolutely."

"And you'll wear the jewelry."

"No problem."

Amused, his lips curved. "Will you always be this accommodating?"

"Not a chance. Don't get used to it."

Minutes later, Ben unlocked the suite and escorted Ruth inside. Joe and Sam followed them while Nico and Trace went to their room.

Ben pulled out his electronic signal detector. In Ruth's room, the chaser lights changed from green to red. Gut tightening, he turned on the lamp and searched for the source of the new electronic signal.

He found a small camera perched between the dresser and the mirror in a section draped in shadow. Blood boiling, he detached the camera pointed at Ruth's bed and disabled it.

He checked the signal detector again. The chaser lights were still red. Another camera or a listening device? Ben found a listening device attached to the back of the nightstand. He dropped the bug into a glass of water. One final check of the signal detector showed the chaser lights were green.

What about the rest of the suite? If the spymaster was smart, he'd wire the whole suite.

He returned to the living room and signaled Joe to check the rest of the suite. He held up the glass with the bug and the remnants of the camera.

Grim-faced, the spotter grabbed his own signal detector and swept the living room. He found a bug and camera near the wall art. After disabling both, he continued through the kitchenette and into his and Sam's room. He returned minutes later with a third camera and bug. After disposing of the last of the electronics, he said, "We're clear."

"How did someone get in here to set this up?" Ruth asked.

"Stole a master key card or bribed a maid." Ben wrapped his arm around her shoulders and hugged her. "It's easier than you think. Your room is clear if you want to shower."

"What about you?"

"I'll be on the couch." He dropped a quick kiss onto her mouth. "No heroics, I promise. By the way, does this charity shindig include food?"

"Of course. No self-respecting charity fundraiser is complete without awesome food to thank people for parting with their money."

"Good to know we won't starve." He nudged her toward her room. "Go. Take advantage of your downtime. I'll be here if you need me."

As soon as Ruth's door shut, Ben made his way to the couch and lowered himself to the cushions. Just in time. A couple more minutes on his feet and he might have embarrassed himself by wilting like a flower on a hot day.

"How bad is the pain?" Sam crouched in front of him.

"Enough that I want to puke."

"I can give you something stronger."

"Not unless it will wear off by the time the party starts."

"What about over-the-counter medicine? You can take that along with the other pain medicine without an interaction."

Ben nodded. "Yeah, I'll take that." He didn't mind grousing at his teammates. Ruth didn't deserve his attitude. She felt bad over his injury. He didn't want to stoke her guilt.

A moment later, Sam returned with the caplets and a soft drink. "The carbonation helps the meds dissolve faster." Once he'd taken the pills, she helped him stretch out. "Rest. After the party, you need to sleep."

"I'll sleep better on the jet." The sooner he whisked Ruth out of here, the better. They were on borrowed time and Ben would rather face down his enemies on home turf than in a land where Fortress had more enemies than friends. "Do me a favor, Joe."

"Name it."

"Call Zane. Ask him to pull security footage from the hallway at the time of the fire and the area near the laundry room. I also want the security footage outside the suite. If we're lucky, we'll see who added the electronics to our suite."

"No problem. Sleep, Ben. Sam and I will watch over you and your woman."

That was the last thing he heard before sleep took him under.

CHAPTER THIRTY

Since she wasn't due to report for her next modeling job for another two weeks, Ruth filled her plate without guilt although she chose whole foods rather than processed carbs.

She glanced at Ben, relieved he appeared stronger. Sleep gave him a second wind. Of the two of them, she seemed to be the one feeling the worst effects of the long day and short night.

They eased through the crowd to the table where Autumn and her boyfriend sat with Joe and Sam. Nico and Trace stood against a nearby wall, watching the crowd and the doorways. Joe and Sam were also alert and watchful. Ruth prayed the precaution was unnecessary.

She was ready to fly home. Maybe the Fortress jet would be ready to leave before tomorrow morning. Although she'd love a moonlit walk on the beach with Ben, she'd enjoy many beach walks in the years to come.

Tito Monterro was funny and charming and madly in love with Autumn.

"How did you and Tito meet?" Ruth asked her friend.

"Tito served as master of ceremonies for a fashion show in which I was participating. We struck up a conversation after the show and he asked me out for coffee afterward." Autumn smiled. "That was the first of many dates when we could find time between our jobs. After two months, he invited me to attend one of his games. I had so much fun watching him play baseball. We've been shuttling back and forth across the country and even out of the country ever since. What about you and Ben? Is it serious between you two?"

Although he was engaged in conversation with Tito and Joe, Ben's hand squeezed hers briefly. How on earth did he keep track of her conversation as well as his own? Multitasking must be his superpower.

"I love him."

Autumn squeezed Ruth's free hand. "I'm so happy for you. Since I've been with Tito, I can't help but want all my friends to find the love of their lives, too."

Ruth glanced at Ben. Yes, that was the perfect description of the man by her side. Ben Martin was the love of her life. She knew that with absolute certainty that he was the only man for her.

As though Ben felt her gaze, he turned toward her, eyebrow raised. "Everything okay?" he murmured. When she nodded, he brushed a soft kiss over her mouth and shifted his attention to the men's conversation.

A commotion caught her eye. Tom and Sapphire had cornered Rich Eisenhower a few feet away. The agent shook his head. When the two continued to press their point, Rich raised his voice. "Roxanne is the darling of the fashion world. If she wants the contract, she has first choice. Always."

Sapphire fired back something, anger flashing in her eyes.

"Get over it. Roxanne paid her dues, but you're getting there. I've made good things happen for you, haven't I, honey? You and Tom? Your time will come." When Sapphire gripped Rich's arm, the agent shook off her hold.

"We're done here. Enjoy the night. We'll talk more later." He walked to the buffet line to grab a plate.

Sapphire glared at Ruth, said something to Tom, and the couple moved to the open bar.

"Watch your back around them," Autumn said.

"Why?"

"Sapphire feels like she should have been offered several of the contracts you were awarded. Tom, too."

"Are they angry enough to hurt me?"

Autumn's expression grew troubled. "Based on what I heard last night at Cinco de Mayo, they'd cause problems if it meant they took your place in the job market."

Not exactly confirmation, but a good indication of intent. "Have you noticed suspicious behavior from them?"

"Like what?"

"Bringing gifts to the job site or leaving notes on my dressing table."

A frown. "Now that you mention it, I did see Sapphire dropping off flowers and a note. I assumed she grabbed your delivery from a security guard."

"What about Tom?"

Autumn shook her head. "He hasn't received as many contracts lately. The fashion designers are requesting younger-looking men. Sapphire bragged about Hollywood screen testing him for roles in movies and television shows, though."

Hmm. Was Sapphire responsible for the stalking episodes? "I hope that works out for him."

Autumn smiled. "He wouldn't wish you well if the situations were reversed. I'm glad I won't be dealing with this much longer."

Conversation drifted to other topics. By the time they finished dinner, almost two hours had passed.

Ruth glanced toward the door and noticed a man staring at her. Her breath caught. Oh, man. Ernie Gorman.

Tito said something to her, drawing her attention for a moment. When she looked again, Gorman was gone. Had she imagined him?

"Ruth." Ben's hand tightened around hers. "What's wrong?"

"I thought I saw Ernie Gorman near the door."

"I don't see him."

"I might have imagined him standing there."

"Don't second guess yourself, sunshine." Ben slid his phone from his pocket and shot off a text. Seconds later, Nico glanced at his phone. Immediately, he gave some kind of hand signal to Trace, and the two of them left the ballroom.

What if she'd been mistaken? Ruth didn't want to waste their time. "Can we leave Mexico tonight after the party?"

"If you want to leave, I'll make it happen."

"I want to go home."

He brushed her mouth with his. "I'll be back after I make a call." Ben glanced at Joe and inclined his head toward Ruth. After his teammate nodded, Ben rose and left the ballroom.

"Where's Ben going?" Autumn asked.

"To make a phone call."

An unsteady Sapphire stumbled and staggered to their table. The model steadied herself with one hand on the back of Autumn's chair, a drink in the other hand. "I hope you're happy, Roxanne." Her speech came out slurred. "You're blocking everybody else's success to fatten your own purse and bank account. What about the rest of us, huh?"

"I'm sorry you feel that way, Sapphire. You and Tom are terrific models. I hear photographers and designers compliment you all the time."

The model frowned. "But they give you the contracts. It's not fair."

"You're drunk," Autumn said flatly. "Go sleep it off, Sapphire."

"Oh, shut up. You don't count anymore. You have Tito's money. You don't need these contracts. We do." She turned bleary eyes still sparking with anger and jealousy toward Ruth. "What are you going to do about it?"

"I don't control the offers. Talk to Rich. He has more pull than I do."

"That's not good enough. You're the industry darling. Rich said so. You could do something good for the rest of us, but you won't. You're too selfish."

Tom hurried to Sapphire's side. "Come on, baby. Let's go. You're causing a scene and not in a good way."

"We deserve the top jobs, not her. Look what she did on this job. Gone all the time and pretending to be sick. We deserve top billing and nothing we did the last few weeks made any difference."

Nothing they did? Did that mean Sapphire and Tom were the stalkers?

Joe straightened. "What does that mean?"

"Nothing. Can't you see she's drunk?" Her boyfriend paled, sweat beading on his forehead. "Shut up, Sapphire. We need to go."

"You shut up! I've got one more thing to say to the great Roxanne." Sapphire lifted her glass and threw the liquid contents into Ruth's face.

Autumn gasped.

"Get her out of here," Joe snapped.

"Sorry, man. She didn't mean any harm," Tom said.

Ruth lifted her napkin and blotted her face dry. She stared in dismay at her shirt. Sapphire's frou-frou drink was pink and quickly staining her white shirt.

"Come on," Autumn said and tugged on Ruth's hand. "We have to rinse that out before the stain sets."

Sam stood. "I'll go with you. I've got this, Joe."

Her husband dropped back into his chair. "You have five minutes before I come looking for you."

She waved and followed Autumn and Ruth toward the restrooms.

"I hope there isn't a line at the sinks." Autumn pushed open the door to the women's restroom and tugged Ruth inside. Surprisingly, the room was empty. "Fantastic. Take off your shirt. If Joe was serious, we'll have to hustle to finish before he arrives."

"Oh, trust me. He wasn't kidding. He'll bang on the door at the five-minute mark." She handed Autumn her shirt. "Please tell me you aren't planning to soak the whole shirt. I refuse to walk into the ballroom looking like an ad for a wet t-shirt contest."

"No sweat. There's a hand dryer in here. We'll use that to dry the material."

Not convinced that would work, she figured Sam would ask one of her teammates to sacrifice a t-shirt for the sake of Ruth's modesty if the dryer didn't fix the problem.

She glanced back at the door. Where was Sam? She hadn't been far behind them.

"The stain is gone." Autumn lifted the wet shirt to show Ruth. "Now all we have to do is dry the material before Ben or Joe burst in here."

The door to the hallway swung open.

Ruth swung around, expecting Sam. She was wrong.

CHAPTER THIRTY-ONE

Ben returned to the ballroom and wound through the milling crowd. When he was near his table, the crowd thinned enough to notice that Ruth was gone. Frowning, he covered the remaining distance in a few strides. "Where's Ruth?"

"In the bathroom with Sam and Autumn. You missed the excitement," Joe said, disgust in his voice. "Sapphire had too much to drink and confronted Ruth."

His eyebrows rose. "What happened?"

"Sapphire threw her drink in your lady's face," Tito answered. "Autumn took Ruth to rinse her shirt."

Joe glanced at his watch and frowned. "They've been in the bathroom more than five minutes."

"Give them a couple more minutes before you hunt them down," Tito said. "Might have been a line or something."

"Yeah, you're probably right." Joe waved Ben to his seat. "Be comfortable while you wait."

His gaze drifted toward the hallway where the restrooms were located. Ruth was fine, he told himself. Sam was with her. Why did he feel uneasy?

Nico and Trace came to the table.

Ben's gaze shifted from one teammate to the other. "Any luck?"

"Nothing." Nico glanced around. "Where are Sam and Ruth?"

"Bathroom. One of the other models threw a drink in Ruth's face."

Trace scowled. "Who?"

"Sapphire." Joe held up his hand. "She was drunk, Trace. However, from a few things she said in her ranting, I think she and Tom were the ones giving Ruth the unwanted gifts. They blame Ruth for not stepping aside and allowing them to have the top contracts."

"That's ridiculous. They have to earn the top spot. If they're as good as they think they are, Ruth wouldn't have to step aside."

"Think they're responsible for the strawberry-laced water?" If so, Ben would be paying them a visit once they were stateside. Ruth would have died if she didn't have the epinephrine.

"Wouldn't surprise me," Joe admitted. "Tom was pale as a ghost and sweating."

"I'll find out once we're home. Ruth wants to leave tonight. I just talked with the pilot. He's readying the jet as we speak."

Trace brightened. "Awesome. I'm more than ready to see my wife."

"Same here," Nico agreed. "As soon as Ruth returns, we'll pack our gear. If Tom and Sapphire are the stalkers, Ruth won't have to worry about them once Ben has a heart-to-heart talk with the models."

Trace's expression darkened. "He won't be talking to them alone. I have a few choice words to share with them."

Even if the models were responsible for stalking Ruth, Davidson was a danger to her until Ben found and dealt with him. He dragged a hand down his face, flinching as his stitches pulled.

Was his mother still in Davidson's harem? She'd be in her late fifties now and the prophet preferred young, beautiful women. If she remained with Davidson, Ben doubted his mother was a favored wife. What woman wanted to be one of many wives of one man?

Joe glanced at his watch. "What's taking the women so long?" He slid his phone from his pocket and typed in a message. He scowled when his text went unanswered. "Sam didn't respond. I don't like this."

Ben was moving before Joe finished his sentence. He should have followed his instincts. Although his teammates didn't spot Gorman, Ben believed Ruth. Was Gorman responsible for Sam's silence?

Praying he was wrong, he dodged several fundraiser guests and hurried toward the women's bathroom. Before he reached the door, a woman in a white blouse ran into the hallway and straight into Ben's chest. He caught her as she stumbled back.

Autumn grabbed his upper arms, terror in her eyes. "He took Ruth. You have to find her."

His stomach tightened into a knot. "Who took her? Was it Tom?"

She shook her head. "I don't know him, but Ruth did."

"Where's Sam?" Joe demanded.

"She never came into the bathroom."

"Give me a detailed description of the man who took Ruth," Ben said to Autumn as Joe searched for his wife. "It's important, Autumn. Her life is at stake."

"He was big, taller and broader than you are."

"Hair and eye color?"

"Black hair and brown eyes. He looks like he spends a lot of time in the sun."

"Did Ruth call him by name?"

She shook her head. "Please, you have to find her. He had a gun and threatened to shoot me if Ruth didn't go with him."

Ben pulled up a picture of Gorman on his phone. He turned the screen toward Autumn. "Is this the man who took her?"

"Yes! You know him?"

"Did he indicate where he was taking Ruth?"

Another head shake. "I gave her my jade shirt because hers was wet when Gorman burst into the bathroom."

"Ben!"

He glanced down the hall. Joe stood in a doorway near the exit. Dread coiling in his gut, he ran toward his friend.

"Sam has a bomb strapped to her chest."

Ben pushed past the spotter and entered a janitor's closet. Sam's hands were secured behind her back with duct tape. A vest with wires running from three bricks of C-4 into a ticking digital timer had been strapped to her body with a truckload of duct tape. "Get Nico."

"Ben...." Joe's voice cracked, desperation in his eyes.

"Do it. We have to clear the ballroom and I need my gear bag. Clock's ticking, Joe. Make sure Autumn and Tito leave."

With another glance at his wife, the spotter dashed from the room. A minute later, Nico strode inside. "What do we have?"

"Enough C-4 to flatten a city block and ten minutes to disarm this bomb."

"Can you handle it?"

Sam's gaze locked with Ben's. "If you can't, get Joe out of here, even if you have to knock him out to do it."

"Forget it, Sparky," Joe snapped as he rushed back in. "I'm not leaving you."

"We aren't losing anyone," Nico said. "I don't want to train a new medic and spotter. What do you need, Ben? Trace went for your bag."

"We don't have time to evacuate the hotel. Clear the ballroom and hope for the best. Gorman kidnapped Ruth. Have Zane activate her trackers. If we can't rescue her, another team needs to go after Ruth." He moved closer to Sam to study the bomb.

"Take care of this firecracker so we can rescue Ruth," Nico ordered.

Ben's lips curved. "Yes, sir." Ben visually traced the wires leading from the C-4 to the detonator and the timer. "How are you holding up, Sam?"

"Just peachy." She scowled. "I can't wait to get my hands on Gorman."

"How did he take you down?" Sam wouldn't have been easy to subdue.

"Sleeper hold. When I woke up, I was in this closet, trussed up like a Thanksgiving turkey with this vest on."

"You'll be fine." Joe knelt beside his wife. "If anyone can dismantle this thing in time, it's Ben."

"Piece of cake." Ben winked at the medic. "It's the least I can do since you sewed me up today."

Trace carried in Ben's equipment bag. "What else do you need?"

"Help Nico clear the ballroom."

"Don't mess up, Martin."

"If I do, you'll be the first to know."

With a quick salute, Trace left.

"Anything I can do?" Joe asked.

"I'll need an extra pair of hands. Mirror my moves exactly, Joe. If we're not in synch, we'll trigger the device."

"Let's do this. I need to hold my wife in my arms."

Ben understood that. He wanted to hold Ruth, but his woman was in the hands of a thug who worked for Ben's worst nightmare. He shoved that aside behind a mental wall for the moment. Once he freed Sam, Ben and his teammates would go after Davidson and his merry band of thugs.

He dug out the tools he and Joe needed, grateful that he'd been training Joe in the fine art of EOD. Nico's orders for each member of Shadow to double up on skills would pay off in spades today.

After handing Joe a set of tools, he and the spotter went to work. Keeping an eye on the timer, he gave Joe instructions for handling each stage as they mirrored each other's movements.

Wiping sweat from his forehead with his forearm, Ben looked at Joe. "Here's the tricky part. We have to clip six wires in order with no more than two seconds between snips to stop the timer."

"What's the order?"

"Blue, red, green, white, black, red. We still have to mirror. If we're out of synch or get the order wrong, you can't name your firstborn child after me."

A quick grin from Joe. "Wasn't planning to do that anyway." He sobered and glanced at Sam. "I love you, baby."

"I love you, too. Don't screw this up. I have long-term plans with you."

Joe nodded at Ben. "Let's do this."

They each gripped a pair of wire cutters and hovered near the blue wire. "Ready?" When Joe nodded, Ben said, "Just like we've done in practice sessions, buddy. I'll call out the colors and we snip together."

With a silent prayer for all of them, he called the wire colors and matched his cutting motion to Joe's. When they snipped the final red wire, the timer froze at five seconds to detonation.

Ben blew out a breath and braced himself with a hand on the floor. Thank God.

"That was close," Nico said from the doorway. "Good job, both of you. You all right, Sam?"

"Get this thing off me," Sam said.

Joe grabbed a Ka-Bar from Ben's bag and sliced through the tape securing his wife's hands, then started cutting the rest of the tape securing the vest to Sam's body.

"Good thing you're wearing long sleeves. Otherwise, you'd lose a layer of skin."

"Just get it off."

Nico crouched on the other side of Sam while Ben collected his tools and stored them in his equipment bag. Between Nico and Joe, they peeled tape from Sam's arms. Removing the tape from her wrists left several raw places.

Once the vest was removed, Joe gathered Sam into his arms. "Gorman is a dead man," he muttered, his expression fierce.

"Oh, yeah," Ben agreed. The question was whether he or Joe would get their hands on the thug first.

"What do we do with this thing?" Nico motioned toward the vest. "We can't leave it here."

"What did you tell the hotel manager?"

"Gas leak. The fire department should arrive any minute. We need to be gone before someone discovers it's a false alarm."

Ben secured the vest in his bag. "We'll take it with us. I can think of a few good uses for this C-4 at the Eden compound."

"Move out," Nico said. "Gorman has a head start on us and we still have to recon the compound and come up with a plan to free Ruth."

"The odds won't be in our favor," Ben warned.

"When are the odds ever in our favor?" Nico led them to the exit door and called Trace.

The operatives gathered in the underground garage after retrieving their gear and Ruth's belongings from their rooms. Ben rode with Nico while Sam and Joe piled in with Trace. As they left the city, Ben called Zane.

"Yeah, Murphy."

"It's Ben. Tell me you have her."

"The trackers are working. You have about five hours before the batteries run out."

"Where are we headed?"

"Toward Juarez at the moment. From the speed she's moving, I think Ruth is in a helo."

Huh. That was new. Davidson was either scoring potfuls of money from his gullible followers or making bank on the prostitution and human trafficking arm of his business.

"Do we have assets in the area, Z?" Nico asked as he passed a slower moving vehicle.

"Maddox diverted Durango. They'll be on the ground in another hour."

"Find them an airstrip as close as you can get to Juarez." Ben's hands clenched. "We can't leave Ruth in Davidson's hands for long. He won't be able to resist taking her for his newest wife. I can't let that happen to her."

Silence greeted his statement, then, "I hope you're kidding," the tech wizard said, voice flat.

"It's his standard operating procedure."

Zane growled. "I'll see what I can find. I'll let you know as soon as Durango lands. I've also sent you a link to follow Ruth's trackers."

"Thanks, Z. Ruth and I owe you."

"Bringing her back home safe and sound is thanks enough."

"Zane, have Maddox contact Rafe Torres. Tell him we need fed involvement yesterday," Nico said. "Once we clear out the vipers in Eden, a lot of innocent American civilians will need help."

"Copy that. Later." Zane ended the call.

"Hurry, Nico."

His team leader depressed the gas pedal to the floorboard and the SUV shot ahead.

"*I'm coming, sunshine.*" Ben stared at the blinking cursor indicating Ruth's position. "*Hold on for me.*"

CHAPTER THIRTY-TWO

Ruth flexed her wrists, hoping for more play in her bonds. Unfortunately, the thugs who kidnapped her from Casa del Mar were experts in restraining prisoners. At least Gorman and his buddy had zip tied her hands in front of her.

She peered into the night, straining for a glimpse of a road sign to indicate where Gorman was taking her, but the SUV moved too fast and the roadway had few lights.

Her gaze settled on her bracelet. She prayed the trackers worked. Otherwise, even if she freed herself, Ruth had no way to contact Ben. Gorman confiscated her phone and turned it off so Zane couldn't trace her location. After taking her from the hotel, he and his buddy drove to a private airstrip and shoved Ruth into a helicopter. Her pleas to the pilot for help met with deaf ears and a punch to the gut from Gorman in retaliation.

Both thugs were armed and willing to use force to control her. She already had bruises to show for her last attempt to free herself before being forced into the car. "Where are you taking me?"

Buckner, the thug beside her, smiled. "Paradise."

Right. If that was the case, these two bozos were snakes in the garden. "You don't want to do this. Kidnapping is a federal offense."

"On the contrary, Roxanne," Gorman said with a quick glance at her in the rearview mirror. "We volunteered for this assignment."

"Who sent you?"

He chuckled. "Don't worry. You'll find out soon enough."

"You're taking me to Jeremiah Davidson?"

"I guess your traitor boyfriend told you about the prophet."

"What do you think?"

That brought a frown to his face. "I think you need an attitude adjustment and if the prophet can't take care of it, I'll be glad to offer my services."

"The man I'm dating is a firm believer of retribution."

Gorman scoffed. "You think that threat scares me?"

"He'll be your worst nightmare."

Buckner growled, balled his fist, and drew back as though to strike her again.

"No," Gorman snapped. "The prophet doesn't want anyone but him to touch her."

"He's not here, is he? Besides, the prophet wouldn't let her disrespect us like that."

"You're both going to be in hot water." Ruth gave a soft laugh. "I bruise easy."

"We'll tell the prophet you didn't cooperate." Buckner sounded nervous.

"Too bad for you," Ruth taunted him.

"Shut up, lady, or we'll tie a gag on you," Gorman growled.

Afraid to push her luck too much, Ruth fell silent, exhilarated by her small success. Anything she could do to cause dissension in the ranks had to be a good thing.

A short while later, Gorman drove up to a closed gate in a concrete block wall. Another thug wearing a handgun approached. He stared at Ruth. "That her?" he asked Gorman.

"Yeah. Open up. The prophet's expecting us."

When the gate swung open, Gorman drove through. The gates clanged shut behind them.

Fighting her fear, Ruth remained silent as the car slowed to a stop.

Buckner threw open the back door and dragged her across the seat and out of the vehicle. "Causing trouble will make things harder on you. Do yourself a favor and watch your mouth. The prophet don't tolerate backtalk from anyone, especially women."

She looked back at the closed gate. Too far to run from these two men and too high to scale.

Gorman grabbed her upper arm on the opposite side and the two men led her toward a large building. "Forget it, Roxanne," Gorman murmured. "You won't escape."

The thugs escorted her into the building and led her across a wide-open space to a darkened hallway.

At the end of the hall, light spilled under a door. Gorman knocked on the wooden surface.

A moment later, the door opened. A tall, well-built blond man stared down at her, then glanced over his shoulder. "It's the woman, sir."

"Bring her to me."

Blondie stepped back, and Gorman and his buddy forced Ruth into the interior of a plush office.

A barrel-chested man with graying hair came around a massive desk, his gaze traveling over her body in slow motion. When his attention returned to her face, his expression had undergone a subtle change. Curiosity had morphed into satisfaction and attraction.

Although sickened by his attention, Ruth refused to look away.

"Welcome to Eden, Roxanne," he said, voice smooth as honey. "I'm the prophet and that is how you will address me. Failure to obey me in everything will result in swift punishment." Davidson lifted his hand and ran the tip of his forefinger down her cheek. He smiled. "I understand why men wish to possess you. You are exquisite, my dear. A treasure beyond price."

Davidson trailed his finger down the side of her neck, over her shoulder and down her arm until he lifted her bound hands to his mouth and kissed her knuckles. "Your skin is like silk. I wonder, beautiful Roxanne, how much Barrett loves you. Will he be willing to die for you?"

Cold chills raced up Ruth's spine. Ben had warned her that the prophet wanted him dead, but she'd hoped he was wrong. If saving her meant giving up his life, Ben would sacrifice himself in a heartbeat. Ruth loved him too much to let that happen.

The prophet smiled, a hideous yet beautiful smile of possession and want. "Soon, my sweet, you will take your place as my wife. We will wait for Barrett's arrival. He won't be able to resist trying to free you. He'll fail, of course. Once he is my prisoner, I'll take my time exacting retribution for the murder of my son. Your man will beg for mercy long before I free him from this life. He will die knowing you belong to me. When I tire of you, I'll give you to my inner circle."

Davidson signaled the two thugs who had kidnapped her. "Take her to the Den and restrain her while we wait for her lover." He paused, then a slow smile curved his mouth. "Send Maren to attend to her needs."

Gorman and Buckner glanced at each other before murmuring, "Yes, Prophet," and leading her from the office. The two men marched her across the compound to another building. Gorman opened the front door and dragged Ruth inside. Buckner turned on the overhead light.

Ruth stared at the chains with manacles hanging from the ceiling with more sets attached to each wall. Whips, knives, and poles were strewn about the large room. In the center stood a stained table with restraints at the four corners. A bloodstained column with more restraints stood at the far side of the room. The concrete floor had drains at strategic places.

This must be the place Davidson sent his disobedient followers for punishment. Ruth clenched her jaw. The prophet intended for her to wait in this place as bait for Ben, a place he planned for her Navy SEAL to die.

"What do we do with her?" Buckner muttered. "The prophet won't like it if we chain her."

Ruth glared at the men. "You're both dead if you hurt me."

Gorman rolled his eyes. "I'm more afraid of the prophet's punishment than your boyfriend's retribution."

She scanned the room again and understood why the big man hesitated to anger his boss.

"Set the chair on the other side of the table," Gorman told his partner. "We'll secure her to that while we wait for Barrett to show."

After Buckner positioned the chair, Gorman pushed her onto the seat and tied her ankles to the chair legs with zip ties. He grabbed a knife and sliced the plastic tie around her wrists, then secured her wrists to the arms of the chair. He glanced at Buckner. "Bring Maren."

Minutes passed before the outer door reopened and Buckner returned with his hand clamped around a woman's upper arm. The woman looked tiny compared to the muscular man, her hair long and graying. Her head bowed, she shuffled along in sandals and a shapeless dress.

Ruth's heart went out to the woman who looked beaten down by life. Had she been one of Davidson's wives or was she one of the commune women?

"You are to attend to Roxanne," Gorman ordered Maren.

She nodded, eyes still downcast.

"I'll be outside on watch. Buckner will remain." He turned toward Ruth. "If you try to escape, you and Maren will be punished."

The older woman's breath caught.

"You're a monster," Ruth said.

Gorman sneered. "You don't know the meaning of the word, but you will." He stalked from the room.

Buckner folded his arms across his chest and leaned against the wall by the door, his attention locked on Ruth and Maren.

Fantastic. Nothing like being under scrutiny for as long as it took Shadow to find her and mount a rescue. Ignoring the cretin by the door, Ruth shifted her attention to the older woman hovering nearby, hands clasped together in a tight grip. Fear? Maren had reason to be afraid. "My name is Ruth."

The woman froze for a moment, then lifted her head to stare at Ruth. "Why do they call you Roxanne?"

Ruth looked into familiar eyes. Ben's eyes. Davidson was truly evil. "Roxanne is the name I use for my work. I'm a model."

"You shouldn't have come to this place," Maren whispered. "You're not safe."

"Davidson had me kidnapped."

A subtle flinch. "Why?"

"He's using me as bait to draw the man I love into a trap, a man you know very well, Mrs. Barrett."

Maren's eyes widened. She glanced over her shoulder at the thug glowering at the two of them and moved close enough that they wouldn't be overheard. "How did you know my name? Who is the man?"

"Your son, Cameron. He goes by the name Ben now."

The woman's face drained of all color. "No. He mustn't come. The prophet will kill him."

"Ben is a hard man to kill. I have only one question for you."

A frown. "What?"

"Will you help him or betray him again?"

CHAPTER THIRTY-THREE

"Do you have a death wish?" Josh Cahill, Durango's leader, scowled at Ben. "Your plan is lousy, Martin."

He didn't like the operation himself but what choice did he have? Ruth had been in Davidson's hands too long. If she was involved with someone different, the crazy cult leader wouldn't have waited to make her his. Because she was Ben's, the old man would want to taunt him to twist the knife deeper.

Nausea churned in his gut. What if he was wrong? "You have a better idea?"

"I thought being a SEAL taught you patience."

He shifted closer to the Delta Force soldier. "Davidson has had Ruth for four hours. If your wife was in his hands of a known rapist, would you wait to hammer out a perfect plan?"

"Of course not, but I hope I'd be smart enough to have a good plan and listen to good counsel. This is a suicide mission for you."

"After surviving what Hugo Torino did to Ruth, I can't let Davidson destroy what she's reclaimed."

Josh dragged a hand down his face. "All right. Before we take on the whole camp, let's swing the odds in our favor. Are all the men in Eden armed and trained? If they are, we'll need more help."

"From what I've been able to learn, Davidson kept to his standard operating procedure. Thirty to forty armed men carry out his orders and protect the encampment. No one else will be armed. The civilian men don't know until they're inside Eden that the only way out is death. No one is allowed to leave."

"You did," Nico said, voice soft.

"As far as I know, I'm the only one." What did that mean for his mother and sister?

Josh's second in command, Alex Morgan, shook his head. "How can people be that gullible?"

Nate, their EOD man, grimaced. "It's why we have job security."

"Let's go over the plan again," Nico said. "If no one offers suggestions to make the mission safer, we go with what we have."

Thirty minutes later, Quinn, Durango's spotter, said, "Are you sure this is the only way, Ben?"

"Offering anything else in a bargain won't work. The prophet wants me because I killed his son."

"The guard rotation changes in an hour," Trace said. "We need to be in place with the explosives assembled and ready."

Nate's mouth curved at the mention of explosives. "Sounds like fun. You brought C-4 to the party, Ben?"

Joe scowled. "Davidson's lackey strapped a bomb on Sam at the hotel. We brought the C-4 with us."

"Need help assembling surprises for them?"

Ben gave Nate half of the C-4. "Assemble bombs for the front and back gates and the power grid plus the backup generator. I'll take care of the bombs for the vehicles and armory."

He looked at both teams. "Don't forget. There are innocent families here, including kids."

"We're not the ones you should worry about," Rio, Durango's medic, reminded him. "The armed guards inside the compound are the danger to the families."

"That's why we take down the armed guards as soon as possible," Josh said. "Alex, you and Trace find high ground and set up. Nate, you won't have time to place all the bombs by yourself. Need a hand?"

"Joe is cross-training as EOD," Nico said. "He'll place bombs on the vehicles, backup generator, and front gate."

Nate's eyebrows rose. "I'll take the back gate, power grid, and armory."

Ben and Nate worked side-by-side while their teammates checked equipment and watched the compound for signs the Fortress operatives had been detected. By the time he and Nate finished, it was time to begin the first phase of the operation.

After giving Joe bombs and last-minute instructions, Ben turned to Nico. "I'm ready."

"Check your comm gear. We need to know what's happening so we can ride to the rescue if you need us."

Their aid wouldn't matter if Davidson decided to shoot him in the head instead of torturing him with Ruth as witness. Ben tapped his ear and tested his reception and transmission. Perfect working order. "I'm set."

"Don't make me listen to you die," Trace murmured over the comm system.

"Copy that," he replied although his odds of seeing another sunrise were slim. "If I go down, get Ruth out."

"Better not come to that, Martin."

Ben smiled at his friend's bad-tempered response.

Nico handed him the keys to the SUV. "I transferred the bags in the cargo area to the second SUV. Wait until I give you the signal before you make your move. I want your word, Ben. No going rogue and working off the timetable."

His jaw clenched. Everything in him demanded he storm the gates of Eden and free the woman he loved. What Nico asked would be nearly impossible. However, more than his and Ruth's lives were at risk. His teammates and Durango were also at risk.

"Yes, sir."

Nico squeezed his shoulder, signaled Josh, and the two team leaders melted into the shadows.

While Ben waited for Nico's order to proceed, he returned to the SUV. Fifteen long minutes later, Nico said over the comm system, "In place. Ben, go. We've got your back."

"Copy that." He was counting on his teammates. Drawing in a deep breath, he cranked the engine and drove on the rutted road toward the compound's front gate.

When the headlights illuminated the gate, a man with a muscular build planted himself in the center of the road, hand resting on his sidearm. "Gate guard has training," Ben murmured. "He's former military or law enforcement."

"Spec ops?" Nico asked.

"Negative."

"Copy. Cameras?"

"Guard house, corners of the compound wall. Can't see the back corners from here. Trace?"

"Cameras on the corners at the back of the compound. Big blind spots in coverage."

"Two cameras mounted in the trees at the front," Alex murmured. "Ten and two."

Silence, then Trace said, "Copy. Same in the back. I missed them."

"Focus, Trace." The short reprimand came from Nico.

"Yes, sir."

"No extra surveillance on the east side," Quinn said.

"Same on the west," Josh added.

"Copy that," Nico said. "Ben, give us as much intel as possible without alerting Davidson or his cronies."

Ben slowed as he approached the gate. "Anybody have a fix on Ruth?"

"Possible location," Rio murmured. "East side, large building lit up light a Christmas tree lot. Thermal imaging shows someone seated in a chair near the back wall. Two other figures inside. One smaller figure standing close to the seated one. The second appears to be a guard near the door."

"Copy," he whispered and stopped less than a foot from the glowering guard. Ben kept his hands in view as the guard moved toward the driver's window.

"This is private property. Turn around and go back."

"Davidson is expecting me. Tell him I'm here."

The man sneered. "He's selective about granting an audience, especially when he's...busy."

"Don't let him provoke you," Josh murmured. "Trust your gut, not your heart."

His gut said the guard knew who Ben was but enjoyed throwing his weight around. His heart wanted to tear apart this man and the rest of the human traffickers in Eden with his bare hands. "Call him. Now."

The guard frowned, but pulled out his cell phone. He spoke briefly into the instrument, listened a moment, eyes narrowing at what he heard. The guard's jaw clenched as he slid the phone into his pocket. "You'll be met inside the gates and searched before you're allowed to see the prophet. If you resist, the guards will shoot you." The man retreated to the guard house and a moment later, the gates opened.

He drove inside the walls and the gates shut behind him. Ben scanned the compound and pinpointed cameras on various buildings. He informed his teammates of the camera locations as well as the positions of guards. Once Fortress disabled the power grid, the cameras would go down.

As he exited the SUV, he glanced at the building where Ruth was likely being held. Soon, she'd be free, and he and Ruth would plan their life together. Ben looked forward to their Zoo date and a host of others as he courted the woman he longed to marry.

Two large, well-armed men walked toward Ben. One pointed a weapon at Ben's chest. "Hands away from your sides, legs spread. If you move, I'll kill you."

"Get on with it. I have business with Davidson." He widened his stance and held his hands away from his body. "How long have you been part of Eden?"

"Long enough to not give you information." He grinned. "The prophet has several things to say to you."

The second thug searched Ben for weapons. He remained motionless, waiting to see if the thug detected the weapon secured in one of his tactical boots.

Not detecting anything suspicious, the guard glanced at his buddy. "He's clean."

"Take me to Davidson. Now."

A smirk from the dude holding the weapon on him. "You shouldn't be so eager to see the prophet. He has painful plans for you."

"Tell me something I don't know."

The second guard shoved him toward the large building to his right. "Move."

Keeping his hands visible, Ben followed the hooligans' directions to a dimly lit hallway with light streaming from one room. Knowing Davidson, he was in his office. Conducting business in that room always gave Eden's leader a sense of power and control. No matter where Eden relocated, the prophet's office was always the same. Plush, decadent, and private.

One of the guards knocked on the door. A moment later, a man opened the door and stared at Ben with hatred in his eyes as he addressed the two flunkies. "You searched him for weapons?"

"Yes, sir. He's clean."

The interior guard, a blond Adonis, shifted out of the doorway and motioned for Ben to enter. As he passed, Adonis warned, "If you make a move on the prophet, I'll kill you and gladly take the prophet's punishment."

Ben ignored him as his gaze locked on Davidson. The prophet looked much as he had twenty years ago except he now sported a fine head of silver hair and a neatly trimmed beard. If you didn't look into his eyes, you might think he was someone's grandfather instead of a rapist and human trafficker.

Davidson rose from his chair. "Twenty years I've hunted for you to make you pay for killing my beloved son," he said, voice low and rough. "Now, you're finally in my possession and retribution is at hand, Cameron Barrett. Don't waste your breath begging for mercy because you won't receive any."

Ben remained silent, knowing the old man would fill the silence with his own rhetoric. Every minute that he spoke gave his teammates and Durango time to prepare for the next phase of the mission. The prophet waxed eloquent about the methods he planned to use to punish Ben before allowing him to die.

When Davidson wound down, he placed his hands palms down on the desk and leaned toward Ben. "Have you nothing to say for yourself, Barrett? Are you such a coward that you tremble in fear before me?"

"Where is she?" The prophet already knew Ben was involved with Ruth. If he didn't care about her, he wouldn't have shown up and allowed himself to be captured to save her.

Satisfaction gleamed in the prophet's eyes. "Where all sinners go to be punished."

Rage tightened his gut. Had he miscalculated? If Davidson had hurt Ruth, Ben would kill him.

"Ice in your veins," Nico whispered. "Don't let him destroy your focus."

Voice even, Ben said, "You took her to the Den?"

"She's beautiful. Silky skin and honey-sweet kisses. Once she's properly trained, she'll be a worthy wife." Davidson straightened away from the desk. "You took my son. I will take your woman. Once I tire of her, I'll give her to the inner circle."

"Ben, hold." This order came from Josh.

He held tight to his temper through sheer grit and military discipline.

"If your friends come, we'll kill them."

"You don't have to worry about the worthless cowards. They refused to help because the odds weren't in our favor."

"Another example of your poor character and judgment. You chose disloyal friends." A frown. "How did you know where we brought Roxanne?"

He smiled. "I followed the money flowing from perverts like you who profit from the pain and suffering of women and children."

Adonis slugged Ben in the gut. He rocked back a step. Whew! Adonis packed a punch. Good thing Ben had been prepared for the blow.

The prophet flicked a glance at the guard. "Take him to the Den. Use the center manacles and chains to restrain him. I will begin his punishment soon. Make sure Roxanne has a clear view of Barrett. Chain her to the wall in front of him. She needs to learn what happens if she disobeys me."

"Yes, Prophet."

"If Barrett resists or tries to escape, Roxanne and her attendant will be punished."

"Yes, sir."

Ben's hands fisted but he didn't fight back when the guard slugged him again and shoved him toward the brutes who had escorted Ben to the office. Thug One and Thug

Two took up position on either side of him and clamped a hand on his upper arms. The trio led him outside and toward the building with light glowing in the windows.

"I guess the prophet doesn't worry about the light bill. The Den is lit up like a beacon."

"Copy that," Nico whispered.

"Shut up," snapped Adonis. "You should pray for mercy instead of smarting off."

Mercy wasn't in the cards for him or from him on this night.

"As soon as you confirm the package is there, we move," Nico murmured.

"How long before the prophet arrives?" Ben asked Thug One.

"Are you that anxious to die, Barrett?"

"Nope. Just want to know when to prepare myself and Roxanne for his arrival."

Thug Two smirked. "The prophet will treat your woman as she deserves. He's very skilled."

As they moved closer to the Den, Ben caught the restless movement of a guard standing watch. Gorman. "I've been looking for you, Gorman," he said, voice soft. "You took something of mine. I want it back."

The Texan chuckled. "And instead, we caught you."

"I surrendered. Big difference. Where is she?"

"Inside, waiting for a real man to arrive. Too bad she has bad taste in men."

"Get inside." Adonis shoved Ben toward the door. "We must prepare for the prophet's arrival."

Suited Ben fine. He was anxious to see Ruth.

Gorman turned the knob and threw open the door. A large man moved into view. Seeing Ben with the terrible trio, the other guard motioned for them to come into the building.

Ben walked inside and scanned the room. Typical Den equipment, equipment he'd been introduced to many years earlier. Unfortunately for him and the rest of the boys Silas had bought, the prophet's son also had his own personal tools to train those who belonged to him.

What wasn't standard in this den of pain and suffering was the beautiful woman zip tied to a chair at the far end of the room. "Ruth."

She struggled against the ties. "Ben!"

"Move, Barrett." Another shove from Adonis.

Ben walked closer to Ruth when he finally got a clear glimpse of the older woman standing near her. His heart sank and he stopped abruptly. "Mom."

CHAPTER THIRTY-FOUR

"Your mother is in the Den with Ruth?" Nico demanded.

Since Ben couldn't answer his team leader's question directly, he directed his response to his mother. "Mom, I hoped you had escaped from Eden."

"No one escapes." Her gaze locked onto his. "Except you. You shouldn't have returned. The prophet wants to kill you."

"I couldn't leave Ruth in his hands."

Tears glimmered in her eyes. "Now you will both die in this place."

"Is Lydia still here?"

Tears spilled. "She died in childbirth."

Pain speared Ben's heart. His beautiful sister's light had been snuffed out too soon. "I'm sorry to hear that."

"We move on my signal," Nico said.

"No," he whispered. Ben moved toward Ruth but Thug One and Thug Two shoved him to a set of manacles attached to a thick, heavy chain suspended from the ceiling.

Adonis strode to a table filled with knives and selected a Ka-Bar. He palmed the weapon, grabbed Ruth's hair, and yanked her head back, pressing the edge of the knife to her throat. "Remove your shirt, Barrett."

He froze. "Move the knife away from Ruth's throat."

"Locked on target," Trace murmured.

"Hold," Ben whispered. The prophet wasn't here yet. If Trace fired too soon, Ben would lose his chance to capture the human trafficker. He grasped the neckband of his black t-shirt and tugged it over his head. He dropped the shirt to the ground.

"You know the drill, Barrett. Get into position," Adonis ordered. "Gorman, Buckner, string him up, then do the same to the woman."

"She's done nothing wrong," Maren protested. "Surely the prophet wouldn't punish her."

"Shut up, old woman. These are the prophet's orders."

"Mom." When she looked at him, Ben shook his head. "Don't."

Thug One activated the mechanism to lower the chain and manacles. When they were in position, Thug Two shoved Ben forward and secured the metal around his wrists. Seconds later, his arms were stretched over his head. The stitches in his back tugged but he ignored the bite of pain. Chances were good that Sam would have to redo some of her work before the night was over, provided he survived his encounter with the prophet and his eager cronies.

Buckner walked to one of the equipment tables and picked up a whip. He snapped it experimentally. "Should we soften him up for the prophet?"

The muscles in Ben's back spasmed as memories of previous encounters with a whip such as this one crowded into his mind. He could handle what might come, but the violence would traumatize Ruth.

"No!" Ruth struggled against Adonis's hold.

"Stop, Ruth," Ben said, voice sharp. If she continued to struggle, Adonis could cut her carotid artery without meaning to.

"Ben." Distress filled her voice.

"Trust me."

With equal parts fear for him and fury at Adonis in her eyes, she went still, her gaze locked on Ben. Her hands fisted in silent rebellion.

Adonis moved the knife away from her throat. He addressed Buckner. "The prophet wants to punish Barrett himself. He deserves to draw the first and last drops of blood."

Buckner looked disappointed but dropped the whip on the table. "What about the woman?"

"She gets a front-row seat to her lover's punishment and death." Adonis held the tip of the knife against Ruth's throat. "If you try to escape, Barrett and his mother will suffer and so will you. If you want to spare your lover an extra day's worth of excruciating pain, you'll cooperate."

Ruth looked at Ben as she responded to Adonis's threats. "I won't run."

Fear for her safety and pride in her strength filled Ben. He got the message. No matter what happened, she wouldn't leave him even to save her own life. He wanted to kiss her senseless for her loyalty and shake her for her stubbornness. Based on how he felt at the moment, Ben figured kissing her senseless would be the first order of business when he had Ruth back in his arms.

Adonis sliced through the zip ties holding Ruth to the chair. "Stand up."

When she looked at Ben, he gave a slight nod. If the Fortress operatives failed to free Ruth, the blond thug would report any disobedience to the prophet who would take great pleasure in administering corrective measures.

Adonis yanked Ruth to her feet and forced her to the wall restraints in front of Ben. He shoved her back against the wall and secured her wrists above her head. "Gorman, get back outside and keep watch. Even though Barrett claims his friends won't help, I don't trust anything he says. Stay alert."

"Yes, sir." Gorman followed him out the door, leaving Ben, Ruth, and Maren under the watch of Buckner.

The remaining guard glared at Maren. "Sit in that chair and don't move."

"Didn't the prophet say that I was to attend to the woman?"

"She don't need a thing so sit down and shut up before I make you obey."

Ben tore his gaze away from Ruth's for a moment. "Mom," he murmured. "Do as he says."

Maren ceased protesting and sat. Her breath caught when she noticed Ben's back. "What happened to your back, Cameron?"

"Silas and military service. Take your pick."

"But you have stitches."

"Got too close to a knife this morning. I'm fine." For the moment.

Through the comm system, Nico said, "A white-haired man with a beard is making his way toward the Den."

"Copy," he whispered. Ben shifted his attention to Ruth. "Be ready," he murmured. With Buckner listening to every word, he couldn't give her a more pointed warning that his team was preparing to launch their attack.

She held his gaze with her own steady one. "I love you."

Man, what had he ever done to deserve this woman? In the midst of a room of pain and death, she still gave him her trust and sought to encourage him to be strong no matter what was ahead for them both. "You own my heart, sunshine."

"Shut your mouth," Buckner snapped. He pointed a finger at Ruth. "You're going to regret that. I'll be sure to report your disloyalty to the prophet." When Ruth didn't look at him or respond, the guard sucker punched her in the stomach.

She moaned and sagged against the restraints.

"You're a dead man," Ben vowed.

"Big talk from a coward hanging from the ceiling."

The door opened and Davidson walked in. He'd changed into a dark shirt and pants, what the community thought of as his discipline uniform. Any time he walked through the compound wearing those clothes, community members averted their gazes and prayed they weren't the recipient of the prophet's ire.

Satisfaction gleamed in Davidson's eyes at the sight of Ben in chains. He flicked a glance to Maren. "Don't move from that chair until I release you."

"Yes, prophet," she whispered, head bowed.

"Joe, Nate, on my command," Nico murmured through the comm system.

The operatives acknowledged the order.

"Hold," Ben whispered. Neither Buckner nor Davidson was close enough for him to take down.

"Negative," was his team leader's response. "We need you functional for this to work."

Frustrated, Ben willed Buckner to move away from Ruth and toward him. He stared at the remaining guard, hoping Buckner would see the look as a challenge to his authority.

The guard's face reddened. "Prophet, assisting you in disciplining the traitor would be my honor."

Oh, yeah. Ben's mouth curved in a mocking smile, egging him on. That's exactly the response he was looking for.

Davidson eyed Buckner speculatively, then gave a slow nod. "You may not use a whip or knife. That privilege is mine. Other than that, you're free to do as you wish until I'm ready to begin."

As the gloating guard stalked toward him, Ben looked at Ruth's horror-stricken face. "Don't say a word, baby." If she protested or begged Davidson to spare Ben, the prophet would hurt her. At the moment, her silence was the only tool Ben had to protect her.

Buckner smiled broadly as he balled his fist. "I'm going to enjoy this."

"A civilian family is in the line of fire," Alex murmured.

"Copy," Nico whispered. "Hold tight, Ben."

The guard slammed his fist into Ben's gut. One of his stitches popped and blood began to seep from the wound on his back as Buckner continued to pummel Ben. When the thug punched him in the face, Nico began the ten-second countdown.

Davidson cupped Ruth's face and turned it toward him. "This is what happens to those who fall from my favor. Remember this lesson well." His hand trailed down her throat toward the buttons of her blouse. He flicked open the first, then the second and third.

Ben jerked on the chain, rage an acid in his gut. No! He wouldn't let the prophet assault Ruth no matter if Ben screwed with the Fortress plan.

Buckner landed another blow, this one directly on the knife wound. White-hot pain detonated in Ben's side as more of his wound ripped open. Seconds later, a massive explosion rocked the compound.

The prophet jerked around, shock on his face. "What...?"

The lights winked out and the Den fell into total darkness.

Davidson swore viciously. "Stay with the prisoners while I find out what's going on." A door opened.

"Yes, prophet," the guard responded, and the door closed again.

Perfect. Those two words gave Ben the location of his quarry. He grasped the chain with both hands and wrapped his legs around Buckner's neck. A strong twist and jerk, and the guard's body dropped to the floor. He wouldn't be getting up again.

"Stay in the chair, Mom," Ben said as he freed a tool from his watch band. "Sunshine, are you still with me?" He slipped the thin piece of metal into the lock and went to work on the mechanism.

"I'm okay. What's happening?"

"Fortress. Anyone have eyes on Davidson?" he asked his teammates. All the responses were negative. His jaw clenched. His nightmare would never be over if they couldn't locate the prophet.

More explosions rocked the compound. He mentally ticked off the targets. The motor pool, the gates, the ammunition supply. Although civilians weren't allowed to wander the grounds during the night unless the prophet called for them or they had a job, the continuous explosions would draw the innocents out into the open.

The manacle's locking mechanism gave way and Ben was free. "Ruth, I'm coming toward you." Working from memory, he skirted Buckner's body, scooped his shirt from the floor, and tugged it over his head, ignoring the intensified pain.

She gasped. "You're free?"

He chuckled. "You have such faith in my abilities." Knowing she'd be skittish, he murmured, "I'm right here," before grasping the manacle securing her to the chain attached to the wall. A moment later, the lock gave. She fell against him and wrapped her arms around his neck, holding on tight.

"I've got you." Ben took a few seconds to hold her close, pressing a kiss to the side of her neck. He smiled when she shivered in reaction. "I have the package plus one," he informed his teammates.

"Copy," Josh acknowledged. "Hold position. Nate and Rio are headed your way."

"Copy that." With one hand holding Ruth against him, Ben used the other to retrieve the knife he'd secured in his boot. "I need a gun. I'm feeling naked over here."

Nate chuckled. "Got you covered. One minute."

Sporadic gunfire sounded throughout the compound.

"What's happening, Cameron?" Maren's voice shook.

"My friends and I are cleaning out a viper's nest."

Silence, then, "I don't understand. Who are these people?"

"We work for a private security firm that specializes in rescuing hostages and human trafficking victims, and counterterrorism."

"Why are they here?"

"To help me free Ruth and expose Davidson and his cronies as sex traffickers."

His mother gasped.

Nate's voice sounded over the comm. "Ben, coming in soft with Rio."

"Copy." He placed his body in front of Ruth. He trusted the two operatives, but Ben had learned early in his military career never to take safety for granted.

The Den's door swung open and two men entered. The man in the lead flicked on a small pen light. "Alex and Trace will have a corridor clear for our exit shortly," Nate said. "Do you need medical assistance?"

"I can wait."

The second man moved closer. "Let me be the judge of that. Can't have you passing out at your woman's feet and embarrassing all of us."

Ben snorted but slid his knife back into his boot. "Weapon?"

"Here." Nate handed him a Sig with four magazines.

Rio set his bag on the ground. "Where, Ben?"

"Back and ribs. Popped a few stitches and I might have cracked a rib or two. The rest of the injuries will wait until we're on the jet." He turned his back to the medic and hitched up his shirt. "Nate, my mother, Maren Barrett, is sitting across the room in a chair. Mom, my friend Nate is coming to get you. Let him help you. I don't want you to fall."

A rustle of movement was followed by Nate's low, soothing voice as he spoke to Ben's mother.

Rio whistled. "Popped a few stitches, huh? How many did you have?"

"Thirty-nine," Sam said over the comm system.

"Most of them have been ripped out."

"Patch him up," Josh ordered.

"Copy that." The medic dug into his bag. "Ruth, my name is Rio. I'm the team medic for Durango. Would you like to give me a hand?"

"Anything."

"Rio, no," Ben snapped. "She doesn't need to see that."

Her soft hand cupped his jaw. "I'll handle it." She pressed a kiss to the side of his neck. "What can I do to help you, Rio?"

"Hold this pen light so I can do a quick fix on Ben's back."

A moment later, she gasped. "Oh, Ben! Buckner did so much damage."

"I'm okay, baby. I promise. I've handled worse."

Rio worked fast to close the wound. "That's the best I can do for now. Josh, do I have time to check Ben's ribs?"

"Thirty seconds."

"Copy." The medic pressed on the ribs Ben indicated. "Both are cracked. I'll use tape to help with the pain, but you're still going to hurt."

"As long as I'm functional."

Fifteen seconds later, Rio tugged down Ben's shirt. "Don't get involved in a wrestling match. This is a quick and dirty patch job."

"I'll do my best." Whether or not he could comply depended on the guards.

Nate escorted Maren to Ben's side. "Josh, Nico, the packages are ready to roll."

"Copy that," Nico acknowledged. "Ten seconds."

"Mom, I'm getting Ruth out of here and I want to take you with us. Will you come with me?"

"I haven't worked in over 20 years, Cameron. I won't be able to find a job and I have no money. How will I live?"

"Leave that to me but you have to make a decision because we're leaving right now. Are you coming with me?"

"I want to go but I don't have a passport or ID."

Thank God. He'd been afraid the prophet's brainwashing would make her refuse to leave the Eden community. "I'll take care of it. Nate?"

"I've got her. Worry about yourself and your lady."

"Thanks. Here's how this is going to work, Mom. When we leave the Den, you listen to everything Nate tells you. If he says to drop, you hit the dirt without hesitation. He'll protect you and get you out of here. The Eden guards will try to stop us from leaving. No one will prevent me from freeing you and Ruth. Do you understand what I'm telling you?"

"I understand. I'm ready."

"Nico, we're ready."

"Trace, Alex?"

"Go," Alex murmured.

Nate said, "Rio, take point."

With his mike bag on his back and a Sig in his hand, Rio moved to the door and eased it open to peer outside. "Clear," he murmured, and slipped outside.

Clasping Ruth's hand with his left, Ben tugged her outside into the compound with Nate and his mother on their heels.

CHAPTER THIRTY-FIVE

Ruth did her best to keep up with Ben as they hurried through the compound. Multiple fires burned in various parts of the commune. People ran from one place to another. Screams and shouts filled the night. Pandemonium reigned.

Ben grabbed Ruth and dropped to the ground with her. To her left, Maren was on the ground with Nate covering her body with his own. Rio opened fire. A man with a gun bearing down on them toppled to the earth and didn't move.

A moment later, she and Maren were on the move again. Ben, Nate, and Rio set a fast pace toward the back of the compound.

"Down!" Ben ordered at the same time as Nate shoved Maren to the turf and dived on top of her, weapon up and aimed to their right.

From the darkness, four guards emerged with guns in their hands. They aimed and fired at Ben and Rio. The operatives' aim was true. Their bullets hit two of the guards while the other two kept firing.

Dirt kicked up near Ruth as the bullets from the guards missed their marks.

Close by, a child screamed in terror.

Ruth raised her head enough to scan the area for the child. Her eyes widened in horror when she spotted a little girl running straight toward her.

"On your six," Nate yelled and shifted the aim of his weapon to the approaching danger.

Oh, man. At least ten Eden guards ran full tilt toward the operatives, Ruth, and Maren. The girl was running into the line of fire.

Ruth scrambled to her feet and, keeping low, ran to scoop the child into her arms. She heard Ben yelling her name, but she couldn't let the girl die. Ruth ran toward a low stone wall, climbed over, and sank to her knees. She laid the child on the ground close to the wall and curled her own body around her.

"You're safe now. My friends will help but we have to stay quiet."

"I want my mommy."

"I know, sweetheart. We'll find her when the noise stops. It's not safe to look for her right now."

"When?"

"Not long." Ben and the others wouldn't let this fight drag out long. The fires would draw attention to the compound. Someone was bound to report the glow to the authorities. Fortress couldn't be here when law enforcement arrived. "What's your name?"

"Serenity."

"Your name is as beautiful as you are. I'm Ruth. How old are you?"

"Six."

"What's your favorite thing to do?"

"I like books."

"Me, too." She heard rustling behind her and prayed one of the Fortress operatives had arrived to protect her and the child. No doubt Ben knew where she was. Even in the middle of a gun battle, he'd keep track of her.

Ruth wrapped herself tighter around the child. "Stay quiet," she whispered and strained to listen. With the screams, shouts, and gunfire, she couldn't detect more movement behind her. The skin at the back of her neck felt as though spiders crawled on her. Not good. Ben told her to trust her gut. Her gut screamed that trouble was stalking her.

She turned her head to scout for a new hiding place. Every place that looked viable also left her and Serenity exposed to gunfire before they reached safety.

Frustrated, she loosened her hold on Serenity and got to her hands and knees. She had to find a safe place for Serenity. "Stay here," she whispered.

"Don't leave me!"

"I'm not, sweetheart. I'm looking for a safer hiding place."

Serenity raised her head. When she looked behind Ruth, her eyes widened in terror.

Ruth started to turn when a hard hand grabbed her hair and dragged her to her feet.

"If you scream, I'll shoot you and then the girl."

Davidson. Once Ruth was upright, the prophet shoved a gun against her side. "Serenity, don't move. I'll deal with you later. Come along with me, Roxanne. I have some old business to finish."

He wrapped his arm around her waist and dragged her against his body to use her for cover, and moved them toward the fighting.

Afraid he'd hurt Serenity, Ruth went without resistance although she slowed their progress as much as possible.

The prophet retaliated by digging the barrel of the gun deeper into her side. "You don't want to make me more angry. You'll be severely punished for this rebellion. By the time I'm finished, you'll know who your master is."

He dragged her out into the open about twenty feet from Ben. "Barrett! Come to me or Roxanne pays the price."

Ben took in the situation at a glance. He moved closer to Ruth and Davidson, weapon up and aimed at the prophet. "Let her go, Davidson. This is between you and me."

The prophet laughed. "I hold the prize. You should have taken your punishment like a man. Now, I'll kill you and Roxanne will suffer every hour of agony meant for you. She won't die, but she'll wish she had died in your place before my anger subsides."

Davidson was crazy. Didn't he realize Ben had more friends throughout the compound and his guards were losing the fight?

"You want me dead? Fine. Come get me." Ben spread his arms wide. "I'm right here. Unless you're too weak to take me on without me being trussed up like a turkey. Let Ruth go and we'll settle this right here."

"You must think I'm a fool. The moment I let her go, you or one of your friends will shoot me. No, that's not how this is going to work."

Ben lowered his arms although he retained possession of his weapon. "What's the plan?"

Davidson shifted the gun from Ruth's side to aim at Ben.

Heart rate accelerating, Ruth kept her gaze on Ben. At this distance, the prophet wouldn't miss. Unlike his teammates, Ben wasn't wearing a bullet-resistant vest. Although Ben was an excellent shot, he couldn't fire because her body provided cover for Davidson.

"I shoot you and your terrorist friends leave Eden or you can save yourself, but Roxanne and your disloyal mother will die. You choose. Your life or theirs."

"No contest. I offer my life freely for the women."

Pain lanced Ruth's heart. She couldn't let him die. He was everything to her.

"Sunshine, do you remember our training last month?"

Her breath caught. The last time she'd been in Nashville, Ben had invited her to his home to train in his gym for a couple of hours. That's all the time she had to spare. They'd worked on one skill. "Yes."

"You may not address her," Davidson snapped. "You speak only to me."

"Do you trust me, baby?"

"With every breath I take."

"Now!"

Ruth slammed the back of her head into Davidson's nose. He cried out and let go of her to clutch at his face. She rammed her elbow into his gut, then punched her fist into his groin. When air exploded from his lungs and he bent reflexively, Ruth kneed him in the face and shoved him away from her. She spun and raced toward Ben.

"Down!"

Ruth hit the ground as a gunshot echoed in the night. A heavy weight fell on top of her. A heartbeat later, the weight was gone.

"I've got him," Rio said. "You check on Ruth."

Familiar hands turned Ruth and gathered her close. "Are you okay, sunshine?"

She wrapped her arms around Ben's neck. "I am now that I'm back in your arms. Is he dead?"

Ben turned his head. "Rio?"

"He's still alive for the moment. If you've got something to say to him, better do it fast."

"Barrett." The prophet groaned.

Ben stood, bringing Ruth with him. He started to turn them away from the fallen man.

"Wait."

He hesitated. "Save your breath to ask forgiveness from your Maker, Davidson."

"Is this what you wanted? Revenge?"

"I didn't want revenge."

"What, then?"

"Redemption for a boy unable to save his mother from a monster." He gathered Ruth close to his side and they strode away from the fallen man.

A moment later, Rio joined them. "He's gone."

Nico jogged toward the operatives as Nate stood and helped Maren to her feet. "The guards are down. It's time for us to go. Zane's been monitoring emergency services communications in the area. The compound will be overrun with law enforcement and firefighters in ten minutes."

Another Fortress operative Ruth hadn't met walked up with Serenity in his arms, her face buried against his neck. "I need to hand this little one to her mother before we leave."

A dark-haired woman ran toward the pair, calling the girl's name. When the man handed over Serenity, the mother broke into tears, thanking him for saving her daughter.

The man held up his hand. "It wasn't me. Ruth saved her. I'm just the delivery man."

Serenity's mother turned to her. "Thank you. We were separated in the chaos. I'll never be able to repay you for saving my daughter."

"I'm just glad she's safe."

"Time to go," Nico insisted. "Jet's waiting."

Ben looked down at Ruth. "Let's go home." He glanced at his mother. "Are you ready?"

She nodded. "Is the prophet...?"

"He's dead."

Another nod, then she looked at Nate. "Your wife is a lucky woman. Will I be able to meet her sometime?"

He chuckled as he turned her toward the back gate. "I'll tell her you said that. We'll look you up when we're in town the next time." Nate escorted her from the compound.

"What about our bags?" Ruth asked Ben. She didn't have anything of value except clothes that could be easily replaced. Ben, however, had his work gear with him. Leaving that behind would prompt too many questions she was sure he and Fortress didn't want to answer.

"They're in the SUV."

"Gorman took my phone."

"I'll get it," Nico said, and ran toward the Den. He returned within a minute and handed Ruth her phone.

As they left the compound and walked the quarter of a mile to the vehicles, they were joined by what looked like another full team of operatives as well as the rest of Shadow.

Sam caught up with Ben. "How much damage did Buckner do?"

"Enough that I'll be off work rotation until Ruth is finished with her contracts." He grinned. "Relax, Sam. Rio's patch job held. You can work on me once we're wheels up."

When they reached the vehicles, Nate tucked Maren into an SUV with him and a couple of his teammates after glancing at Ben for permission. As Ruth slid into the backseat of another SUV hidden in the woods surrounding the compound, emergency vehicles raced past their location with sirens blaring and lights flashing. Nico and the other drivers cranked the engines and drove in the opposite direction of the compound.

"Are you sure you're not hurt?" Ben asked Ruth, voice low as he held her tight against his side. "Buckner hit you pretty hard."

"My stomach is tender, but it's nothing compared to what he did to you." She turned her head to look at him. "Why did you tell me not to say anything when Buckner beat you?"

Ben brushed her lips with his own. "If I didn't make it and Fortress failed to free you, Davidson would have hurt you for rebelling against him. Asking you to keep silent was the only way I could protect you if something went wrong."

Tears stung her eyes. "But you could have freed yourself."

"I would never leave you in that place to save myself."

"I love you, Ben."

Another kiss from her wounded warrior. "You are my life, Ruth Monihan. Without you, my life has no purpose."

A loud sigh came from the front of the SUV. "Do you mind?" Nico groused. "You make me miss Mercy more than I already do. Have a heart and knock off the sappy romance until you're alone."

With a grin, Ruth lapsed into silence and rested her head against Ben's shoulder, about the only place she figured Buckner hadn't hurt.

Ben laughed at his teammate. "Suck it up, Rivera."

Nico growled although his eyes twinkled with amusement when he glanced into the rearview mirror. "Call Maddox. He's waiting for an update."

"Yes, sir." Ben grunted as he slid his phone from his pocket. He hit speed dial and put the phone on speaker.

"Maddox."

"It's Ben. You're on speaker with Nico and Ruth. We're away from Eden and headed for the jet."

"Davidson?"

"Dead. We rescued my mother as well, sir. She agreed to come home with me."

"Excellent. Injuries?"

Nico answered before Ben could speak. "Bullet kissed Quinn's side. Ruth has bruises from rough treatment. Ben got the worst of it. One of Davidson's guards worked him over before we got to him."

"Ben, how bad?"

"Enough to keep me sidelined for a while," he admitted. "Cracked ribs, bruised kidneys, and popped most of the stitches Sam used to close a knife wound."

"I want an updated report from one of the medics when you're on the jet."

"Yes, sir."

"Ruth?"

"I'm here."

"How are you?"

"I'm fine. What I experienced is nothing a few days of rest won't cure. I'm more concerned about Ben."

"He's tough and so are you. You'll both heal. Ben, you're off rotation until you have a clean bill of health from one of our docs. The jet pilot has instructions to fly you into Bayside, Texas to be checked out by Sorenson."

Ben groaned. "Aww, sir. You wouldn't do that to me, would you? He's a sadist."

That brought a laugh from Maddox. "Oh, you bet I would. That's the price you pay for being injured on a mission. Enjoy your time in Sorenson's tender care. Nico, make sure I get that update on Ben and Quinn."

"Yes, sir."

Maddox ended the call.

"Who's Sorenson?" Ruth asked.

"A man who loves pain," Ben groused.

Nico laughed. "Don't let him fool you, Ruth. Ted Sorenson is one of the best trauma surgeons in the country and he works for Fortress as one of our on-staff doctors."

"He's also a vet." Ben's lips curved at the corners. "As in he treats animals, too. That's the only thing I enjoy about my visits with him."

"That's because you don't see him unless you're banged up," his team leader pointed out.

"Yeah, yeah. Rub it in. Just wait until you're the reason we have to stop in to see Sorenson. I won't let you forget this."

It took Ruth a while to figure out that Nico ragged on Ben to keep his mind off the pain. The Mexican government didn't waste money on road repairs and the potholes had to feel like craters at the speed they were traveling. Nico and the other SUVs moved at a fast clip down the rutted road.

Sooner than she anticipated, Nico turned off the main road onto a side road that was in even worse shape. Watching Ben, Ruth asked Nico, "How much longer? Ben's in a lot of pain."

"Two minutes. Hold on, Ben."

"I'm fine."

He wasn't. Sweat beaded on his face and every rut made Ben flinch. His hand was clenched so tight, his knuckles showed white against his sun-darkened skin.

Finally, Nico skidded around a corner and raced to the Fortress jet. "Go, Ben. Get Ruth inside. I'll take care of the bags." He slid from the SUV and hurried to the cargo area as Ben opened the back door and tugged Ruth out.

"Straight to the back of the jet. Sam will want to start working on me as soon as she's inside."

They sped up the stairs as the other SUVs screeched to a stop. Operatives spilled out and retrieved bags. Just before Ruth walked inside the cabin, she glanced over her shoulder to see Nate rushing Maren toward the stairs. Good. Now Ben wouldn't worry about his mother.

Ben led Ruth to the back of the jet and into a bedroom. He stopped just over the threshold, wrapped his arms around her, and pulled her against his chest. His mouth captured hers for one hot, deep kiss after another.

"Get a room," Rio teased as he walked inside with his medical bag. Sam followed with her own bag.

"I did," Ben said. "You walked in uninvited."

"We need to get your shirt off." Sam slid her bag from her shoulder and came up behind Ben.

"You don't have to stay for this, sunshine." He lifted her hand to his mouth and kissed her palm. "You're been through enough already."

"You need someone to hold your hand when Sam and Rio come at you with needles."

He flashed her a grin despite the pallor of his face.

Together, Sam and Rio worked Ben's shirt loose from the wound on his back. Sam scowled when she saw the extent of the damage in the lighted cabin.

At that moment, the jets powered up.

"Cover the bed, Rio." Sam unzipped her bag as the other medic draped the bed with a plastic cover.

That done, Rio motioned for Ben to the bed. "On your right side, buddy. We'll work on the rest of you after we take care of the stitches." When Ben eased down and stretched out as directed, the medic glanced at Ruth. "Sit where he can see you. Ben needs a distraction while Sam and I work our magic."

As she settled on the bed, the jet began to move. Soon, they were in the air.

"Ben, you don't have to worry about Ruth's safety for a few hours. I'm starting an IV with antibiotics and pain meds." When Ben started to protest, Rio pointed a finger at him. "Can it. Buckner did a number on you and the repair will be painful. There's no need to distress your lady. Let go and let us do our job."

Clenching his jaw, Ben gave the medic a slight nod.

"How do you get uncooperative patients to do what you tell them?" Sam glared at Ben. "My teammates argue with my treatment recommendations."

Rio grinned. "Being a foot taller than you helps."

Sam rolled her eyes, then hooked Ben up to the IV Rio had prepared. She and Rio cleaned Ben's back, then used lidocaine to numb the wound.

Rio straightened. "I'll check Quinn while the lidocaine works. I'll be back in a few. Don't start the fun without me."

"Fun for who?" Ben asked.

The other team's medic chuckled as he left the room.

Sam continued to check Ben while Rio was gone. "Ruth, I know Buckner nailed you with at least one punch. Were you hurt during the abduction or before Ben showed up?"

"A few bruises. I'm fine, I promise."

"Ice packs," Ben ordered Sam. "She has to work soon."

"Yes, Dr. Martin. I'll get right on that."

"Brat," he growled.

Shadow's medic grinned.

Rio returned a few minutes later with his bag. He donned rubber gloves. "We ready, Sam?"

She pinched various places along Ben's back. "Feel anything?"

"Pressure." He sounded sleepy.

"That's what we want. You can either look at your girl or go to sleep."

His eyes were already closing. "Don't leave me, Ruth."

As if she would. Nope, the handsome operative had her heart. "Never. Sleep, Ben. I'll watch over you."

With a slight smile on his mouth, he fell asleep.

CHAPTER THIRTY-SIX

Ben glared at Sorenson. "Let me out of here, Doc. Your dogs are driving me nuts." That was a lie, but he couldn't stay in the doctor's recovery room another day. The walls were closing in on him. Worse, he was afraid to fall into a deep sleep. What if he woke up screaming, a good possibility since his confrontation with Davidson and his cronies? Despite having the means to free himself from the chains, being restrained had reawakened nightmares.

Not only that, his mother was stuck in this clinic with him and Ruth. He wanted to get her to Nashville and settled in a place of her own as soon as possible. Time for her to find out who she was without Davidson's abuse, the woman she might have become after his father's death if not for the influence of a man who lived to manipulate and hurt others.

Knowing what she'd been through, he'd already had a few conversations with Maddox about counseling for his mother. She'd need help transitioning back into society after the cloistered confines of Eden not to mention the years of trauma she'd suffered at Davidson's hands.

His boss had arrived at the Bayside clinic three hours after Ben and the others landed. While Durango, Nico, and Trace had returned home, his teammates Joe and Sam remained behind with him and the women. Maddox and the Grays provided security while Ben concentrated on healing and making sure Maren and Ruth were all right.

The surgeon had won Ruth over immediately. Even though he gave Sorenson a hard time on principal, Ben owed the doctor for convincing Ruth and his mother to let him check them for injuries and persuading them to talk about their experiences in the compound. He didn't know what they discussed in their one-on-one meetings in the office, but Ruth and Maren were more at peace when they returned from the sessions. Who knew the hard-nosed vet with a soft spot for animals was also capable of soothing traumatized women?

Sorenson glowered at Ben. "Don't try to con me, Martin. I've seen you sneaking down the hall to the animal recovery room off and on for the past two days. What's the real reason you want away from my stimulating company?"

He'd have to give the other man something. As a former operative, Sorenson had seen almost everything. "I can't breathe here."

The doctor's eyes narrowed. "Not buying it. Try again."

Ben dragged a hand down his face. Fantastic. He should have known the taciturn surgeon would see right through him. "If I fall into a deep sleep, there's an excellent chance I'll wake up screaming."

Sorenson rolled his eyes. "Is that all? Come on, Ben. Your girlfriend is strong enough to handle your night terrors. From what she's told me, Ruth has some of her own from time to time. She'll have more for a while after her experience with Davidson. She understands what you're going through."

"My mother won't. She already feels guilty for taking me to Davidson's commune when I was a kid. Mom doesn't need to know how much the past scarred me."

"I think you're underestimating Maren." He left without agreeing to release Ben.

Sam walked in five minutes later with a tray of food. Her eyebrows soared at the expression on his face. "Who rained on your parade?"

"Ha ha." Ben swung his legs over the side of the bed and stood. "Where's Ruth?"

"In the kitchen making brownies with Maren. Joe is with them." She smirked. "The ladies think chocolate will sweeten your attitude. Since I love chocolate, I didn't bother telling them that their efforts were a waste of time."

He frowned and took the tray from her hands. "What's this?"

"Comfort food. Chicken pot pie and baked apples." The medic sat on one of the chairs at a nearby table. "Want to tell me what's going on besides your normal sour attitude when you're healing from an injury?"

Ben set the tray on the table and took a seat beside her. "Being in Eden reawakened memories of my first experience in the commune. If I go to sleep, I'll probably wake up screaming. Mom doesn't know I have PTSD and I want to keep it that way."

"Does Ruth know?"

He nodded.

"I can't guarantee I'll be able to convince Sorenson to release you. If I can't, I'll talk to the boss about sending Maren to visit Nate and Stella." She smiled. "Your mom and Nate have a mutual admiration society going. He freed her from Eden and he says she reminds him of his favorite aunt."

The tension wracking his frame eased somewhat. "Thanks, Sam."

The medic patted his arm and walked to the door. "Eat. Sorenson's wife made the meal for us. I'll see what I can do to spring you from jail."

Ben tucked into his meal and polished it off quickly. Since he was at loose ends again except for walking, Ben made his way down the hall to the animal recovery room to see the Westie hit by a car and brought in for treatment by a citizen who found him by the roadside. According to Sorenson, the dog didn't have tags or a chip, and no one had claimed him despite the clinic posting his picture on social media two weeks earlier.

After glancing around to be sure he wasn't being watched, Ben slipped into the room and closed the door. The Westie raised his head and thumped his tail. "Hey, buddy. How do you feel?"

The dog whined and edged closer to the crate door.

Ben eased down on the floor and released him. The white-haired dog limped out and crawled onto Ben's lap, licking any part of his face that he could reach. Chuckling, Ben cradled the dog on one arm and gently stroked his fur. "You're a sweet boy. You need a name. Got any suggestions?"

The dog barked.

"Wish I was fluent in dog vocabulary." Ben continued to pet him for a few minutes, considering various dog names and discarding all of them but one. He glanced down at the dog. "How about Yoda?"

Another bark.

"Glad you approve, Yoda." When the pain in his back grew too great to ignore, Ben stood with Yoda in his arms. He glanced at the crate. No. Yoda didn't deserve to be caged because someone had abandoned him. Sorenson wouldn't mind if he spent time with the dog in more comfortable surroundings. Probably.

Cheeks hot, he went to the door and eased it open a crack. The coast was clear. With silent steps, he returned to the human recovery room and eased down onto the bed. His continued weakness irritated the daylights of out him, but Sorenson had assured him that the weakness was from blood loss and he'd be at full strength soon.

Swinging his legs onto the bed, he reclined against the pillows and settled Yoda at his side. The Westie gave a sigh, snuggled close, and drifted off to sleep. Hmm. The dog had a good idea. A nap sounded good. He closed his eyes and let himself drift off.

Sometime later, footsteps approached his room and stopped in the doorway. Ben turned to see Sorenson with his shoulder propped against the jamb. "What?"

"I wondered if the Westie had learned how to open the crate door. I see now that he had help. How's he doing?"

"Seems like he's comfortable. He didn't like being a prisoner." Ben hadn't liked being a prisoner, either.

"If I can't find a permanent home for him, he'll have to go to a shelter soon."

Ben scowled. "Dog jail? Have a heart, Doc."

"I'm not having any luck finding his owner. Since he was dumped on the side of the road, I'm also not looking too hard to find them. Do you know someone who might give him a good home?"

Ben and Yoda looked at each other. "Maybe," Ben muttered. "Can he travel?"

"He'll need to be checked by a vet in another two weeks to see if his leg has healed enough to remove the cast. Other than that, he's in good shape. Do you know of someone who will take him?"

"Depends." He wanted Yoda, but his job demanded that he travel. He'd need help caring for the Westie. "I need to talk to Ruth first."

A slow smile spread across the vet's face. "I'll get her."

Two minutes later, Ruth walked in with a small plate of brownies and a glass of ice water in her hands. Her mouth dropped open. "Who is this?"

Ben drew in a breath and dove in, feet first. "His name is Yoda and he needs a home. I want him but I'll need someone to watch him when I'm on deployment. If I don't take him, he'll go to dog jail."

She set the plate and water on a rolling table away from the dog's reach. "Are you asking if I mind helping with Yoda?"

"He's a good boy and nobody deserves to be a prisoner."

Ruth reached out her hand for Yoda to sniff. She smiled when he licked her fingers. "He's a sweetheart. I'll be happy to help with him."

Relief flooded Ben. "Thank you, sunshine. Where are your last two photoshoots?"

"Orange Beach, Alabama, and Gatlinburg, both places we can drive to and find a hotel that is pet friendly."

He scratched between Yoda's ears. "You hear that, boy? No dog jail for you. You've got a home now."

Yoda barked.

Ben chuckled. "Now all we have to do is convince Sorenson to spring me from jail and we'll go home with the most beautiful woman in the world." He looked at Ruth, sobering. "Are you sure you don't mind sharing responsibility for this little guy?"

"I'm sure." She bent and kissed Ben. "He makes you happy. How can I say no?"

"I don't deserve you, Ruth, but I'll do everything in my power to make sure you don't regret taking us both on."

He glanced at the door as Sorenson returned. "Yoda has a home with me, Doc. Now, when can we go home?"

Sorenson grinned. "Tonight. I want to watch both of you for a few more hours. I'm releasing you into Sam's care. You do everything she says to the letter or I'll have Maddox ship you and Yoda back here. Clear?"

"As crystal."

When the sun went down, Sorenson checked both Ben and the dog one more time. "You aren't to go on a mission for at least four more weeks, Martin. My prescription for you is to relax, eat, and sleep as much as you can for the next two weeks. Give your body a chance to heal. After that, light workouts for a week before you ramp up the activity level the fourth week. Spend some time with your dog and your woman."

Ben threaded his fingers through Ruth's. "That's an order I'll be happy to obey."

"Good. Now, get out of here. I don't want to see you back in here as a patient for a long time. If I do, I won't be nearly as nice as I've been this time." Sorensen squeezed Ruth's shoulder. "Take care of yourself, Ruth. You have my number if you need to talk."

"Yes, sir. Thank you."

After Sorenson left, Ben bent and captured Ruth's mouth in a long, deep kiss. When he came up for air, he smiled. "Come on. Let's get Yoda and Mom and go home."

CHAPTER THIRTY-SEVEN

Christmas Eve. Tonight was the night. Ben reached for the box with a trembling hand. Scowling, he shoved the box into his pocket, and glanced down at Yoda. "You ready?"

The Westie barked.

Ben grinned as he clipped the red leash onto Yoda's matching collar and led the dog out to the SUV. Six long months he'd waited to give both himself and Ruth time to work through the trauma they'd suffered in the Eden compound. He didn't want to wait another day.

As he drove toward Ruth's house, Ben placed a call to Otter Creek to the one man he trusted to give him unbiased advice.

"Lang."

"Marcus, it's Ben." When he heard laughter and the clink of glasses and silverware in the background, he winced. "Sorry. I didn't mean to interrupt your holiday activities."

"No problem, my friend. What do you need?"

"I'm on my way to Ruth's. I want to ask her to marry me tonight, but I don't want to pressure her if she's not ready for this. I don't want to hurt her."

"Ruth is a strong woman. I don't think you have anything to worry about. You can trust your gut and your heart, Ben."

The operative gave a huff of laughter. "Great. My gut is tied in knots for fear that she'll turn me down and my heart is racing faster than an Indy race car on a straightaway."

The Otter Creek pastor chuckled. "You'll be fine. Both of you have been through a trial by fire and come out the other side stronger than steel. I think you already know what her answer is going to be. You've been dating for six months and dancing around each other six months before that. Did you bring your wingman?"

"You better believe it. Say hello to Marcus, Yoda."

The dog barked.

A laugh sounded in the SUV's cabin. "If you have the ring and the dog, how can Ruth resist? Best of luck to you, Ben. Shoot me a text later tonight and let me know what she says."

"Yes, sir. Thanks, Marcus. For everything." For more than he could say. The pastor had spent numerous hours with him and Ruth, helping them come to terms with their pasts in order to move into this new phase of their lives.

"Both of you would have gotten there eventually. I just moved you along the path a little faster. Later, my friend." The pastor ended the call.

A short time later, Ben parked in Ruth's driveway. The white lights of her Christmas tree glowed in her living room window, a beacon in the night, drawing him to the woman of his dreams.

He glanced at Yoda. "I'm counting on you, buddy."

The dog whined and wagged his tail.

Blowing out a breath, Ben slipped the ring from the box, and shoved it deep into his pocket. He exited the SUV and walked to the front door with Yoda. Before he rang the bell, the door flew open and there she was. Ruth Monihan stood in the open doorway, a vision of beauty in black pants and a bright red sweater. The best thing was her smile of welcome.

She brushed his mouth with hers, then bent to pet Yoda before stepping back. "Come on in. Trace and Bridget will be here in a few minutes. Bridget was finishing the last of the cookies she's baking. They're picking up Maren on the way here." Ruth closed the door behind them.

At least he didn't have to beg her to marry him in front of his teammate and her sister as well as his mother. If Lang was wrong and Ruth turned him down, Ben would have a chance to get himself together before the others arrived.

"Do you want some coffee? It's fresh."

"In a few minutes. I need to talk to you."

Ruth looked puzzled. "Are you okay? You seem nervous."

He wrapped his hand around hers and led her to sit on the couch beside him. "I have something to ask you, but I need to tell you some things before that." Man, he was going to die before he got to the all-important question.

"You can tell me anything, Ben. I hope you know that."

"I love you, Ruth. Even though I fell for you the first moment I saw you, I never thought I had a chance. I know I'm not good enough for you and never will be. You're everything I'm not. You're the light to my darkness, my strength when I'm weak, my heart and soul. Without you, I'm lost and have no purpose."

"Oh, Ben," she whispered, her eyes sheening with tears. "I love you so much."

"I really hope you mean that, sunshine." He shifted to kneel on one knee in front of her and slid his hand into his pocket for the ring that reminded him of her, one that symbolized his love and devotion. He lifted her hand and held up the ring for her to see. "I adore you, Ruth Monihan. Will you do me the honor of becoming my wife?"

"Yes!"

Thank God. He slid the ring on her finger and gathered her close for a heated kiss. The doorbell ringing and Yoda barking brought them up for air. "I'll get it."

She laughed. "Good. I don't think my legs will hold me up at the moment."

Ben staggered when he got to his feet, prompting more laughter from Ruth. He winked at her and opened the door to admit his mother, Trace, and Bridget.

Bridget took one look at her sister's face and shoved her tray of cookies into her husband's hands. She hurried to Ruth. "What happened? Are you okay?"

Ruth smiled and held out her hand with the engagement ring. "Look."

Her sister squealed and hugged her. "Congratulations! It's about time Ben manned up."

"Hey!" Ben protested. "I was giving her time to get used to me, all right?"

"Good job, buddy," Trace said and clapped him on the shoulder.

His mother hugged him, tears in her eyes. "I'm happy for you, son. She's a wonderful woman. I hope you two have many years of happiness together."

"Thanks, Mom." His words came out strangled.

"How soon is the wedding?" Bridget asked.

"If I had my choice, it would be tomorrow." Ben smiled at Ruth. "However, I think Ruth will want a day or two to plan and buy a dress or something."

The women laughed.

"I think Valentine's Day." Ruth hugged Yoda who had hopped onto her lap. "I think that should be perfect."

He'd already waited a year for this woman. He could wait six more weeks. Maybe. Perhaps his new mission should be persuading her to consider a date earlier than

February 14. He was a SEAL and SEALs never failed to complete a mission. Loving Ruth was going to be the sweetest, most important mission of his life.

ABOUT THE AUTHOR

Rebecca Deel is a preacher's kid with a black belt in karate. She teaches business classes at a private four-year college outside Nashville, Tennessee. She plays the piano at church, writes freelance articles, and runs interference for the family dogs. She's been married to her amazing husband for more than 25 years and is the proud mom of two grown sons. She delivers occasional devotions to the women's group at her church and conducts seminars on personal safety, money management, and writing. Her articles have been published in *ONE Magazine*, *Contact*, and *Co-Laborer*, and she was profiled in the June 2010 Williamson edition of *Nashville Christian Family* magazine. Rebecca completed her Doctor of Arts degree in Economics and wears her favorite Dallas Cowboys sweatshirt when life turns ugly.

For more information on Rebecca...

Signup for Rebecca's newsletter: http://eepurl.com/_B6w9

Visit Rebecca's website: www.rebeccadeelbooks.com